Reeta Singh was born in 1974 in the United Kingdom. The daughter of first generation, East-African Indians, she grew up in an idyllic market town just outside of London. She studied at an all-girls secondary school before completing Bachelor of Science in genetics at Newcastle University and passing out with 1st class honours degree. She then went on to study medicine, at Leicester University, and embark a career in pediatrics. On meeting her husband, she opted to become a GP to serve a deprived community in North East Lincolnshire. It was here where she had her first dog closely followed by two children. She practiced clinically for her own community and helped serve patients who were difficult to doctor, and she also taught medical students for a number of years before leaving the NHS and emigrating to North America.

In 2015, she moved with her own family to Canada where she took a career break to raise her children, have two more children and embark on a new career as a writer.

Sanjog, her debut novel, was written overlooking the Atlantic waters of her new home, Halifax, Nova Scotia, where she now lives with her husband, four children and a dog. Her first novel is a tribute to her father and mother.

This book is dedicated to our fathers—they, with soft grey-brown eyes and they, with the smell of diesel on their hands, and smell of whiskey on their breath. They were, are and will always remain to be our heroes.

Dr Reeta M K Singh

SANJOG – A NOVEL

AUSTIN MACAULEY PUBLISHERS™
LONDON • CAMBRIDGE • NEW YORK • SHARJAH

Copyright © Dr Reeta M K Singh (2020)

The right of Dr Reeta M K Singh to be identified as the author of this work has been asserted by her in accordance with section 77 and 78 of the Copyright, Designs and Patents Act 1988.

All rights reserved. No part of this publication may be reproduced, stored in a retrieval system, or transmitted in any form or by any means, electronic, mechanical, photocopying, recording, or otherwise, without the prior permission of the publishers.

Any person who commits any unauthorized act in relation to this publication may be liable to criminal prosecution and civil claims for damages.

This is a work of fiction. Names, characters, businesses, places, events, locales, and incidents are either the products of the author's imagination or used in a fictitious manner. Any resemblance to actual persons, living or dead, or actual events is purely coincidental.

A CIP catalogue record for this title is available from the British Library.

ISBN 9781528908665 (Paperback)
ISBN 9781528908672 (Hardback)
ISBN 9781528959018 (ePub e-book)

www.austinmacauley.com

First Published (2020)
Austin Macauley Publishers Ltd
25 Canada Square
Canary Wharf
London
E14 5LQ

So many people have helped in this massive quest to go from clinician, having had every bit of creativity well and truly quashed, to author. There have been those who are obvious, and named here, but also those who have stood on the sidelines and cheered me along! I am grateful to each and every one of you, named and unnamed. But to name a few, here we go:

To Nancy, who tirelessly read every single chapter I sent her and told me when I was giving too much away or not enough. You were one of my first real friends in my new home. Thanks for all that you did, helping with meals when I was too pregnant to cook, helping with children when I was too distracted to offer them fun, helping with boxes of Kleenex and a listening ear when life threw yet another curveball. Thanks for putting aside your own thoughts to comfort me. Thank you, my dear, dear friend for being absolutely rock solid.

To Mama Baroni, for lobster and wine and a place by the sea, and for giving me Nancy.

To Grammar School parents and library mums, for listening to my endless tales, my moaning, and explaining to me how to navigate Canadian weather! For encouraging me so much to believe in myself and reach for the stars! Your cheering from the sidelines has been truly awesome!

To Zoya who could see the picture in my mind that translated to the front cover. You have amazing talent and I am so thankful you loaned it to me.

To Paige and Deb for the makeover and photo shoot; you made this mum into a star! Thank you.

To Whitney, who rejected me but still believed in me to get this book published; who told me to keep at it because it truly is a great manuscript, just not for children, or cookery, or Canadian enough! Thank you for the time you gave me when you had no reason to!

To Linden and Stephen, Eleanor, Ashley, Kevin, Shaun, Carol, Katie, Heather, Kelly, Candice, Phyllis, Ashely, Kayla, Wilma, Deanna and all other teachers who helped my children flourish, even when I was wilting.

To Leicester Medics 2001, we can be whoever we want to be! Thanks for making me who I am!

To Micky and Anj, thanks for being there when I could not.

To my three *masis*, Ani, Pami and Ranjan; and *masas*, *mamas* and *mamis*, *buas*, *phuphars*, uncles, aunts and cousins. The length and breadth of this family is limitless! Thank you for all the stories and all the encouragement and divulging all the family secrets, historical and about food, to allow me to write this.

To Austin Macauley Publishers, who gave me a chance.

To my dearest husband, who believed that I could do this when I did not; who gave me so much inspiration with his stories of life growing up in India; who has a Punjabi saying for everything; who has been my best friend throughout this whole experience and; despite not reading it, knew all about it. Thank you for all the adventures in Canada and home, a lifetime of literary inspiration in just a few years. Thanks for all the cups of tea and for all the hugs. Thanks for showing me how to laugh and how to wait. My heart is yours forever.

To Gracie, Jonah, Naomi and Jacob: my four beautiful babies. You are the best kids ever. Dream big and don't be scared to fail, because the best success comes from failure; we are here with you always. Be there for each other every day and don't forget to be thankful; you are truly blessed.

To my mum, thank you for everything you have ever done and continue to do. Thank you for being such a strong woman who showed me that life is what you make of it, so make it with love and be determined. I have never known anyone like you with so much strength and dignity. You have shaped me more than you will ever know. Thank you.

To my God, who has blessed me with every spiritual blessing in Christ Jesus and made me His own because of His endless grace and mercy.

And finally, to my dad: my friend, my inspiration, my mentor. No one could have done it like you did. And no one could have shown me how to be rich and humble like you have. I love you dearly.

Family Tree
Farida Begum
Rizwan Khan
Kuljeet ("Bhabi)
Sukdev
Harjinder
Baljinder
Paramjeet ("Biji)
Baldev Singh ("Pita-Ji)
Ranjeet
Simran ("Parjai")
Feroz Khan
Shaheeda Begum
The lost baby
Balbinder Kaur
Kuldeep Singh
Satvinder
Meera
Santosh
Mya
Jai
Sareeta
Raja
Preety
Ravi
Nishu
Annie
Dharam
Kiran
Ash
Sonia
Rishi
Ricky
Mandeep

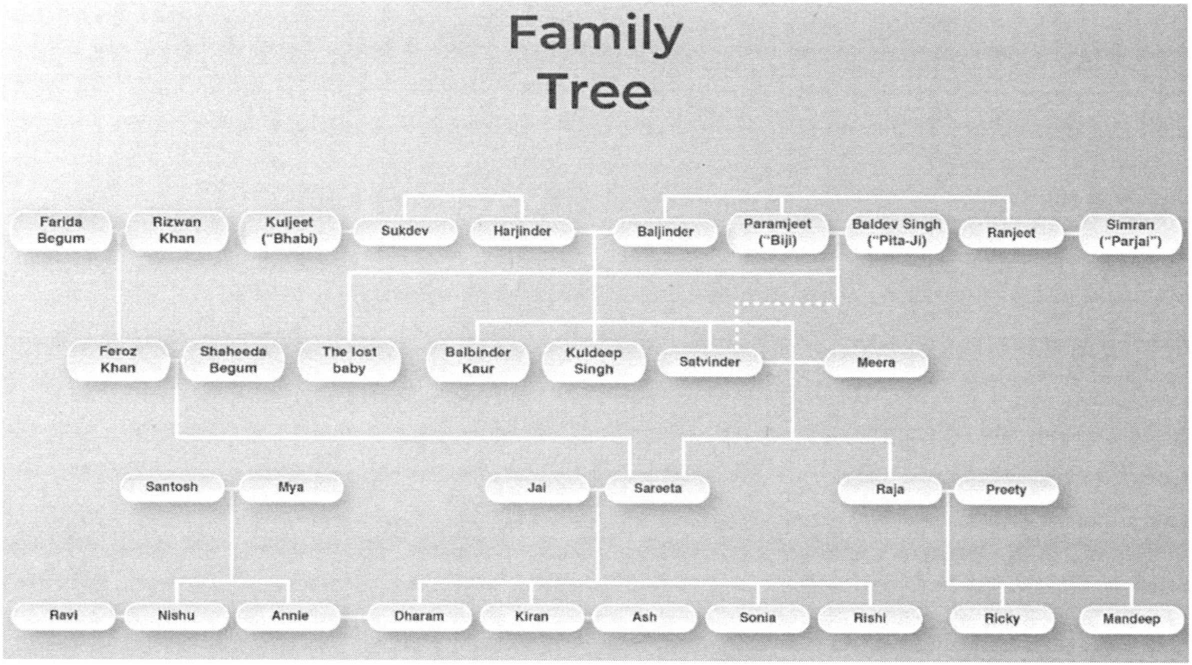

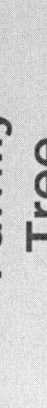

Chapter 1

Atlantic Canada, 2017

That day, the day of the wedding, should have been perfect. There was really no reason why it should not have been with all the planning and days of preparation. At that moment, the sun was just beginning its dip, a peachy coral yolk, misplaced in its aqua nesting bed. The view from the hotel was fantastic: an expanse of grey-blue, cool and alluring, reaching out to nowhere forever. Apart from the sun, there was nothing obscuring that view, no rocks, no islands, no artifact. Just as God himself had intended, a calmness unmatched, underwater worlds unseen.

Sareeta looked out for a minute and almost lost herself in her thoughts without trying. It was brief, so brief before the noise around her dragged her back to her duties. Today was her eldest son's wedding day. The near and extended family had come together for this and she felt both very privileged as well as extremely exposed. The formal wedding rites, both Sikh and Christian, had been taken care of and the reception was about to begin. She could hear the *bhangra* music resonating from the main hall, a music that she had come to associate with weddings alone. She quickly scanned the room, full of guests in sparking *saris* and glowing *sherwanis*, tottering on jeweled heels and flat *jutti*, glasses clinking filled with tiny bubbles and orange crimson delights.

The colours of the drinks matched the setting sun, the bubbles matched the air of anticipation around her and she had a sense of absolute peace at that moment although she had no right to. Like the sea, it was as if God himself had intended this. She looked at her father across the room, sitting in his wheelchair looking lost in the ocean of jewels and she knew what he was feeling.

It was a noisy and busy occasion and he was not used to these events any more. The music was loud and there were too many people chatting around him saying things like "How is your wife these days? I heard she had another baby?" and replies like "Oh yes, aunty-*Ji*, she would have loved to come but you know hard it is with three small children now". Followed by "That is so true, *beta*. But I am glad that you came. Such a shame though, it would have been nice to see her."

It left him trying hard now to think of who these people were. Whose daughter or daughter in law was she, the one with the three children? Would he even know who that was or would he be better off asking himself whose granddaughter she was? He wouldn't have chosen to come to a wedding if his wife had asked him. Not really, he hadn't really ever enjoyed weddings, although he was not a grumpy man. He just found them tiresome and overly extravagant these days. He was bored of all the post-wedding commentaries on how there were too many or not enough people. The women just traded notes on where that beautiful *sari* came from or whether they thought her jewellery was real or artificial. The men talked business for a short time and then just looked at the scenery. Everyone just waited for the food which was always criticized regardless of cause. Not hot enough, not varied enough or simply, just not enough. But he had to come to this wedding. It was his grandson's wedding.

What a prince Dharam was, he thought.

Tall, broad shouldered like his father, radiant in his golden *sherwani*. He looked like a proper Sikh, even though he had short hair and a trimmed beard. He looked the image of his father and Satvinder felt a pride rising up in him; yes, Sareeta and Jai had brought up a very fine son.

Satvinder thought back to his own wedding day and how different that had been. None of today's glamour and style. It had been a simple wedding, for a few friends and family; most boycotting it as it was a 'love marriage' not arranged and entirely unacceptable in his family back then.

He remembered he had not worn a suit or *sherwani*, but he could not remember what he had worn. Although he had uncut hair, a full beard and turban, he lacked the status that Dharam carried today. He considered how unpolished he must have appeared compared to how beautiful she looked in her simple red and gold sari. He remembered its colour; it was just right, the red was just perfect on her being neither too scarlet nor too crimson. She looked like a newly budding rose, the way it looks when you can just see the colour beginning to peep out of its green casing and you have that anticipation of the beauty and fragrance will be there very soon. Apt because roses were always her favourite flowers, then and now. He remembered the gold embroidery on her chiffon sari: tiny peacocks and flowers were just as they should have been on her, delicate and intricate just like her. Her hair had been high at the crown with a short fringe; it was the fashion back then. Her sari blouse was short, revealing her beautifully sculpted nape and back – just enough but not too much.

He remembered the way she walked and smelt and…"*Sat sri akal,* Uncle! So good to see you, Uncle. You're looking well. You must be so proud of Dharam!"

His daydream ended and he looked up to see his cousin's son. "*Sat sri akal,* Beta, yes, I'm very proud."

Sareeta arrived. "Dad, here you are! Oh Hi, Jaggy, how's things? So glad you could come, where's *bhabi*?"

"Oh, she's somewhere around, I think. Hey, this is a great do, Saru. Great wedding."

"Thanks, Jaggy, took a lot of time to get it right! Anyway, I think we are ready to eat. Do you know where you are sitting?"

"I'll find it. Chat later?"

"Sure. I'll get dad to his table."

Sareeta swung him around and headed off into the Hall. "Are you okay, Dad? Bearing up? I know it's a lot for you today, but you're doing well."

She was close to her dad and now, he was old, frail and tired after his series of strokes and needed a gentle touch. He hadn't found the move to Canada easy; he'd moved too much in his life. India, Kenya, England and now here. He didn't really feel like he had a home or identity any more. She had asked him once where his felt his 'home' was. He had thought and then replied that he didn't feel he had a home as such having left India aged five to be a foreigner in Kenya, then a foreigner in England and now a dependent foreigner in Canada.

"My home is where your mother is," he had said.

She managed to navigate herself and him through the guests, stopping frequently to exchange kisses and compliments before finally finding their table. Her family was already there. Her mother, old now but still with strands of brown hair making her look less than her 70 years. She sat adorned with gold and rubies that rarely came out of the safe. The last time had probably been at her granddaughter Kiran's wedding who had married just a couple of years before her brother today.

Sat next to her was Sareeta's younger brother and his wife. He always looked the same to her, no matter how old he got, he always looked as he did when they were in high school. Still slim and slight, still long limbed and short torso, jigging his left leg nervously as he always did when he was tired. He still had deep-set eyes and always looked exhausted. His wife next to him was quiet and composed. It was obvious to Sareeta that the mass of friends and relatives had worn her down but she was trying to keep an interest in the events of the day. Actually, she could do with a long hot bath and curling up in a soft white-sheeted bed. Their two children sat next to them, teenagers now. Both had their phones out and were frantically tapping away whilst the DJ was encouraging guests to take their seats whilst playing the obligatory *Celebration* by Kool and the Gang.

Next was the bride's mother, quiet, demure, sharp featured but even more sharp minded. It was obvious to all the guests that she was unimpressed with the whole show which she thought was very unlike the society weddings she was used to in her home city of Nairobi.

Then the bride's father, tall and distinguished looking, greying hair and a neat moustache. His suit matched his hair but his red tie added a sense of celebration, however slight. His foot tapped to the music and he seemed pretty much oblivious to the fact that he was a central player in this particular play. Sareeta's own seat was next, and then her husband's. Her lovely Jai.

When they had initially started dating, they had met much opposition. She, the Doctor, had ticked every marital box. She was 'homely yet outgoing', fair, tall and from good stock. Slightly rotund too, her biodata described her as 'heavy build' to which she had always objected but even this was not enough to outweigh the pluses. And it amazed her how many potential mother-in-laws felt that this particular aspect could be conquered with a strict Ayurvedic diet with herbal supplementation and home fitness DVDs. Jai, on the other hand, was neither a doctor, a lawyer nor an accountant, the Holy Trinity of potential husbands if you happened to be a first generation Anglo Indian. He was an engineer, acceptable but not brilliant. But he was tall, good looking and fair, that helped somewhat.

The problem was that he wasn't 'settled', whatever that had meant as it seemed to mean so many things at that time. It had encompassed possessions, properties, job prospects, family, family skeletons and anything else the parents and extended family wanted to know to complete their picture. Jai wasn't 'settled'. His family were not their 'kind of people', his job wasn't 'stable enough' and he had few possessions but none of these included his own house and car. And, he wasn't a Doctor like her.

But he was of the same faith as her which had seemed improbable if not impossible to them. Sareeta had herself converted from Sikhism to Christianity as a child, an act which had both amused and upset her parents. Nonetheless, after 15 years, give or take, they had come to realize that it wasn't a phase she was going through, like when she decided it would be cool to become a vegan (that had lasted all of 48 hours!). Her father had simply chuckled when she had requested that he find her a 'Christian from a Sikh background' just like herself, but here he was. 'Sanjog' they had called it, meaning some kind of predestined fate.

Jai too had converted, in a different country at a different time. His revelation occurred aged 19 in Punjab, India, following which, he cut off his long hair and abandoned 4 of his 5 Ks, keeping hold of his *Kara* to remind him of his great Sikh heritage. He had faced homelessness, persecution and slander from those near and far. And all this whilst religious tension between Sikhs and Hindus, Hindus and Muslims, was running high. Jai had been reconciled to his family before he fled India at the age of 19 but he had yearned to return to his home ever since. He had moved from India to England to Canada and was no longer the not yet settled engineer but one of the East Coast's finest immigrant assets owning miles of real estate and eateries on the Atlantic Coast.

Sareeta looked at him now. His hair, which should have been grey, was jet black. His eyes were still shiny and framed with the most beautiful long lashes she had ever seen on a man but feathered with 'smile lines' as she called them. His shoulders were broad and strong, not a hint of slumping despite his 54 years. His chest was proud and seemed to balance perfectly his slightly expanded waistline, a result of his wife's cooking for which she was famed amongst her friends in Atlantic Canada, and his love of Indian Milk Cake sold in the local Walmart. His smile was like switching on a light bulb in a darkened room and his teeth were still perfectly white and perfectly straight. Only the lines on his face had changed but these too seemed to speak to her of memories, memories of their initial love, memories of their four children, memories of the pain of death they had experienced and losses they had taken time to come to terms with. Every line on his beautiful face told her a story of their past and she admired every single one.

Sareeta's mother was already in her seat speaking to Annie's grandmother next to her reminiscing about life in Nairobi in the 1960s when they were both young women. Meera wore the sari she had worn at Sareeta's own wedding, a beautiful cerulean blue silk with rose gold and bronze embroidery. Though elderly now, she had a class that was her own. The saris she had accumulated over the years were not of the fashion of that moment but classic and timeless. The fabrics and embroideries showed off her wealth. Her hair, now mostly white although it had remained chocolate brown for many years past its best before date, was piled high on her head. Her neck, now with furrows, was still long and showcased the beauty of the jewels adorning it.

She liked the bride, Annie, and Annie's family, not least because they were Kenyan Gujis like her and not from the Punjabi brood into which she and her children had then married. She liked her own clan, the way the ate, sweets meats with savory, their thin *chappatis* loaded with butter, ten to a meal minimum, *daal* and rice at the end of a meal, always. She liked the way they spoke, not crude and lewd like the Punjabis but gentle and mild spirited. She liked the language, singsong like and polite, so much respect intertwined within the words themselves. She was so pleased when Dharam had introduced her to Annie, slim and slight, the right height for him, a fair complexion and had sharp features, in keeping with her clan. Her almond-shaped eyes were dark and mysterious but seemed trustworthy enough.

At the next table sat the happy couple with their siblings, Dharam and Annie looking resplendent in their matching wedding attire. Then Kiran, his eldest sister, with her husband Ash. Next was Sonia Dharam's little sister, six years his junior, she had all the young bachelor eyes on her. Slim and tall like her sister, she was vivacious, full of life and oblivious to all the men trying to get her attention. Her younger brother sat next to her. Just a teenager but already with his father's charm and his brother's style, Rishi giggled with Sonia. They were obviously gossiping about one of the aunties at the wedding, Sareeta could tell. They had a naughty streak when they were together; years of being surrounded by a more adult humour had left them with a penchant for sarcasm.

Annie's sister also sat at the table next to Annie. She was the older sibling, married with two children but for some reason, her husband and children were sat at a different table nearby; Sareeta had heard it had something to do with them being small and too distracting when Annie needed her sister's undivided attention.

The other tables around were dotted with close relatives and some friends although most of Dharam's friends had been relegated to the tables further away from the head and nearer to the bar. Sareeta knew that as soon as he felt he was no longer the main attraction at the zoo, he would nip off and be with his friends. He enjoyed the company of these boys, although he was not much of a drinker himself. And she had liked his friends too, all hard-working professional boys who enjoyed life.

Sareeta had always wanted her children to work hard and enjoy life so she was pleased that his close-knit friends were a group of guys who seemed to be the same. Dharam, unlike Kiran, had few friends but they were very close. He was an innocent and sweet guy that attracted people to himself but in a different way to his sisters who were just plain fun.

When Dharam had first come home with Annie, Sareeta had been anxious. She had heard this Annie mentioned many times recently and was both excited and worried to meet her. She knew, deep within, that this was probably who Dharam had decided to be his life partner. She couldn't tell why she knew, she just did. He had mentioned many of his female friends before and his tall good looks, unassuming personality and general mildness had always ensured a throng of female followers. Sonia and Kiran had also ensured that he understood the female mindset, having made him subject to their many meltdowns over the past twenty odd years. But the way he spoke about Annie was different. Maybe it was the frequent references to her or maybe it was just something in his voice that changed when he spoke of her. Whatever it was, Sareeta had known from the outset that she was the one.

Sareeta remembered that day when Dharam had walked through the door with her. She had been cooking for him, knowing he was arriving any minute. She had made his favourites: Punjabi chicken *masala, jeera pilau, aloo gobi, dahi* and *chappatis*.

Jai had been making fun of her all day as he always did when Dharam came home from Boston. "You've forgotten me again," he would complain, half-jokingly. "Always forgetting me when your prince is coming home!"

"Yes, of course!" she would retort, "You are always here with me, why should I not forget you when he's coming home!"

Days like that were her favourite. Kiran lived close by and Sonia and Rishi were still at home but what she had looked forward to most was days like this when they were all together at her home. The energy that emulated from them was magical and she could just sit and listen to them excitedly telling each other stories about their lives, friends, tease each other about their love interests and more.

And today, Dharam was coming and bringing this Annie with him. The smell of hot oil, cumin, ginger and garlic had filled the kitchen. She hoped Dharam would just find it the smell of home. The cooker, which she had fitted to overlook the lake, was filled with pans of different sizes, all with their own fragrance. It was always the smell of the food that allured her more than the taste. She knew, instinctively, whether her *masala* was good or bad with the smell. Like her home, where from the smell of the air inside, she had been able to gauge the mood within. Ginger, garlic and cumin smelt happiness, peace and homecoming to her. Perfume and pizza meant Sonia had her friends over again. No smell meant emptiness but hope, like when they had first come here after Jai had completed the building work. But today, the smell was that of anticipation and hope mingled with a fear of what, or rather who, was unknown. She couldn't explain why, although the dishes were as she had always made them, the smell was different; or maybe she could.

When they walked through the door, Sareeta quickly cleaned her hands and untied her apron. She had a quick glimpse of her hair and lipstick in the hallway mirror just outside the kitchen and went to greet them. Dharam was just taking off his shoes in the foyer, mumbling to Annie to do the same when he caught sight of her.

"Mama!" he said, coming forward to hug her.

She kissed him on his soft cheek and hugged him tightly. The days of him being in her complete embrace had long gone, now she managed to get her arm around his waist and do an almost full hug. He, on the other hand, enclosed her completely now.

"Mama, I'd like you to meet Annie. Annie, this is my Mama, the Doctor Memsahib!"

"Dharam, don't be silly! Annie, it is an absolute pleasure to meet you. Please just call me Saru," she replied, looking disapprovingly at her son.

"Aunty, it is a pleasure to meet you too. Dharam speaks so highly of you and uncle so I'm very pleased to meet you."

Annie was very pretty, no less than Sareeta had expected her to be. She was about Sareeta's height which was a good height to be. She had very defined features, high cheekbones and forehead. A small nose but a nice shape and proportionate. Her eyes were beautiful. Almond shaped and dark chocolate brown with long lashes. Her soft pink lips were full but not so voluptuous. She looked innocent, like Dharam. She had that perfect figure, a larger bust and narrow hips. She was wearing skinny jeans and a fitted shirt with tall boots. Sareeta could tell straight off that she was one of those women who naturally had style and didn't have to try too hard. She knew she would have liked her a lot more if she didn't have that special relationship with Dharam that made her feel unjustifiably insecure.

Dharam himself looked glowing, somehow more alive but also completely content. She couldn't argue with it. It was very clear to her that he had found his match and, sooner or later, the match would become part of her family.

And now here they were, two years later, two families joined, two children married and two left to go. Ash, the 'poodle', as she and Jai called him in secret and Annie added to their own brood. She and Jai had always realized and accepted that the children were never theirs to really keep. They would grow and leave home and marry and she and Jai would be alone again, as they had been all those years ago. But they wouldn't be strangers thrust together again after a lifetime of child rearing, she had made sure of that by enforcing date night on them every week. They would be more like old friends reunited with common memories and references; like when she met her old classmates from medical school.

The rest of the reception passed in a blur with feasting, *bhangra* and too much alcohol. By 9 o' clock, guests were slowly drifting away, exhausted by the five days of events that had preceded. By 11 o'clock, the DJ had begun to pack up and the waiters were busily clearing the tables, anxious to get done and get home. Dharam and Annie had long gone. Jai was settling the final bill with the caterer and her parents had retired to their room as soon as the couple had left. She took off her sequined heels and rested her feet on the chair opposite. Sonia and Rishi also sat at the table, picking at the crumbs of the cake plate left on their table.

Jai returned and sat down.

"All done," he said. "Shall we go up?"

"No, Dad!" Rishi and Sonia complained in unison. "We wanna know what happened at Annie's house!"

Kiran had driven some of Annie's relatives back to her parent's cottage which they had hired for the wedding formalities before they returned to their native Nairobi the following week.

"Yes, darling, we need to wait for Kiran to come back. I want to know how it went too!" Sareeta added.

"Okay, okay. We'll wait. All she's doing is dropping them off though, there won't be any gossip that you lot love," he knew his wife and children well.

"Hey, Mama," Sonia caught Sareeta's attention, "did you see Bobby Uncle? What did he bring with him?!"

"His girlfriend, obviously!" retorted Rishi

"Yeah! Well, I wasn't sure if it was his girlfriend…or his granddaughter!"

"Hey, kids, don't be rude!" Sareeta smirked because the same thing had crossed her mind too. "Uncle Bobby is good looking, rich and lonely. He's bound to have certain women after him. So don't make fun of him! Loneliness is a terrible thing."

"I'd sure like to be that lonely!" mumbled Rishi, eyes firmly on his phone

"Heard that!" said Sareeta

Jai chuckled and shook his head. Sareeta glanced at him and tried to give him her typical disapproving look but she knew she couldn't; he's always had this notion that his boys should 'enjoy life', just as all Punjabi men did. His daughters, on the other hand, should never be subject to any man that had any ounce of desire for the female kind and Punjabi men were the worst.

Just then, Kiran rushed through the mass of empty banquet tables hurriedly trying to get to the others. The urgency of her rushing indicated that there was indeed some gossip she was bringing with her from Annie's house. Sareeta sat up, taking her feet off the chair on which they were resting whilst the others looked expectedly toward her.

She was clutching something in her hand, a piece of paper or a photograph of some sort; whatever it was it had that yellow tinge that old things have. In her other hand, she held her heels by the straps in order to quicken her pace to the group.

"Guys," she said short of breath, "you'd better take a look at this!"

Punjabi Chicken Curry for Dharam

You Will Need

1 whole chicken, skinned and cut into 10-12 pieces (2 drumsticks, 2 thighs, each breast piece cut into 2-3 pieces, 2 winglets)

½ cup vegetable or sunflower oil

2 large white onions finely chopped

1 400 grams can of chopped tomatoes

1 garlic bulb, 2 inches ginger and 2 green chillies blended into a paste with some water

2 tsps. whole cumin seeds

2 tsps. salt

2 heaped tsps. ground cumin
2 tsps. ground coriander
1 heaped tsp turmeric powder
1 tsp chilies powder
1 tsp *tandoori masala*
4 cups water
1 tsp *garam masala*
1 tbsp. fresh cilantro leaves chopped

What to Do

Take a large *karahi* or heavy based casserole and heat the oil

When it is hot but not smoking, add the cumin seeds and let the sizzle and spit – this takes about 30 seconds.

Now add the onion and cook until golden

Then add the ginger/garlic/chilies paste and cook all together until a deep mahogany colour. Add a splash of water if there is any sticking.

Add the tomatoes and continue to cook until the *masala* is pulpy – this takes 10 to 15 minutes. Again, add a splash of water if there is sticking.

When the oil begins to separate from the *masala* (golden oil sizzling around the edges of the tomato *masala*), add the spices except for the *garam masala* and continue to cook for another 2 minutes.

Now add the chicken pieces and coat them with the sauce. Cook the chicken in the sauce for 10 minutes, stirring often – this is called '*bhuno*' and ensures the sauce is penetrating the meat.

Now lower the heat and cover the chicken. Cook on a low heat until the chicken is cooked through (about 40 minutes) stirring every 10 minutes or so.

Now add the water, bring to the boil and simmer with the lid off until the sauce is thicker, this take about 10 to 15 minutes.

Sprinkle over the *garam masala* and cilantro and enjoy.

Chapter 2

The piece of paper in her hand was indeed a photograph, small and curled at the edges. Kiran handed it to Sareeta. It was yellowing around the edges, grey and sepia.

In it were four people. A middle-aged man; he looked quite tall and robust, a Sikh man sporting a fine neat beard and moustache that curled at the edges. He wore a safari suit with thick belt and white turban and had strong, though slightly bowing, legs.

Next to him and slightly shorter was his son. The boy looked 18 or 19. He was slim wearing a white shirt and grey or brown pants. He had thick black framed glasses and a cheeky smirk on his face. There was no mistaking that it was Sareeta's father.

Next to him stood a little lady, maybe in her mid-forties. She didn't smile and looked somewhat haggard. She wore a simple *salwar kameez* with the *duppata* over her head and large gold loop earrings. She also had a tiny nose stud and was much smaller than her husband stood next to her.

Sareeta recognized the parents in the picture as her grandparents on her father's side. She had actually seen this photo many times before as it was framed, along with all the other family photos, on her hallway wall. But this one had an addition that she had not seen before; in the arms of her grandmother was a baby.

"Where did you get this from, Kiran?" Sareeta asked as the photo was handed round.

"It was the strangest thing, Mama. I was at Annie's house while her Mom was making me tea (she insisted!) and this old lady comes up to me and presses this into my hand! I barely had time to look at it and she'd gone."

"So you don't know who it was?" asked Sareeta

"Well, I asked Annie's sister, who said it was her Mom's old nanny who they regard as family now. She flew over with them from Kenya. Apparently she's as old as death but Annie's mom was practically brought up by her so she had to be here for the wedding. She must be 80 at least!"

"Did she say anything to you when she gave you the photo?"

"She mumbled something, I couldn't quite make out, but it sounded like 'find baby' or 'my baby' or something like that."

Jai handed the photo back to Sareeta.

"What do you think?" she asked him

He shrugged his shoulders. "I don't think it's anything. It's probably his cousin or something. I wouldn't worry about it. Come on, let's go to bed, Saru, I'm exhausted."

"Yeah," added Rishi, "you know that's the trouble with you people, you always need to make a conspiracy out of a crisis!"

"Well, a) there's no crisis b) it's in our genes and c) you're also one of you people!" retorted Sonia. "Come on, guys, we'll do the post wedding dissection tomorrow. My feet are killing me!"

Sareeta gathered her things and got up. She was still clutching at the photo when her and Jai arrived into their room and climbed into bed. Within minutes, Jai was snoring contentedly but Sareeta kept staring at the photo, feeling that there was something not right.

The photo was the exact same one they had hung up on their wall minus the baby. She knew that her dad's family had moved to Kenya in 1952 when he was five years old. He had told her that the British Government had given incentives for professional Indians to move to Kenya. His father had been a teacher and made quite a name for himself in Kenya.

When Satvinder had moved to England to study, his mother and father had followed. But they had died very shortly after the move, his father first and his mother a few months later. Sareeta had not really known them.

Most of Sareeta's family were East-African Indians since her mother had also been born and grew up in Kenya. They had a culture and cuisine of their own, the result of Indo-Paks being thrust together in a foreign land. There seemed to be less of a divide between clans and religious groups although she had understood that, socially, they had remained separate. Most

Indian immigrants to Kenya had gone as labourers to build the railway from Nairobi to Mombasa but her family were different.

On her father's side, there had been teachers, engineers, doctors and businessmen investing in the various fields. Her mother's side were cloth merchants, importing cottons and silks and selling them to the European gentry and the vastly growing Indian communities. The communities had grown and East African Indians formed one of the largest diaspora in England where she had grown up.

Their way of cooking had always fascinated her, maybe because she was acutely aware that she had to learn to re-cook following her marriage to the more traditional north Indian fare that her husband, and more importantly at that time, her in-laws, were accustomed to. The fusion element in the food had always interested her too, the use of African staple foods like cassava and maize. The spices also seemed to have blended and some spices which would normally be found in South Indian cuisine had made their way into most everyday dishes she had eaten at home although neither her mother nor father had ever even visited South India.

Her mind had wondered too far and she brought herself back to the predicament in front of her. Something made her feel uncomfortable inside; she felt prickly and unsettled. She knew, despite what her husband and head had quite sensibly pointed out, the baby in the photos had some family significance and she needed to find out. The most obvious thing to do was to ask her dad the following morning in a casual, nonchalant kind of way. With that in her mind, and the exhaustion of spending the last eight hours in three-inch, jeweled stilettos, she put the photo on the bedside cabinet and switched off the light. She fell asleep quickly, listening to the gentle hum of her snoring husband next to her.

The following morning, the dining hall of the hotel was full of bleary-eyed relatives and friends excitedly regaling tales of the previous night. The silks and taffetas were exchanged for denim and stretch fabrics and the pointed heels for flat pumps and sneakers. Sareeta, in all the post wedding dissection, had all but forgotten about what had seemed so important the night before.

The day after a major family function was so much more intimate than the actual event she thought. She had time to talk to her aging aunts and uncles and share niblets of gossip with her cousins. In the time it had taken to demolish 400 pancakes, 800 rashers of bacon, 75 English muffins, 300 slices of Scottish smoked salmon, 400 breakfast sausages, a gallon of maple syrup and a mountain of hollandaise amongst various other breakfast items, Sareeta had learned that various extensions of the family unit had gone off to college, got married, divorced, had babies, left the country, changed sexual orientation, bought businesses, cars, boats and much more. Her head was reeling.

Her parents had not shown for breakfast and she had not noticed until now.

"Hey, kids," she spotted Kiran, Rishi and Sonia huddled in a corner with a pot of coffee and a plate of pastries "Have you seen your *Nana* or *Nani* this morning?"

"I saw *Nani* this morning," replied Sonia "I knocked for her thinking she may want to come down with us. But she said *Nana* wasn't feeling good and had ordered tea in their room."

"Oh, what was wrong with Dad?"

"She didn't say but I think he just wanted some quiet time, he looked really tired yesterday."

"I'll just pop up and see them then," replied Sareeta and turned away from the group to head up the elaborate central staircase just outside of the hall.

As she arrived at their door, she could hear raised voices behind it. The door was slightly ajar, maybe they had been ready to head out. She pushed it a little but did not go in.

"Why did you think no one would ever find out?" She heard her mother's voice.

"It was years ago, Meera, it was a terrible time. You don't know what we went through back then," her father replied

"I know, *mere jaan*," Meera always referred to her husband as 'my darling', "but it was wrong and you know it. We should have told them a long time ago. They deserve to know."

"Look, what we did, we did for them. She's had a good life, we've given both of them everything. We did nothing wrong. It's best we just forget about it, I don't think she would have said anything to them, I don't think she even knew who we were."

"Yes, but what if she did recognize us? She's the only other one who knew. And you know she always thought we shouldn't have done it. I can't believe it, *mere jaan*, I just can't believe it. I thought it was forgotten!"

Sareeta heard her mother break down into soft stifled sobs. Instinctively now, she knocked and pushed wide open the door.

"Hey, what's up? You didn't come to breakfast, is everything okay?"

Her parents looked at each other and at her. After what seemed like many minutes, although it can really only have been a few seconds, her father took a deep breath.

"Sit down, *Beti*," he said, "I have a story to tell you."

Meera's Mogo Chips – An East-African Indian Dish

You Will Need

2 Cassava
Large pot of boiling salted water
4 cups vegetable oil
1 lemon
2 tsps. salt
2 tsps. chilli powder
1 tbsp. fresh cilantro chopped
Tamarind sauce to serve

What to Do

Peel the cassava (mogo) and cut into wedges approx. 2 inches by ½ inch – the same size as potato wedges

Plunge into the boiling water and simmer until tender – approx. 10 minutes

Drain and cool

Heat the oil in a *karahi* or large chef's pan to medium hot. Break off a tiny piece of mogo and put in the hot oil to check if it is hot enough, it should sizzle straight away and remain floating at the top.

Then add all the 'chips' to the hot oil and deep fry until golden brown and crunchy on the outside.

Drain on kitchen paper and transfer to a place.

Sprinkle over the salt and chilli powder and squeeze over the lemon.

Finally sprinkle over the chopped cilantro and enjoy hot dipped into a tamarind sauce.

Chapter 3

India, October 1947

"Push, *Memsaab*, I can see the head!" The birthing attendant was ready with the razor to cut the cord and cotton sheet to swaddle the baby as she reached between Baljinder's knees, ready to receive the head.

Baljinder was young but having her third child. This time was different from the others; she was alone. Riots had terrorized her village, her family and friends had fled, food was scarce and she too had taken the terrifying train journey across the border trying to reach an area of safety, swollen with her seven-month pregnant belly and her other two children in tow.

She had been happy before in her village, her small but growing family, her life with her husband and two children, the joy of this third child coming. But then the lines had been drawn and they were on the wrong side. She had heard the rumours of the troubles in Lahore, even before the boundaries were decided. She had listened with increasing fear as she heard the tales of Sikhs and Hindus being stabbed and killed, arson attacks on their business and numerous injuries in the sectarian violence.

It was after this that her husband Harjinder had decided she needed to go to Delhi with their children.

"I'll close things here and then follow you," he had said. "Don't worry about me, I'll be coming but let me see what I can do here. We can't live off your brother; we need some things of our own."

But he hadn't come and she didn't know if he would.

She didn't want to leave Sindhiwala; she had come as a young bride and made it her home. She couldn't say how old she was, her birthday was 1st January but she didn't know what year. But she knew she had only become a woman in the real sense of the word recently. She had remembered the pain of being cleaved from her parents' home, the only home she had known, and being brought to Sindhiwala by her new family.

She didn't know Harjinder, she'd never seen the man with whom she would share her most intimate self with until that day. But she had liked him immediately. He had kind eyes and a gentle spirit. He spoke softly to her and treated her respectfully that first night.

She hadn't known what to do, her mother had warned her that it would hurt but she must not make a sound. She had said that this was her marital duty and the service of the woman to the man. The man would protect her, clothe her and feed her and she must in return be his right hand. She must revere him as a God, never look at him disdainfully and serve him in the bedroom as in the kitchen. She should respect her new mother and father and her new brother-in-law and sister-in-law. She must recognize that she has a role in her new family to make herself helpful, willing and never to bring shame to her own family.

Harjinder had not made love to her that night. He had spoken softly to her, asking her questions about herself. What did she like doing? What was her favourite colour? What food was her favourite? By the time they had fallen asleep, she realized he knew all there was to know about her but she had asked him nothing. The next night, he had taken her into his arms and his smell was already familiar. She boldly explained to him that he knew everything about her but she knew nothing of him. So she asked the same questions.

Even today, she remembered every single one of his answers. He liked playing cricket in the summer when the evenings reduced the earth to a balmy coolness. In the monsoon, he liked reading Ernst Hemingway as the rains hammered down, making the garbage from the gutters float like lotuses on a pond. And in the winter, he would wrap up warm and go with his friends and brother for hot fresh *jalebis* from the *mithawalla* in the village. He described the warm steam and sweet cardamom smell coming straight out of his banana leaf bag as their crunchy sticky spiral treasures nestled within. His favourite colour was red because red was the colour of passion and he felt that whatever one did in life, one should at least do it with passion. And his favourite food was *mattar paneer*, the softness of the homemade *paneer*, the sweetness of the peas shelled that day and the spiciness of the sauce.

By the end of the first week, she was in love. And it was only then that he gently caressed her shoulder, covered them with slight kisses and slowly worked his way down her arms, stopping at the inside of her wrists before loosening her braid and letting her hair fall over her nakedness. He was gentle with her and guided her as if he had no right to her although she was his right completely.

She fell pregnant within a few months and Kuldeep Singh was born healthy and strong. A year later, she was pregnant again with Balbinder Kaur. Gandhi-*Ji* and Nehru had been imprisoned for two years when she was carrying Balbinder and the Muslim League had taken centre stage in Indian politics. She had never been involved with the men's discussions over politics, preferring the confines of the family kitchen and the familiarity of the young children around her, her own and her nieces and nephews. But she remembered overhearing Harjinder talking to his brother and other people from the village in hushed tones, Muslims, Sikhs, Hindus sitting together. Friends.

"They're saying a separate country for the Muslims, what will that mean for us? Should we also be having a separate land? And separate land for Sikhs too? We've always lived together and lived well, we are brothers, Bhai Saab, no!" One of the villagers spoke to Harjinder

"Yes, but Jinnah has already passed the resolution Kumar Saab," Harjinder had replied. "I'm not so sure that Gandhi-*Ji* can do anything to stop this. Independence may mean partition of the country. Jinnah has said independence and divide."

"Yes and why not? We will still be brothers but you must know we are oppressed here; we are not free to be ourselves. Gandhi-*Ji* himself is a Hindu so don't you think preference will be given to his own? No, no, we must have a separate land where we can be free to practice our way of living. Our identity is Muslim. Jinnah-Saab is right, we cannot exist as one nation when we are a minority," she heard Fariq-Bhai speak.

She had left before she could hear much more but it was after this that Harjinder started speaking more about moving to Delhi. She didn't know the intricacies of what was happening but she knew that the peace around them had been disturbed. Harjinder and her brother-in-law were more distracted and pensive, the village women began to stick to their own kind more and the children were encouraged to play in the courtyard with the gates closed rather than out in the gullies like they used to. Her *Bhabi* had told her that times were changing and India was changing. Their role was to make sure the men were fed and the children were kept out of the way.

"It's men's work, Bali-*Ji*," she would say. "We must just make sure that they have nothing else to concern them, everything here should run smoothly."

In 1947, when both independence and partition had been agreed and sectarian violence was increasing, Harjinder had put her and the children on the train to Delhi. He had held her tight before she boarded the over-packed train and she had strained out of the small window trying to get the last glimpse of him as walked away.

Baljinder's sister-in-law had already fled back to her own village, fearing the worst and they did not know if she had arrived. Harjinder and her brother-in-law had stayed back in Sindhiwala hoping, against hope, that they could salvage something and start up new in the newly formed India.

But now she was here, in Delhi, in her brother's house, not knowing where Harjinder was or if he would return. Baljinder thought that she would have felt something in her spirit if he had been killed. She had convinced herself that he would come. She would wait and when he came, he would find his wife and children waiting for him. But she was all too aware the money he had sent her with was running out and she didn't know how long her brother could keep her and her children. She didn't know what she would do, how she would feed them, clothe them, keep them.

Satvinder was born healthy that morning, cold and damp in Delhi. Her brother's wife, her *Parjai*, had not attended, resentful of the extra mouths to feed when food was already stretched to maximum. She had reluctantly sent for a birthing assistant but had pre-warned Baljinder that she herself would be paying for the privilege. The birth of Kuldip and Balbinder had been such joyous events with Harjinder and his brother pacing anxiously outside in the courtyard whilst her sister-in-law had mopped her brow and rubbed her back. But today, there was no rejoicing, no tears of joy, no slapped backs and pegs of whisky to celebrate. Satvinder was born and all stayed quiet. Baljinder looked at the sleeping infant in her arms and cried.

October came and went and with it rumours of atrocities as thousands of Hindus and Sikhs fled Pakistan and thousands of Muslims fled India. Baljinder heard stories of trains loaded with corpses arriving in Delhi, the carriages seeping with the blood of her kinsmen. She tried to switch off, not wanting to think or know if Harjinder was one of them. She heard of babies being hacked out of pregnant mothers' abdomens and breasts cut off and placed in bags. She heard stories of rape, abductions, infanticide. She felt sick; she felt lonely; she felt lost; she felt poor.

Her brother's wife mocked her daily. "How long will you live off us?" she would say. "You are still young, there will be some men who will give you a few *annas* for five minutes of you."

October turned into November and still no word from Harjinder. The winter passed slowly and the violence continued. She continued to hear of tragedies and heard her sister-in-law wailing one afternoon.

"*Parjai*, what's the matter?" asked Baljinder.

"What is it to you? Why should you care? You're here eating our food, breathing our air, living like some Maharani! Why couldn't it have been you? *Hai Bhagwan*!!" she started banging her chest. "*Hai Bhagwan!*"

Baljinder later discovered that her *Parjai's* sister, for fear of being raped or forced into conversion, had thrown herself into the village well. Already full of bodies, she had not drowned but been hauled out, raped and killed. No one knew what happened to her three-year-old daughter and seven-year-old son.

Baljinder knew deep in her heart that Harjinder may never return. Her brother may have been willing to keep her but her *Parjai* would not. She had to find strength and make some future for her children, for herself. By now, she did not particularly have any stamina or will to live but she had no option to die; she was alive, for now she was safe, she had children and no husband, she had to make a plan.

In the spring of the following year, Satvinder was six months. He was nursing some but had started to take rice mixed with milk. He was starting to sit on his own and he slept well. He was a happy baby, full of laughs and smiles. Her brother, Satvinder's *mamma*, loved him. His *mammi* tolerated him but the depression had come over her since the news of her sister and she mostly just sat in her room weeping as Baljinder did the household chores.

It was in that season that Baljinder's sister and brother in law came to visit from Dehradun. As children, Baljinder and her sister Paramjeet had played together, her sister being only a year or two older than her. Since their respective marriages, the sisters had known little of each other as their lives were now one with their husbands and not their own any more but they had heard news of each other, usually from their brother. Baljinder knew that Paramjeet had married a teacher and landowner although she herself had been unable to attend the wedding as she was late in her pregnancy and the wedding was to take place very quickly after the families had agreed. She felt that Paramjeet must have been somewhat happy and safe in Dehradun, away from the atrocities that were ravaging Punjab and Delhi. She knew that they had some land and a small house, they had tenants farming the land and they were happy. But there was one thing that plagued this young couple; Paramjeet was barren and destined to stay that way.

It did not take long for Baljinder to decide to give Satvinder away to her sister. Kuldeep and Balbinder would need to stay with her. In a few years, Kuldeep could work and Balbinder would be able to help with the household chores. She may be able to convince her *Parjai* to keep them on that basis; they would, after all, be cheaper than keeping the servants she currently had. And without a baby to look after, Baljinder herself could work harder in the house and maybe *Parjai* could dispense of the servants straight away.

On a bright spring morning in April, Baljinder took some rice and milk and mixed it in a tiffin. She wrapped some clothes and swaddling for Satvinder in a large cotton sheet. She brought up the four corners and knotted the cloth and handed it to Paramjeet's husband. She took her baby her arms.

He was smiling and gurgling, *kajol* framing his big brown eyes and his hair freshly massaged with coconut oil. She smelled him for the last time and handed him over to her sister.

"Be safe, *Puttar*," she whispered, "be safe and be happy."

A week later, Harjinder walked through the door.

Harjinder's Mattar Paneer

You Will Need

4 litres whole milk
2 tbsp. white vinegar of lemon juice
1 tsp. salt
4 cups vegetable or sunflower oil + 2 tbsps. extra for *masala*
2 cups shelled peas
1 large onion
6 tomatoes chopped
6 cloves garlic, chopped finely
2 green chilies chopped finely
1 tsps. cumin seeds
Pinch asafetida
2 tsps. Salt
1 tsp. chili powder
1 heaped tsp. turmeric
1 heaped tsp. cumin powder
1 heaped tsp. coriander powder
2 cups water
1 tsp. *garam masala*
1 tbsp. cilantro leaves

What to Do

In a large pan, heat the milk until simmering but not boiling. Add the vinegar/lemon and salt.

The milk will separate into curds and whey.

Place a muslin over a colander or sieve and pour the milk mixture through, the curds will collect and the whey fall through.

Bring up the corners of the muslin and squeeze over the curds to squeeze out extra whey. Place a plate over the curds still in the muslin on the colander and place some heavy weight on the plate, leave to drain for another 30 minutes – the *paneer* is made.

In this time, you can shell the peas and chop the garlic and vegetables.

Now heat the oil to medium hot.

Unwrap the *paneer* and cut into bite-sized cubes. When the oil is hot, deep fry the *paneer* cubes in batches until they are golden brown, set to one side.

In a large *karahi*, heat the 2 tbsps. oil. When hot but not smoking, add the whole cumin and let it splutter, this will take about 30 seconds.

Now add the onion and fry until golden. Add the garlic and chopped green chili now and continue to fry for another 5-7 minutes until all is browned.

Now add the tomatoes and continue to cook for another 7 to 10 minutes, the tomatoes will cook down to a pulp with the onion mix.

When you see oil sizzling around the edges, you can sprinkle over the spices, adding a splash of water if you get any sticking. Cooke this out for a further 5 minutes.

Add the water and let the sauce bubble. Reduce the heat and simmer until the sauce is thicker. It can be as thick or thin as you want, you may want to simmer longer (for a thicker sauce) or add more water (for a thinner sauce). (Harjinder prefers his thick as he likes to eat it with *chappatis*.)

Now add the *paneer* cubes and peas and simmer for a further 10 minutes until the peas are cooked through.

Sprinkle over the *garam masala* and fresh cilantro.

Chapter 4

Atlantic Canada, 2017

Sareeta looked at her father. He looked troubled but calm at the same time. Although he had not yet started on his story, she felt nauseous. She knew that, whatever was coming next, it would change her life irreversibly.

"I was only five when we left Dehradun," he started. "Most of the trouble had passed but that doesn't mean life was easy and there was peace. I don't remember much of my life there but my father would tell me the stories. Dehradun had some troubles though not as bad as Delhi and Lahore. The years before we left, he had been confronted by Muslim mobs demanding he take off his turban and cut his hair. He was rescued by our Muslim neighbours. Other things had happened to him and *Biji* but he told me he had managed to keep safe. The communities protected each other and there were still good people on both sides protecting their friends. One year, something bad had happened. He didn't tell me too much but I remember his words well. He cried as he told me, he felt bad about something, I knew. 'Beta,' he had said to me, 'no matter how much you dress a donkey in fine linens, he will always find his way back to the mud.' I didn't know what he meant. I didn't know what he meant."

The old man broke down into tears; Sareeta's mother came and placed her arm around him. "Stop it now," she said gently, "we don't have to go any further."

Sareeta said nothing. Her years as a physician had taught her that if she wanted an answer, not to speak; the silence would be broken by the other party.

Satvinder composed himself.

"It turned out that *Biji* had been able to have a child before I came to them. She had married in 1945 and had a baby girl in 1946. One night, she had been at home. The troubles had just started. Your Dada had been at the school and she was at home with the baby. He had wanted to come home early but there was work to be done and by the time he left, it was dark. From a distance, he could make out the smoke rising from his *kothi* but by the time he reached the big house, it was too late. The field had been burned and the house was on fire. He ran in and found her in the corner of the room. She had blood over her salwar which was ripped.

"Your Dada carried her out of the flames and lay her on the ground; she was half dead. He shook her to find out where the baby was but she didn't say anything. The tenants who farmed the field took them in to their home and cleaned her up. She didn't say anything for days and refused to eat. She just wept. She never revealed what had happened to her but it was clear to the town's folk what had happened.

"The child was never found, there were no remains in the big house. Although *Biji* never spoke of what happened, she would not allow your Dada to do any funeral rites for their daughter.

"Over the next couple of years, your Dada rebuilt the house and the farm with the tenants; they had farmed that land for many generations. They tried to carry on with their lives as if nothing happened. She never talked of that night and neither did he. I came to them the next year and after a while, we moved to Kenya. No one spoke of what happened but I knew that *Biji* cherished me more that an adopted son would deserve."

Sareeta spoke, "How do you know this, Dad? If no one spoke of it?"

"When your Dada died, we had to sell his estate in Dehradun. I was 20 and had been married for a few months."

"So you'd moved from Kenya when exactly, Dad?" Sareeta asked, confused

"I went to England when I was 19 and your mother came over and we married in 1967; we were very young.

"I went to Dehradun to do the formalities after *Pita-Ji* died; I went alone. The tenants had been there for many years and I met the son of the tenant who had the land and the house when we left for Kenya. They had taken the *kothi* too as caretakers.

"We had a great night, his wife had cooked up a feast fresh *sabzi*, *pilau* rice, fresh *rotis* in the tandoor and they had even killed a chicken to make us *tandoori* chicken. I remember the smell of the coal. It was a cold night but his wife was out lowering chicken into the tandoor and bringing it out charred and smoky; it was and is the most beautiful chicken I have ever had, so moist, so smoky. And then he brought out a bottle of rum. I didn't take any, of course, but he kept taking peg after peg.

"It was then that he told me that the man who had violated our family had died. I didn't know what he meant. He told me that his father had told him the story of what had happened to *Biji*; he was a good few years older than me so remembered some of the events himself. Rumours had been rife in the town for many years because the Khan family had been one of the few Muslim families not to leave for Pakistan. 'And why should they?' he had said to me, 'Rizwan Khan was himself the leader of the mob.'

The Khan family was synonymous with wealth, power and prestige. They were big landowners around Dehradun and had many tenants as well as farming their own land. They used to lend money to the poorer folk and were the arbiters for their own communities. Rizwan Khan had inherited the land from his ancestors and the thought of giving it all up to move to the newly formed Pakistan just was not going to happen to him.

"The tenant told me that he and *Papa-Ji* were great friends before the trouble, they had grown up amongst the same paddy fields and played cricket together on the streets. They had both served together in the Indian army. There were also rumours that both *Papa-Ji* and Rizwan Khan had wanted to marry *Biji* but she had, of course, chosen your Dada. Her family would never have allowed her to marry anyone other than a full bearded Sikh.

"When the troubles started in Lahore and Delhi, Rizwan Khan understood that he may lose his family's inheritance and would not allow that to happen. He had spoken to *Papa-Ji* about leaving as the trouble may come to Dehradun but *Papa-Ji* had refused; he would not listen and he would not go; *Papa-Ji* was a very stubborn Sikh man. The tenant told me that there had been a big fight between Rizwan Khan and your Dada and Khan had vowed to have his day, and his revenge, on *Papa-Ji*.

"No one could be sure, he had told me, but Rizwan Khan was thought to have taken *Biji* himself and damaged her so badly that she could no longer have any children. He had taken her child and burned the house and crops, leaving her inside for dead.

Your Dada rescued her body but her soul may as well have burned as she was beyond repair."

"What happened to the baby?" Sareeta asked

"The tenant said the rumour was baby was taken to Pakistan by Rizwan Khan."

"Why didn't Dada do anything? Why didn't he go to the police? Why didn't he find this Rizwan Khan?" Sareeta was protesting although she knew there was little point.

"*Beti*, what could he do? Riots were happening everywhere, police had no control and some even said they were instigating the riots. Children were being taken, women raped, arson and destruction all over. Dehradun was affected less, but that does not mean it was not affected. *Biji* never spoke about it and your Dada could have left her or kept her; there was chaos in those times. It wasn't that he chose to do nothing, he had nothing to choose. His daughter was gone, his property burnt to the ground, his wife destroyed. No one would dare accuse the Khan family, they owned most of the land and had many tenants and workers. Even if your Dada had gone to the police, they would not have done anything, the Khan family were not to be touched. He did what he could do; he carried on. And when opportunity came, he left."

"Dad, I've seen the photo," she confessed. "Who is the baby?"

Satvinder said nothing but tears dropped slowly from his brown-grey eyes.

"Sareeta, I think Dad has had enough now," Meera spoke, "I don't think he should speak any more."

"No, I want to finish," Satvinder said.

"After I found out about what had happened to *Biji*, I was numb, then angry. Then I started to think about it all, our move to Kenya, my life there, the depression that *Biji* suffered from, how she became so anxious when I wasn't in her sight and it seemed to make sense, everything except the baby. They had moved to Kenya to try and blot out what had happened to them in India. It was a new start, no memories, no explanations. But I wondered why Kenya and not India. My father was never happy in Kenya, he longed to go home but we never did, not even once to visit. I thought that he had never returned to see his brothers or visit the farm and the tenants. We made a new life for ourselves there. By the time he died in 1967, he was well known and respected; he had set up schools there and led the scouts. He even met the Queen when she went to visit."

"I remember you telling me, I think I've seen that photo too," Sareeta interjected.

"I met the tenant a few days later and we spoke. I asked him why *Pita-Ji* had not come back. 'Saab,' he had said to me, 'he came back every year for many years. He would come to the farm and check. But he never seemed interested. He stayed in the house; we had always kept a room for him. Every evening he would take a walk to the town. He sometimes asked us questions about what had happened to certain families and where they had gone.'

"'Did he ask about Rizwan Khan?' I had asked him. The Tenant had looked away; he had not wanted to answer my question. He tried to tell me that he could not recall and then that it did not matter anymore. Eventually, he agreed. 'All the time *Saab-ji*,' he had said to me, 'all the time.'

"My father stopped visiting in the mid-1960s; the tenant could not tell me the year but he remembered the time well because it was the year Rizwan Khan's grand-daughter disappeared and Khan's son, Feroz, came to the farm in search of her. He came to the farm and terrorized the tenants but they told him nothing. 'The town's folk protected Singh-Saab,' he told me, 'and Feroz Khan left without knowing anything.'

"They never found the girl. The Khan family returned to the farm a few times and tore the *kothi* apart, questioned the tenants but the towns' folk, Sikh men, always came and got them out and back to the town."

"The baby, Dad, what about the baby?"

"The baby girl in the photo just appeared one day when *Pita-Ji* had returned from a trip to Mombasa. Or rather, I thought he had been to Mombasa because I remember him taking trip there every year. Now I know that it was not Mombasa but Dehradun. *Pita-Ji* explained to me that this was my cousin and she was now going to live with us."

"Who is she, Dad? Where is she?" Sareeta asked anxiously.

"The girl did not stay with us for long, the servant girl in the house said she would find a home for her. My father told me not to ask any questions but that it was better for all of us. I remember

Biji weeping all the time while she was with us. The baby used to cry a lot and *Biji* would weep over her saying she was sorry and to forgive her. I was glad when she went, we returned to some kind of normality. I guess I knew all along that she wasn't my cousin but I knew not to ask or even to wonder about it."

"Where is she, Dad?" Sareeta was shaking now, the nausea was rising and the pit of her stomach felt empty.

Satvinder sighed deep. He looked at Meera whose eyes were full of tears of sorrow for her husband and for the news that he was about to reveal to his daughter. He looked up at her. His eyes were red and he had dark shadows underneath. His skin, which had once been pink and ruddy, now had a pale yellow-grey twinge. His cheeks which had been full were now sallow. He looked directly into his daughter's eyes.

"The servant girl is the one who gave Kiran the photo. And the baby in the photo…" He looked at his wife one last time and she slowly nodded. "The baby in the photo…is you."

The Tenant's Wife's Tandoori Chicken

What You Will Need

1 whole chicken, skinned and cut into 10 pieces

First marinade

1 bulb garlic and 3 inches ginger ground into a paste with some water
Juice of 1 lime
2 tsps. black salt

Second marinade

2 cups fresh yoghurt (homemade)
1 tsp. salt
2 tsps. chili powder
2 tsps. ground cumin
2 heaped tsps. *tandoori masala* (homemade)
Wedges lime
Chaat masala for sprinkling (homemade)

What You Will Need to Do

Clean the chicken pieces in cold water and prick all over to allow the marinade to penetrate.

Place in a bowl and add all the first marinade ingredients, mix well. Leave this for a minimum of twenty minutes up to two hours.

Add the second marinade ingredients and mix well. Leave to marinate overnight if possible or minimum four hours.

About an hour before cooking, place coals at the bottom of the tandoor and leave to heat – this takes about 45 minutes and the coals should be white.

Skewer the chicken, 3 or 4 pieces can go on one skewer depending on the size of the tandoor, and lower into the tandoor.

Turn after approximately 10 minutes and again after another 10 minutes to ensure all sides have some charring and smokiness.

Serve hot squeezed with fresh lime and *chaat masala*.

Chapter 5

Rawalpindi, Pakistan, 1946

"Here, just take her. The runt from the dogs!" Shiraz Khan almost threw the baby at the maid.

In her surprised arms, the baby screamed. She was hungry but had no milk and no breast to suckle. The journey from Dehradun had been long, the train had been packed and the passengers had not been permitted to open windows or doors.

Shiraz had travelled alone, leaving his wife and children behind, having only returned to Dehradun at the behest of his cousin Rizwan to carry out an important task. His wife had asked him what madness had entered his head for which he would risk his life and their future. He had not told her, he had not spoken of it, simply informing her that he was going.

But he had been disturbed the night before he had left, pushing the plate of his favoured mutton *biryani* away from him, not even noticing the enticing aroma that rose from the fragrant rice and sweet spices. He had always complimented her on her wonderful *biryanis* but that evening, he had not said a word. She had known then, if she had not already known, what lay ahead of him was not of his wanting but placed upon him and he was under a compulsion to go. It was all that she knew, but it was enough to ensure that the meal intended for the masters of the house became a feast for the servants that night.

Rizwan had explained to Shiraz that their land and property in Dehradun had come under threat by the Indian nationalists in the town.

"We will lose everything cousin," he had explained. "If we don't stop them in their tracks."

"But why involve me?" Shiraz has asked, "Cousin, Lahore, Karachi, '*Pindi*, these are the places to be now. Where we can live with our true brothers and in a land that follows our own

Sharia. Just leave the pigs, my brother, come here. We can start again."

"No, I will not," Rizwan had said firmly. "Don't you understand? This is more than a fight over our land. This is fight for our respect, our name, our forefathers' respect, the very future of our own children! Cousin, our fathers and their fathers before them tilled this land themselves. Their sweat nourished the grain, their might ploughed the land, their integrity, their respect, their honour grew our community. We are more than the landowners. We are the very salt of this community. We cannot leave, we cannot be thrown away after all that our forefathers gave for us to be free here. How will I look at my children's faces knowing that I ran and I took from them what was given to me so easily? No, cousin, I will not do it. We must show these people that they cannot just remove us from our birthright because they want to; they cannot plunder and steal what is ours!"

Shiraz knew he did not feel the same. He had not had the responsibilities nor the rights of his cousin who was the head the family now. Shiraz had been only too happy to move to Rawalpindi, to the small piece of land his family already had there. But he did share some sentiment with his elder cousin. He, not a politician but full of religious fervour, despised the unfaithful polytheistic Hindus whose holy books were full of immoralities and deception.

He feared what living in a country that would be so influenced by fundamental Hindus would be like and what that meant for him and his fellow Muslims. In addition, he had seen with his own eyes what happened when one of them learned a few words of English and threw themselves as servants before the white gentry and he feared what the future may hold even after the British left. He had nothing against the Sikhs and knew Baldev Singh and his family well. It made him uncomfortable to carry out what his cousin had suggested because, inside, he liked Baldev.

"OK, cousin, I will do as you say. But why him? Why now?"

Rizwan could not tell him the truth. He could not tell his cousin what he had only just admitted to himself: the truth that Baldev Singh was not merely a landowner in Dehradun who had wronged him or an innocent just in the wrong place at the wrong time. He could not tell his cousin that he despised Baldev Singh with a guttural hatred so deep and ingrained within him that it had almost been his pleasure to taunt him with threats of taking his property and land into trust.

Baldev had seen his innermost desires and Rizwan had not liked it. Baldev was right about him, Baldev had always been right about him even as children. It was true that he had always wanted what Baldev had, even though he could have had anything. There was something in him that made Rizwan want to have it, whatever 'it' happened to be that day. Baldev was a better cricketer than he but quiet about it. He had ambition and future, the promise of his own success although he should have inherited, like Rizwan, so he himself could never boast. But he didn't boast anyway and Rizwan hated it. His humility was so understated, it was almost arrogant. He walked his fields as a man walks in a park, his hand running through the yellow *sarson* flowers releasing their scent and not as the owner of such a crop who should pick the leaves to check for pestilence. He attracted respect, even though he had no ownership of it like Rizwan's family did. Townsfolk, Hindu, Sikh and Muslim just liked him and respected him and even that for nothing. Rizwan hated it.

And then, there was the girl. How he himself had longed for her with her ample hips and full bosom. The thick wavy hair tied in a long plait with *paranda* at the end matching the colour of her simple *salwar kameez*. Her milky skin, too fair for a girl working in the sun and dark unrevealing eyes, hiding a multitude of dreams and aspirations that he would never uncover. The curves of her waist and rump echoing that of her upper half. But more than this was the rectitude emanating from her. She didn't flirt back with him like the other girls, despite his fanciful ways and Persian features. She hardly looked at him, she didn't want him and he liked to be wanted. She didn't look at Baldev either although Rizwan had guessed his friend's desires for her. But Baldev had got her; he had won the prize and that without even competing. Rizwan hated him.

"Baldev Singh will be the example, cousin, he will be the one we use to show the others that the Khans and all we represent shall not be crushed."

Shiraz knew better than to disobey his cousin. His people were like that, internally they could bicker and fight and not speak. But when a time came to be together against an adversary, they would form together like the fingers of a fist ready to fight against any power, authority or person who would try to come against them. He had taken the train between 'Pindi and Dehradun, some 700 kilometres, for the second time aware of the dangers confronting him. He had arrived safely. He had met with his cousin and the group. Together, the group, some 50 strong had gone to the Baldev Singh's *kothi*.

He had stood outside the gate watching for anyone who may want to disturb the carefully planned program but it was unlikely. The *kothi* was isolated and Baldev was at school. It was a cool evening and he was wrapped in a shawl. First he had heard her pleads for understanding and loyalty in friendship. Then she had begged for his mercy. Then he heard the cries as she had beseeched him to just kill her rather than carry out what he was preparing to do. Finally the screams as he forced himself and then metal objects inside her. Then there was just silence from her and the baby crying in the background.

He had stood and listened, burying the conscience within him that yelled at him to stop what was going on. The background noise of the child crying seemed so insignificant, although had that sound been on its own, he would have found it disturbing and rueful. Now, it seemed like nothing.

The air had been cold that evening but not now. He could see beyond the boundaries of the courtyard the fields ablaze and begin to smell the kerosene in the air. Still at his post, he heard Rizwan order some of the mob to start dousing the *kothi* with kerosene. He had turned to see his cousin stride out of the *kothi*, his clothes dishevelled and *kurta* unintendedly tucked into his *pyjami*, carrying the now screaming infant in his arms. He thrust the child in Shiraz's arms.

"Take her," he had ordered, "take her back."

With that, Rizwan strode off and the smell of burning kerosene filled his nostrils.

Shiraz had not known about the child or that he would be required to take her back to 'Pindi. He didn't quite know what he would do with her. The journey had given him some time to think. He knew that he could not have refused his cousin but Rizwan was not accustomed to being refused. He also knew his wife would not accept the child as her own since she was not a particularly loving mother even to their own children. Her health suffered with the young children around her and her frequency in headaches had increased exponentially since their children had arrived, often forcing her to retire to her room to rest.

But more so than that, she had the same dispassion for the children of India as his cousin. He could enforce that the child was there's to feed and clothe but that was about all; he could do no more to endear the child to her. It was at this moment that Shiraz understood that he could never have any attachment to this child. He knew that she must mean nothing to him; he could not torture himself with thoughts of how she had come to him, what she had lost, what her future now held. He had to dissociate himself and not speak of it. He made a decision never to speak of it, not even to his wife.

The arduous journey had allowed him to be alone with his thoughts and come to terms with what he been involved with, not easily but necessary. He had been fortunate to have a seat on the long journey, the child wrapped in his shawl. He could still smell the kerosene and he could still smell the smoke. When the child had begun to cry, he had not known what to do; he could not quieten her.

"She's hungry," said a haggard-looking woman in the carriage. She had a baby with her too and could not have been more than 25 years. The lines on her forehead spoke of her misfortunes but the stories were so common now the sympathy did not flow as easily as impassivity. "Give her to me."

Shiraz handed the infant over and she lifted the corner of her loose *kameez*. The infant suckled from a stranger's breast and assuaged. When the stranger passed the infant back, she was sleeping and remained that way for the remainder of the journey.

The maid looked at the screaming child in her arms and then at her master.

"She's hungry," he said and walked away.

'Pindi Mutton Biriyani

You Will Need

    1 kg of goat meat on the bone
    2 tbsp. vegetable oil
    2 large onions sliced

1 bulb garlic finely chopped
3 inches ginger finely chopped
4 green chilies sliced finely
1 kg fresh tomatoes chopped
3 tsps. cumin seeds
4 black cardamom pods bruised
Stick cinnamon roughly broken to pieces
2 tsps. salt
2 tsps. turmeric
2 tsps. cumin powder
1 tsp. coriander powder
1 tsp. chili powder
8 cups basmati rice
4 green cardamom pods crushed to expose seeds
Large pinch saffron
1 cup warm milk
2 cups *desi ghee*
4 hard-boiled eggs chopped
1 whole bunch fresh coriander leaves chopped.

What to Do

Firstly, par boil the rice by placing in a large pan with 4 liters of water and the green cardamom pods.

Bring to the boil and simmer for 5 minutes and then drain. The grains should be fluffy and separate but fully cooked through. Set to one side.

Now cook the meat.

In a large *karahi*, heat the oil. When it is hot, add the cumin seeds, black cardamom and cinnamon sticks. Let them sizzle and sputter for about a minute, the aroma should be amazing.

Now add the onions and cook until golden brown, adding a splash of water if needed.

Add the garlic, ginger and fresh chilli and continue to cook until the mixture is dark brown. Again, add a splash of water if needed.

Now add the tomatoes and cook down. This takes about 20 minutes and the oil will separate from the *masala*.

Sprinkle over the ground spices and mix in. Cook for about a minute.

Now add the meat and coat with the *masala*. Cook and continuously stir for about 10 minutes ('*bhuno*').

Now lower the heat and cover. Cook on a low heat until the meat is tender and falling off the bone. This usually takes 1.5 to 2 hours depending upon the size of the meat pieces.

Take a large deep dish. Put the saffron in the milk and let it infuse. Melt the ghee.

Layer 1/3 of the rice over the bottom of the dish. Sprinkle over 1/3 of the saffron infused milk and 1/3 melted ghee.

Now lay 1/3 meat mixture on top.

Now another layer of rice, saffron milk, ghee and another layer of meat.

Repeat again so all the rice, milk, ghee and meat is used.

Cover the dish and place in an oven on a very low heat for 30 minutes.

Take out and run a fork though the rice and meat to fluff up – the rice should still be separate grains and fully cooked now.

Sprinkle over the hard-boiled eggs and cilantro and enjoy with fresh yoghurt.

Chapter 6

Nairobi, Kenya, 1966

"And the child's mother, sir? Where is she?" The Immigration Officer glanced at Baldev Singh's passport.

"She is at home Officer," he replied, "I took the child to see my parents. My wife was too infirm to make the trip."

He nodded and stamped the passport. With a flick of his fingers, the Immigration Officer indicated to his passenger to move on which Baldev did without hesitation. The child, still asleep, was nestled in the crook of his ample sized arm.

Baldev's driver was waiting for him outside with his grey Chevrolet. It was early evening and the sun was touching the horizon. The red earth welcomed him back but he did not feel happy to be home, in the most obvious sense.

When he had arrived in India, the smell welcomed him; it was all too familiar. The earth in India exuded a fragrance that filled his nostrils and penetrated his mind with thoughts of his paddy fields and sheets of yellow mustard plants growing side by side, hot roasted nuts eaten on the roadside and the promise of love from his family and friends waiting for him.

When he returned to Nairobi each time, the red earth tried to welcome him. Welcome him as an immigrant who was bringing with him fortune and hope. But he could not accept it. He could not make this place his home, it felt like betrayal to his native *Bharat*. He could not feel the love of his family and friends, he could not substitute his roast peanuts for roast corn, he could not see fields of yellow promising him a season for his favourite *sarson da saag te makki di roti*.

He knew why he had come to this land, so similar and yet so vastly different. After what had happened to his beloved wife, his love affair with Dehradun has died. He had walked the streets with a heart filled with grief for his wife, his child, himself. His rebuilt house was no longer a home where laughter and warmth abounded; it was an empty shell. His fields, which had harvested the finest basmati rice, now just harvested rice, neither special, nor fragrant, nor pure. Everything had become tainted, his whole world had been defiled and, no matter how much he tried, he could not shake off the feeling.

Rizwan Khan and he had grown up together, eating from each other's mother's dishes, pinching mangoes and lychees from neighbour's gardens and washing off the evidence in the same water. They had laughed and wept together, rivals and brothers, Muslim and Sikh.

As young men, they had teased the girls in the valleys whilst they collected water from the well, circling their long braids with colourful *paranda* ribbons. The boys were mesmerized by the swirling colours of their ribbons and swishy-wishy of their hips. Baldev had been too shy to do anything other than to look and smirk at them but Rizwan had no such timidity.

"Hey, *kanchi*!!" he always used this term when he saw the gaggle of these voluptuous young girls and wanted their attention, "When will you pay as much attention to me as to those ribbons in your hair?"

Some girls giggled and averted their eyes. Paramjeet always lifted her head high and looked in the other direction. How she could look so defiant and so demure at the same time, Baldev had wondered.

"*Yaar*,'" he would say to his friend, "do you want her father to come after you with his *Kirpan*? I've heard he has the biggest sword in the entire state!"

"Bhai," Rizwan always called Baldev 'brother'. "*Hai hai*," he rubbed his chest, "isn't she worth dagger and sword?"

When Baldev's parents had fixed the marriage, Rizwan had been pleased, slapping him on the back as his glowing friend tried not to show his abundant exuberance at the thought of his wife to be.

"Bhai," he had said, "Such a dream girl would be too good for a rascal like me!" He half joked. "You are the half of me that wants to be better so it is right you win the prize. *Inshallah*, I will be blessed with such a treasure as you have."

The paths of the two men took differing courses over the coming years. Rizwan continued in the family business whilst

Baldev became a teacher in the high school and became a father. He loved his baby girl, dedicating every moment that he was not working with playing with her, walking around his field with her and show casing her as his most prized possession. When the troubles began, Rizwan had come over to his house.

"Bhai," he had started, "you and me both know what is happening here. My family have farmed this land for generations; my people belong here. But the times are such that we cannot protect ourselves without force. Mark my words, blood will be shed in the very streets where we have played. You must leave now. I will do what I can to protect your land but I implore you, please go."

"*Yaar*, why should I leave? My family has also been here for generations, our sweat itself has nurtured this soil just as yours has. We are neither Hindu nor Musalman; we have no fight with you, *yaar*. This is my home and this land is my inheritance, I cannot leave it any more than you can," Baldev had replied to him.

"Bhai, understand what you are saying. Blood is going to be spilled. Blood of Hindus and that of Sikhs. Go to Delhi, go to Bombay, go anywhere, just go. I am but one but I am a Khan, I cannot be seen to show mercy to one and not another. I know what you do not, Baldev-Bhai, and I am telling you to go. How can you alone protect all this? There are not enough of you to stop the storm that is coming this way! Just go and leave this with me, start again somewhere, you can teach in Delhi."

Baldev felt his internal temperature rise at Rizwan's words. Maybe it was the way Rizwan had said this, mockingly, carelessly, arrogantly. His heart was thumping in his chest and he began to clench his fists.

"Rizwan, since we have been children, you have always wanted what I have whether toy or food or woman! You could have any kite in all Dehradun but you wanted mine, you could have any mango from any tree but you always wanted the one I picked and even my wife is not free from your desires. Now you want my land too? You want to take my very birthright? I will not let you."

"Baldev, listen to you…"

"I will listen and I will not go. Do your worst, you and your thugs. You cannot take from me. I will defend until the end."

"So be it, brother, you fool! Too many years in your turban has made your brain mush!" Rizwan had got up. "But I swear to you today, I will also defend until the end, but that end will be yours, brother, and not mine!"

Now Baldev was back on the African red soil. Although he had done what he had set out to do, he did not feel the satisfaction; instead numbness. Baldev thought he would have felt something, just something, guilt even, but he just felt indifferent. His driver looked at him and the baby in his arms.

"*Challo*," said Baldev, "let's go."

As he rounded the corner to his house, he could see Paramjeet shelling peas on the verandah. She had on her lap a stainless-steel *thali* already with a mound of potatoes and onions on it. The peas were falling over the vegetables like rain drops on the mountains in Dehradun.

She must have been making *samosas*, he thought, in readiness for his return. She only ever had a vague idea of when he would return and that too only if he had managed to contact the one neighbour in the street who had a telephone to advise her. But she always managed to produce a homecoming meal for him as if she had known his exact coming. Since the atrocity, she had lost the swish of her hips which had enticed him so much, she had lost the air of defiance too and although he could not admit it, he could no longer see her as demure. He almost hated himself whenever he thought of her, such a paradox because he loved her more than himself too.

She had not said anything when he got out of the car with a baby in his arms. She had not asked him anything, she had not questioned the origins of the child, she had not wept, she had not smiled. She looked at him with no hint of curiosity. The breeze had blown the *dupatta* off her head. She pulled it back over, lowered her eyes and departed to the kitchen to make tea.

By the time she returned with the tray, the child had woken and was crying. In anticipation, she had heated some milk and took the baby from her husband. With a small cup, she fed the child while he sat silently, drinking his tea and watching her.

Later that night, Satvinder returned from his evening tuition. Ecstatic to see his *Pita-Ji*, but also ever respectful, Satvinder bowed to touch his father's feet. He blessed Satvinder before he noticed his mother with the baby. Only then was an acknowledgement of the babe made at all.

"This is your cousin, she is staying here, that is all you need to know," Baldev-Singh had said.

Paramjeet tried to look after the child but she knew who she was and why she was there. Over the coming days, she could not forget and accommodate. Her silence turned into weeping, a grief that she could neither understand herself nor explain to anyone else. In a perverse way, she knew that this child was to replace the child she had lost, almost like a gift from her husband. She knew that other children had been taken and given in acts of both love, like Satvinder, and revenge. Some children had been accepted and some despised. Paramjeet did not have it in her to despise this child, who through no wish of her own was here in this foreign land, like Paramjeet herself. But she neither had the capacity to love her.

A few weeks passed and her weeping pervaded everything she did like the smell that rose from the gutters in the height of the summer; starting as a mere trace of odour and increasing over the days to an almighty stink. The servant girl noticed more than anyone else that this baby was destroying the little strength her mistress had left.

"Memsahib," she said one morning when Paramjeet was so afflicted, she was unable even to hand out chores for the day, "let me take her away from you. I know someone who can take care of her, a good family, Memsahib. She will grow up happy."

Paramjeet looked deep into the girl's eyes. The girl was Gujarati, simple and kind. She must have been in her twenties or so. She was unmarried and had no family. Paramjeet knew nothing more about her. After a while, Paramjeet spoke.

"No," she said. "No family will take this child. Only you yourself will have her. You will take care of her and bring her up; you will be her mother, sister, aunty and friend. Only you, I will only give her to you."

When Baldev returned from school that evening, the baby had gone as had the servant girl. Paramjeet stood alone at the stove, stirring a pot of *daal*, her back to her husband. In the same way that she had not questioned where the child had come from, he did not ask where the child had gone. Paramjeet had known the child was taken from the Khans to avenge her lost child,

Baldev knew the child had now been handed over to the servant girl because he had not been able to fill the black hole that was slowly engulfing his wife.

He sat out on the verandah and stared at the red earth. He thought about his life in Kenya, what he had achieved in the short years he had been here. He was celebrated as a fine immigrant setting up schools and scout groups. He was well known in his community and others, a highly respected teacher. They knew him as 'Master Saab'. He had a fine house, respectable family, a good car with a driver and more. He was dressed in fine linens.

Satvinder came out disrupting his thoughts. "*Pita-Ji?*" he enquired, "what are you doing here?"

He looked at his son, a fine young man, soon to leave for England to study. Only now did Baldev feel something for what he had done. Pain and guilt came crashing down on him, looking at the innocent face of his son. It rained down on him, sharp and biting. What had he done? What had he done? How could he have thought this would give him the justice he had searched for all these years?

"Oh, my son," he said as he finally broke down into loud sobs, "oh, my son."

And then he used a proverb that Satvinder had heard before but not referring to his own father. "No matter how much you dress a donkey in fine linens, he will always find his way back to the mud."

Satvinder never forgot his father's words although he had not understood the meaning at that time. It was only over the coming years that he understood that his father wore the outer garments of a respected man, a coveted character, an example of integrity. And yet, he had acted like a country bandit because his inner being desired revenge so much.

After Baldev died, and Satvinder found out the horrible truth of the mystery baby, he knew that only he must put an end to the cycle of bitterness and revenge that had swallowed up both his parents. He made up his mind to find the child and bring her home.

Baldev Singh's Homecoming *Samosas*

What You Will Need
Samosa pastry

4 cups plain flour
Enough warm water to make a soft pliable dough
1 cup plain flour mixed with water to make a paste, the consistency of porridge
½ cup oil for rolling

Samosa filling

1 tbsp. mustard oil
1 tsp. mustard seeds
1 tsp. cumin seeds
4 medium potatoes peeled and cut into small cubes about 5 mm square
1 medium onion chopped finely as the potato
2 cups fresh peas
3 fresh green chilies chopped
2 tsps. salt
2 tsps. cumin powder
1 tsps. *garam masala*, preferably home made
1 tsp. turmeric
Cup of water
2 tbsp. fresh cilantro chopped
1 tbsp. fresh mint chopped
1 litre vegetable oil for deep frying in a large *karahi*

What You Will Need to Do

First, make the samosa shells. Take a small piece of dough, about the size of a walnut and roll into a ball. Repeat so you have 2 balls, flatten slightly to 2 thick discs.

With your fingers, dab oil into the flat side of one disc and sandwich them together

Now roll both together to the size of a saucer.

Because of the oil barrier, you should be able to separate the 2 thin discs (the point of rolling two together is to ensure they are thin).

Cook each disc for 30 seconds on each side on a hot *tawa*/griddle and cut in half – you should have 4 semi-circles.

Continue to do this until all the dough is used and you have a pile of semicircle '*rotiayaan*'.

Now make the filling.

Heat the mustard oil until it smokes and add the mustard and cumin seeds. Let them splutter for 30 secs and then add the potatoes and onions.

Reduce the heat to the lowest and coat the vegetables in the oil.

Sprinkle over all the spices and stir.

Cover and let the vegetables sweat for 10 minutes, adding a splash of water if needed to prevent sticking.

Now add the chopped chilies and peas and water and stir again.

Let the vegetable mixture cook until the vegetables are cooked through and the mixture is dry.

Add the cilantro and mint and mix through. Leave the mixture to cool before filling the *samosas*.

To make the *samosas*, take a semi-circle *roti* and fold 1/3 over. Use your finger to spread the paste on this 1/3 – the side facing you.

Fold the other side over the pasted 1/3 so you have a cone shape.

Take the cone in your hand so the opening is facing upwards and the point downwards, like a funnel in your hand.

Fill the cone with the cooled vegetable filling, leaving about 1 cm all around the open top.

Again, use your finger to put paste all over the 1 cm rim of the cone and then pinch together so you have a filled triangle.

Heat the vegetable oil to medium hot, you can check by taking a tiny piece of dough and dropping it in, it should sizzle and float straight to the top.

Fry the *samosas* in batches until golden and serve with any seasonal chutney that you have, although tamarind chutney is excellent.

Chapter 7

Atlantic Canada, 2017

Sareeta just stared at her father. At first, everything seemed to slow down as if she were watching herself and her parents on a movie with the slow-motion button pressed. The news echoed around her like a bullet ricocheting off the walls of a steel room.

"The baby is you…the baby is you…"

It didn't sink in, it just went round and round and round.

She sat, before she collapsed, on the edge of the bed staring at her father in his wheelchair and her mother stood behind him, her hand on his shoulder. They looked back at her, expectant of a reaction but she couldn't react, she didn't know how to, she didn't know what to feel. It wasn't that she felt numb, she did indeed feel sad, but it felt like the news was unrelated to her. As if someone had just told her some gossip about someone distant she knew; the most unbelievable story but true. But at the same time, she was shaking, she felt faint, she felt sick.

"I need to go," she said.

"Sareeta…" her dad implored, "Sareeta…"

"I need to check on the guests…I need to say goodbye…I've got to pack…" She said all of this without looking at him and then she got up, turned her back on him and walked out.

She wasn't sure how she made it back to the foyer where a small queue of her relatives had collected, waiting to check out. Jai was not around or not that she could see, and she couldn't see her kids either. She scanned the foyer and what she could see of the main hall for them; not that she really wanted to see them or felt overwhelmingly that she needed to; she just needed a focus. She needed to be seen to be busy or someone may talk to her. They did anyway.

"Hey, Saru, good job! What next? You should be a party planner!" Her cousin was talking to her, or who she thought of as her cousin anyway.

"Err thanks, Sandy," she spoke but not really to Sandy. She was still scanning. "Have you seen Jai?"

"No, honey, hey, are you ok? You look kinda pale."

"Yes, I'm fine. I just need to find Jai," she frowned and walked toward the hotel entrance.

In the corner of her eye, she saw Sandy shrug her shoulders and carry on talking to the relatives in the queue.

Down the steps and onto the gravel driveway, across the lawn, the expanse of the ocean was still apart from gentle waves unfurling their white fringe on the sand in front of her. The sun shone, glistening on the still blue water.

The water is so calm, so gentle and so deceiving, she thought.

Dangers hidden beneath the serenity of the ocean and no one knew because the surface looked so calm. But there were currents underneath that could grab someone when they were not expecting it and lure them into death. It could happen in minutes, a whole life gone in minutes. A whole existence just gone.

She couldn't say how long she sat there for but it cannot have been for that long; her guests were leaving and she was needed.

"Mama, we've been looking for you everywhere. What are you doing out here?" It was Kiran. She looked beautiful. She was beautiful. Sareeta had waited for a few years to conceive her first born and when Kiran had finally been born, she could not have been cherished more.

There were many things, along life's path, that Sareeta had felt she was entitled to but children were never one of them. Each child, she knew, was a gift from God. But Kiran she cherished especially, because she was the first and because she was the most longed for. She had worked hard at mothering, trying to have special moments and special memories with each of them, times of intimacies that they could not have as a common reference.

Moments with Kiran like getting her nails painted professionally when she was just 7, going for a grown-up lunch date when she was a teenager and driving her to college without Jai whenever she could. Kiran had become a 'helper-mom' with the others who often confided in their elder sister before their mother. She represented them, and she represented Sareeta.

Kiran's wedding day had been very different to Dharam's, largely because Kiran was not only a painful perfectionist, but also because she had chosen to do much of the planning herself. She had exquisite taste and was well known in the family firm for being the creative one.

If Kiran chose a new product line, it would just take off. If Kiran endorsed a practice, it just worked. If Kiran felt that an individual just wasn't right for the organization, they were not. Her wedding had been perfect with an absolute balance of intimacy and inclusiveness, solemnness and light-heartedness, passion and passivity. Ash had just slipped into Kiran's life almost unnoticed and Sareeta found it hard at times to actually comprehend that there was perhaps another view in their marriage other than Kiran's.

Kiran's natural charisma had helped her in many a tricky situation. She was as sharp as a knife but easily endeared people to herself; you couldn't help but like her. She was reliable, trustworthy, accepting. She attracted people to herself because she genuinely listened to them and was interested. Sareeta often thought she would have made a wonderful physician but Kiran was also wise enough to know that the noblest of professions was not that noble any more.

Instead, she had chosen to become her father's right hand in his company, choosing a smart phone over a pager and pencil skirts over scrubs; she had left those items for her brother Dharam, a surgeon in training. And then there was the undeniable fact that she was stunning, a comfortable life with an emphasis on being well groomed had helped with that.

Her appearance was not typically Indian as she had olive skin, not brown. She had dark brown hair, not black and her eyes were not dark brown but hazel. She was long limbed and athletic but curved. She looked good in anything she wore but even so, chose to wear very chic clothing; she was indeed a head turner.

Being the eldest girl, like Sareeta herself, she had a very special bond with her father. On occasion, Sareeta had caught them out on the porch with her father late at night, having a whisky on the rocks and putting the world, or business, or family, right.

"Shouldn't you be at home, Kiran?" Sareeta had asked her.

"It's fine, Mama, I'm spending quality with Dad."

Jai had smiled smugly, so pleased that he still had a part of his daughter whilst his son-in-law had the rest.

In that moment, with her beautiful, exceptional, special girl in front of her, Sareeta wondered how Kiran would react if she was told that she was not Jai's daughter. And she was not Sareeta's firstborn child.

"Mama? Are you alright?" Kiran looked at her

Sareeta smiled and shook her head lightly. "Yes, yes. I'm fine," she swallowed the lump in her throat. "Where is everybody?"

"Well, Sonia and Rishi are also looking for you and Dad is…erm…I'm not sure where he is actually."

"Well, let's go find them," Sareeta replied, putting her arm around Kiran's waist and kissing her unexpectedly on the cheek for just a little bit too long. "Ignore me, sweetie, I'm emotional."

The hotel foyer was more full of guests checking out than it had been earlier and Sareeta very quickly busied herself with speaking to each of them, exchanging hugs and promises of seeing each other more than just at weddings and funerals.

She saw Jai quickly, a natural instinct after so many years of marriage, as if she herself was a homing device for him. He turned toward her briefly (he had been chatting to a friend about cars, his favourite subject) and smiled that smile. The one that made her feel safe, the one that showed her he cared, the one she had fallen in love with. He had always been her anchor when life had gotten rough for both of them, his love never faltered, never failed. When other things had become so unstable, like when she found herself unemployed, like when her closest friends and allies had turned their backs on her, like when she had miscarried, like when Kiran and Dharam had left home, Jai had always been a constant, a plumb line, a foundation. And now she had received the most devastating news, which she still didn't seem to attribute to herself, there he was again, just being him and just being stable and normal.

Everyone had nearly left and Sareeta should have packed up their room but Jai had already done it; she recognized their cases and suit bags by the concierge desk. She was in no frame of mind to check or ask; she did not want any excuse to be alone in the hotel room so she just accepted that everything was there. The only ones left in the foyer now were Kiran and Sonia chatting whilst Ash was packing their SUV with Rishi helping him. Jai was handing the concierge his car keys who had called a porter to load up his Maybach. Sareeta stood on her own and looked at her family. She had begun to feel lost.

The lift doors opened and Meera wheeled Satvinder out. He looked worn out, tired, grey, defeated. He looked at her with those deep brown eyes hopefully. She looked back and him and her mother who had her eyes full to the brim with tear. Sareeta walked over to them, just a few steps and crouched down so she was level with her dad.

"I love you, Dad," she said, "I love you," and she took his hands into hers and brought them up to her tear-filled eyes. The wetness of her tears spilled onto his dry hands. His face came to the top of her head and he kissed her forehead.

"I love you too," he wept, "you're always my baby."

They didn't have much time to wallow in their acceptance of the truth before they were bombarded by the children.

"Ignore Mama, Nana. She's emotional!" Kiran carelessly mocked. "She's had to give away her prince."

Satvinder quickly wiped his eyes and looked up at his granddaughter.

"*Putter*," he said "losing a child, no matter what you gain in return, always leaves a scar that only family's love can heal. You make sure you all look after your mother."

"Oh no!" giggled Sonia, "Nana's emotional too, I think it's time we got both of them home so they can mourn the loss of their precious prince Dharam together! Come on, Nana."

With that, Sonia shifted herself behind her grandfather and started to move him to the entrance of the hotel and Kiran's SUV. Kiran, Ash and Rishi followed.

"Come on, Mum," said Sareeta to Meera and took her hand.

She squeezed it gently, kissed her mother on the cheek and led her out to the car where Jai was waiting.

The journey home to the lake house took little over an hour and was done mainly in silence, both car's passengers exhausted and lost in their own memories of the previous days.

Arriving late afternoon, Meera busied herself with making tea whilst the men emptied the cars of the luggage for the lake house and Kiran directed them as to each item's final destination. The festivities were all but done except for a meal that night for the family, a few choice close friends and the relatives that had yet to make their way home.

Sareeta was expecting about twenty people which was really no big catering event for her. She had opted for a simple Atlantic salmon coconut curry which both showed off the delights of her Atlantic home, which she took great pride in, and also had a lightness and detoxifying element to it that she felt would be well received after so many days of very rich food.

The climate was still beautiful and she had already arranged with her housekeeper to ensure that the patio overlooking the lake would be set with the large table, patio lamps and citronella candles. The champagne flutes were already laid in trays and jugs of freshly squeezed orange juice and bottles of prosecco were chilling in the pantry fridge. There had been a time once when, if she had been cooking for anyone other than her own family, she would have cooked at least four different curries, rice, flat breads, salads and also an alternative for the non-curry eaters. But over the years, and with Jai's constant affirmation of her, she had become comfortable in her own skin and now kept her meals to one good curry with a starch and a couple of good hearty sides.

By seven pm, the sun was tucking itself to bed on the lake, the candle and lamps giving their warm hue to the table and guest arriving, casually dressed and ready for an informal meal. Most had not eaten since the hotel breakfast so, although plump from the previous day's exotic menus, they were also ready for a good feed.

Satvinder and Meera had already retired to their annex having eaten a simple meal of *daal* and *rotiayaan*; Satvinder did not care for any rich food these days, no matter how 'detoxifying' Sareeta tried to convince him it was.

In the business of the aftermath, she had not spoken to her dad and mum other than to give them their meal, ask them if they needed anything else and bid them a good night. She had taken extra care to kiss them both and tell them that she loved them. It was infrequent that she told them that she loved them, it just was not something that culturally she had been used to saying. But after the revelation of that morning, she wanted to say it and the words had more depth to them.

The food had been eaten and the drinks drunk. Stuffed and lethargic, the guests milled about the patio sharing stories of the wedding day and opening up conversations of family gossip. There was laughing and giggling and many "ohhs" and "really?" and "you must be kidding?!" Sareeta was present in body and listening but unsettled and unusually quiet. No one commented. She had, after all, just married her son. Tables cleared and friends and relatives enjoying the last drops of warmth the late summer evening had to offer, a high-pitched painful wail emanated from the annex. It silenced everyone and then chairs scrapped back frantically as Kiran, Sareeta and Jai got up first to run across the patio and down the steps to the annex. Other family members followed close behind.

Kiran, arriving first, flung open the door which opened straight into the lounge area to see her grandfather collapsed on the floor, on his side, his wheelchair still upright. The TV was still playing CTV news and Meera was knelt on the ground with him holding his hand and begging him to wake up between deep sobs. Kiran crouched down as the other arrived.

"Dad!" screamed Sareeta and knelt done straight away. She took his hand away from her mother and felt for a pulse. "Get him on his back," she instructed Kiran at the same time, "and someone call 911!"

Sareeta's Atlantic Salmon Coconut Curry

What You Will Need

4 salmon fillets, skinned and pin-boned
½ cup mustard oil
1 large onion, finely chopped
6 cloves garlic and 2 inches of ginger blended into a paste with some water
2 green chilies – deseeded and sliced thinly
15 curry leaves
1 tsp. mustard seeds
1 tsp. fenugreek seeds
1 tsp. cumin seeds

3 dried red chilies
200 grams chopped tomatoes (canned)
1 cup water
1 tsp. turmeric powder
1 tsp. chili powder
1 tsp. salt
1 tsp. ground cumin
1 can coconut milk
1 tbsp. tamarind sauce (or a tbsp. tamarind pulp soaked in hot water and drained)
1 bag prewashed baby spinach
2 tbsp. chopped cilantro.

What You Will Need to Do

Cut the salmon fillets onto large chunks, between 5 and 6 chunks per fillet. Set to one side.

In a large *karahi* or deep chef's pan, heat the mustard oil until smoking.

Add the curry leaves, closely followed by the mustard, fenugreek and cumin seeds and the dried chilies. Cook briefly for about 30 seconds before adding the onion.

Cook until the onion takes on some colour and then add the sliced chilies and garlic ginger paste.

Let this cook until golden brown and then add the tomatoes.

Cook this for about 7 minutes, stirring frequently and adding a splash of water if there is any sticking.

When the oil separates from the *masala*, add the spices and cook for one minute.

Now add the coconut milk, water and tamarind and bring to the boil.

Add the bag of spinach leaves.

The sauce is done but if it is too thick, add some more water (this just depends on how thick you like your sauce. Also remember to taste for salt as this is also to your own liking).

Lower the heat so the sauce is simmering and add the salmon piece by piece, making sure each is submerged into the fragrant sauce.

Cook for a further 5 minute to cook the salmon through so that the middle is still slightly pink.

Sprinkle over the cilantro and serve with plain steamed rice.

Chapter 8

Nairobi, Kenya, 1968

"You're where?" Meera couldn't quite believe what her new husband was saying to her over the phone.

She was in England and it was a very typical cold, damp and dark Autumnal afternoon.

"Nairobi," he repeated. "Something came up. I had to come here, Meera. I had no choice. And I can't really explain, this call is costing a small fortune too. I just want you to know that I'm fine, I'll be about another week or so. I'll try and call you again but I've got to go."

Meera could hear the beeping tone the operator gave as a warning that the line was about to be cut.

"Love you!" she said loudly but she didn't know if he got that before the line went dead and she was left wondering what on earth was going on. As far as she had known, he had gone to Dehradun to sort out his father's estate. His father's death had come hard on Satvinder, she had known that much. They had not had an obviously close relationship; her father-in-law had been a very private man, seldom displaying emotion of any sort. He didn't come across as sad so much as resigned to life. Nothing joyful would fill him with happiness and nothing sad had made him weep; he had accepted life as if it was his lot that he could neither love nor change. Maybe his indifference to life had been the reason why he had been one of the few people to actually attend their wedding, most family and friends boycotting it because of the inter-faith element.

Meera and Satvinder had met in Kenya and had been childhood sweethearts. They had kept their relationship a well-guarded secret for many years, considering many options when they had decided their match was a forever one, including eloping, coming clean (Satvinder more keen than Meera), converting (Meera, not Satvinder) and also marrying their respective parent's choice but continuing an affair for the rest of their lives.

In the end, Satvinder had managed to get a place at Hatfield Polytechnic in England to study engineering and Meera a place at a nursing school nearby. They had decided each to make their career plans independently, as far as their parents were aware, and once in England announce their engagement.

Meera's family had disowned her outright, her mother wailing with the disgrace and shame of it all, announcing to the Hindu Gujarati community in Nairobi that her daughter was dead to her and the family. Her siblings had pleaded with their mother to have a change of heart but she had refused, stating that she would rather her daughter had really died than marry a Sikh.

Satvinder's family, on the other hand, took a more sly but equally as devastating approach, demoting him from the golden son role to gossip fodder. Those who were honest enough to admit their disdain no longer spoke to him and politely refused to come to his wedding, making excuses ranging from sickness to downright refusal. The others came for entertainment value and relayed the finer details to those who had decided to stay at home. Satvinder's parents, whilst not overly happy with the union, did attend; he was their only son and they were somewhat dependent now.

The ceremony in the Sikh temple in Shepherds Bush had been simple with Meera and Satvinder cooking the *langar* themselves in the morning and rushing off to get changed ready to get married before noon. Afterwards, there had been no grand reception, no party, no celebration. Satvinder, Meera, Baldev Singh and Paramjeet had returned to the small two-bedroom flat in Hatfield, changed to their normal attire and had tea. Had they not had such a great love for each other, Meera and Satvinder would surely have succumbed to bitterness but they understood that some decisions bear shame to the family, even if that shame is hidden under layers of prestige. They did not want to rub salt into an already quite deep wound and they just accepted that a marriage certificate, promise of a married life and a small degree of acceptance from his parents at least was enough.

Now, several months on, Baldev Singh had passed on suddenly. He hadn't been ill, he had, in fact, been healthy and strong. But then one afternoon, after a heavy brunch of *aloo parathas* laced with shards of cold salty butter, yoghurt and pickle, he had gone for his customary walk around the park near the flat and had not returned.

By early evening when Satvinder returned home from college ready to start his evening shift as a factory packer, Paramjeet was frantic. It was unusual for him to not come home without word and especially unusual for him to miss his afternoon nap after such a heavy meal. She'd scanned the park but had not seen him. She had not known what else to do and by the time Satvinder had returned, she was in pieces. First Satvinder had taken the car and driven around Hatfield wondering if his father's wonderings had led him further afield but he had been able to locate him. He had called Meera at work to see if *Pita-Ji* had any appointments but she was not aware that he had any hospital appointments. In the end, he had called the Accident and Emergency unit at the Queen Elizabeth Second Hospital who asked him to come down.

The doctor broke the news in a very matter-of-fact way explaining that he had been seen by a passerby collapsed, an ambulance had been called and he was pronounced dead on arrival. A post-mortem was to take place. He was sorry. Would they like a cup of tea?

Paramjeet should have been devastated; her partner of over twenty-five years had been taken from her so suddenly. But she wasn't. She wiped the few tears from her eyes with the edge of her *dupatta* and said to her herself, "May God given him peace in death, such as he never had in life."

She got up and walked out of the stark relative's room. A few relatives were called and a simple funeral took place in the same Shepherds Bush Gurdwara. Paramjeet took to wearing white, the customary colour of widows, which for some reason seemed to suit her more than the colours she had worn preceding his death. It was almost as if she had come into her own as a widow.

And now Satvinder found himself back in Nairobi, on familiar streets searching for a child that he had become acquainted with for a few weeks many months before. After his time in Dehradun, he had just known intuitively that he had to find the child. He didn't know why, she wasn't a blood relative, she had not made his mother happy, she was an illegal immigrant and a kidnapped child. His head was telling him it was madness. The privileged information he had should surely be shared with the proper authorities who could trace the child and return her to her Pakistani family. But it just didn't sit right with him. Something about that absolutely reasonable and sensible plan disgusted him. He knew he just wanted to find the baby and he wanted to make her his. Maybe he too felt he wanted to avenge his mother's tragedy. Or maybe the thought of returning the child to Pakistan meant defeat for his father; he didn't know why, he just knew that something in his being yearned him to take the child home with him. What felt right to him was retribution, atonement, justice.

It didn't take him long to track the baby down; there were not many Gujarati servant girls, unmarried, who had acquired a baby in Nairobi. When he found them, Pallu was smashing clothing against the concrete step with the baby sleeping contentedly next to her in a moses basket. *The baby must have been at least 11 months old*, he had thought to himself as he looked at them but she looked scrawny.

"*Choti-Saab?*" exclaimed the girl as he approached. "*Yahan?* You're here?"

"Yes, Pallu. I've come for the girl.

Pallu was shocked. "*Nayhe, Choti-Saab*, I cannot. *Memsaab* gave her to me. She told me only I could look after her even when I told her I knew a good family who would have her, a rich family Saab, they couldn't have their own and they would have loved her. But *Memsaab* said no, Saab-Ji. Now I have her, Saab-ji. I raise her as mine, *Saab-Ji*. I look after another girl, they are the same, they will play together when they are older. *Saab-Ji*, that is why they keep me. I look after the baby and this one and the family let me stay. I cannot give her to you."

"Pallu," he replied, "I must take her with me. It will not be long before her family come here and look for her, of course they know where she has gone. It took me no time to find you and it will not take them long either. And then, what will they do? Do you think they will just leave you? Leave the family you are with? What will happen to the child, they may not even want her back now as their own? I will take her with me and I will keep her safe. I will raise her, Pallu."

"*Saab-Ji, maaf karo*, forgive me. It will be a mistake of you take her. What will you tell her, *Saab-ji*? At least with me she will have a simple life and not ask any questions, I can tell her any story that makes me her mother and she will believe me. And if her family come here, *Saab-ji*, and find me, I will return her. *Maafi karo, Ji,* but it was not right what the Sahib did. It destroyed *Memsaab*. If they come, I will return her and if they do not, I will keep her with me."

"No, Pallu. Whether right or wrong, she is my father's burden and he is no longer here, so she is mine."

"*Saab-Ji*, this is wrong. Please leave her," Pallu pleaded with him but he would not give up or give in. Pallu, aware that even now the authorities and community were turning a blind eye because it was Baldev Singh who had brought the child, realized that she would not have such privileges if she was to be questioned. She was realistic about her place in life's hierarchy and knew that she could give the child quietly in private or be disgraced in public. It was likely that she would be prosecuted if things became ugly because, no matter where in the world one is, even she knew that justice requires money and she did not have that commodity.

Pallu picked the now awake and gurgling baby up from the basket and handed her over. She then carried on cleaning the clothes and turned away from Satvinder. For the second time in her young life, Sareeta was abducted.

It wasn't hard for Satvinder to add Sareeta to his passport since she was already on his father's and he merely explained that his father had died, showed the certificate, and stated that he was now the guardian. He then falsified a birth certificate with his name listed as the father and Meera as the mother, a document which would be useful on his return to England. Her birthday was ten months after his marriage; who could tell whether a baby was 10 months or 12 months anyway?

None of this took long and within a week, he was on the plane headed for England. Paramjeet went as white as the clothes she was wearing when she saw Sareeta in Satvinder's arms but she herself died a few months later, having given herself permission to let go of life and join her husband in eternity. Meera, such was her love for her husband, accepted what had happened more easily than one should expect from one's wife.

She embraced motherhood quickly, explaining to her colleagues that a relative in Kenya had died and her husband was the next of kin. The baby had been adopted and she needed some maternity leave – it was granted. And then they did what they had to do; they cut off all contact with their few friends and moved to a place where they were not known. They announced to their relatives that they had given birth to a baby girl a few months previously who, having not really kept in close contact with the family, were none the wiser that there had been no pregnancy bump and no mother-in-law's baby shower to welcome the conception. After all, when both of your parents have died within six months of each other, when would you possibly announce the arrival of a new life; everybody knows you just don't do that kind of thing. Satvinder found a job in the newly emerging IT profession and Meera stayed at home and brought up Sareeta. If anyone did suspect, no one said anything because given what Satvinder and Meera had already done, nothing could surprise them. The nearest any relative came to the truth, as far as they knew, was to suggest that Meera fell pregnant before the wedding, how distasteful!

Within a few months, any gossip about Sareeta died down, mentioned only at family weddings and functions. Over time, no one really knew if the rumours had any fact base at all; the baby was just accepted as the child of Satvinder and Meera, the granddaughter of Baldev Singh and Paramjeet. And life just carried on its normal business with her growing, a brother being born a couple of years later, schooling, medical school and marriage in that order. The unconventional family soon became well thought of as Satvinder and Meera built their wealth, their daughter and son became a doctor and accountant respectively and other family gossip, divorce and marriage and suchlike, took central stage. Relatives who had passed so much judgement on the family soon had problems of their own to deal with, marriage out of religion and blended families became so common that there really was nothing to comment on any more. By 2017 in Atlantic Canada, it had all had been forgotten. It had not been spoken of, mentioned or speculated about for nearly fifty years.

And then a wedding took place in which an esteemed Nairobi family invited their old Nanny who recognized not only the groom's elderly grandfather but also his rather enigmatic daughter who had once been sleeping quietly next to her as she slapped out the dirty laundry in public. And she thought in her heart, it was time for her retribution.

Aloo Parathas for a Heavy Brunch

For 8-12 *parathas*

You Will Need

4 cups *chapatti* (wheat) flour (I specify wheat flour as *chapatti* flour also comes as a durum semolina flour…better used for pizza crust than *parathas*!)

Warm water (tap is fine) – approx. 3 cups but enough to make a dough

6-7 potatoes, about the size of a lime, boiled in their skins, cooled, peeled.

Bunch of green onions (about 6), or 1 small red onion, chopped finely

Handful chopped cilantro (stalks can be used too if they are not to woody)

2 fresh green chilies, with or without seeds, sliced thinly

2 ½ tsp. salt

2 tsps. black pepper

2 heaped tsps. Ground cumin

1 heaped tsps. Ground coriander

1 tsps. red chili powder

Bowl of *chapatti* flour to roll out the *parathas*

1 cup vegetable or sunflower oil and a pastry brush

What to Do

First, make the dough by putting the flour into a large bowl and adding the water bit by bit until you have a soft pliable dough. You may need more or less water. When the dough is formed, tip it out of the bowl and kneed for at least 5 minutes. It should be soft and smooth. Leave this to rest for at about 30 mins whilst you do the rest.

Crush the potatoes with your fingers or chop them finely with a knife in a bowl

Now add the chopped onions, chilies and cilantro. Sprinkle the salt and spices on top and mix all together well. Your filling is made.

Put a flat griddle ('*tawa*') on a medium/high heat on the stove to heat.

Now, this is where it gets trickier. Take some dough and form into a ball the size of a lime/kiwi. Flatten it into a disc (about the size of a small saucer) with your hands and then coat the disc with *chapatti* flour. I do this by immersing it on one side and then the other; the disc obviously has to be smaller than the bowl!

Roll the disc out to the size of a tea plate, sipping it back into the bowl of flour if it is sticking to the surface.

Now take about a tbsp. of the potato mix (or as much as you think you can use!) and place it in the middle of your disc.

Now, draw up the sides of the disc, like a drawstring purse, over your potato mix and pinch the top together hard. You should now have a ball in your hand with a dough outside and potato inside.

Carefully start to flatten into a disc again with your hands, gently pushing the filling outwards.

Again coat the disc with flour and very gently, using a little pressure as possible, start to roll it out. Turn frequently to ensure it stays round.

The filling may begin to show through the dough but don't worry, the bit of peeping potatoes become crispy when the paratha is pan fried and taste good. Since the potatoes were cooked in their skin, the mix should be dry enough so as not make the dough soggy but keep sprinkling/coating with flour whilst you roll.

Roll out as thin as you dare but try to get to the size of a dinner plate. The technique of rolling out *parathas* takes some time to master so just be patient and keep trying to get it thin. Ideally, it should be no thicker than 5 mm but of course this depends on the chunkiness of the filling too.

Gently try and shake off excess flour by passing the *paratha* from palm to palm

The *tawa* should be hot so now place the *paratha* on it and gently half cook one side (side 1). This takes about 2 minutes. Take a peak whenever you want and if you see the dough half cooked (it starts to change colour from a brown-grey to a creamy-white). Paint the uncooked side facing you (side 2) with oil using the pastry brush and flip it over.

Side 1 is now facing upwards. Brush this oil as before. Leave side 2 to cook fully, about 4 minutes but keep checking. You should hear a very gentle sizzle. Now flip it over and finish cooking side 1, about another 2 minutes.

(Once you get good at this, you can roll out your next *paratha* whilst one is cooking on the *tawa*. It is my firm belief that multi-tasking *parathas* wards off early dementia!)

Place you hot *paratha* on a plate, and add a knob of cold salted butter to middle which slowly melts, a dollop of natural yoghourt on the side and some tangy pickle.

Chapter 9

Queen Elizabeth Hospital, Halifax, Atlantic Canada, 2017

Sareeta and her family sat anxiously in the relatives' room when Dharam and Annie rushed in.

"Kiran called us," Dharam explained.

Although having a few days in the Nova Scotian highlands, Annie and Dharam had chosen not to have a proper honeymoon for a few months. Kiran had called as soon as the ambulance had arrived and Dharam, being like a son to his grandfather, had taken to his car with his new wife immediately. It had taken him a few hours to get there but arrive he did.

"How is he?" Dharam asked anxiously when he walked into the room, wife in tow.

"It looks like he's had another stroke, mum is with him," Sareeta explained, immediately feeling more comforted with her eldest son there.

Sareeta had not practiced medicine for many years now, mainly devoting her time to Sonia, Rishi and her other passions, although previously she had been a very accomplished rising star in the UK National Health Service. Jai had proudly commented on many occasions that she had more letters after her name than in her name.

However, like many doctors in the UK at that time, she had seen her job change beyond recognition with more emphasis on protocols than caring and more time spent developing care plans than actually delivering them. In the end, the rising star had come crashing down after various scrutiny bodies had thoroughly scrutinized her. She had not only lost her job, but had also left the country far behind. Since the birth of her youngest two, she had chosen a different path in life. She had been pleased with her choice, but still, even today, she felt the pangs of a lost dream and shattered expectations. Nonetheless, she had been thrilled when Dharam got his place to study medicine and glad that he had chosen a surgical route which more suited his eye for detail and introverted personality. Annie, also a doctor, had chosen pediatrics and Sareeta had often wondered if that had something to do with Dharam's fascination with her initially as Sareeta herself had been a pediatrician and was a big believer, as well as loather, in the notion that men chose their mothers to marry.

"Is he awake?" Dharam asked. "Can we see him?"

"Not yet. He's stable, awaiting a scan."

The family sat and waited. No one talked much, the emotions of the last few days had taken their toll. Sareeta sat and thought about what had been said that morning. It seemed so long ago although not even twenty-four hours had passed. She looked around at the faces of her children, her brother, her husband and she prayed.

"God," she said in her heart, "Please let him live. Please don't take him away from me yet. Please let me have more days with him to love him and be with him. Let me have time to restore to him what has been lost. Take him, Lord, another day, when there is peace in this family and atonement for the sins committed. Please have mercy on him and also me so that I can have him here a little longer." She knew that her prayer was not exactly biblical, given that she believed Christ himself was the atonement.

But she felt deeply and sincerely that the revelations of the morning could not be buried again once exhumed. The knowledge was out there and what had happened in the last few hours to her father had meant, to her at least, that there was unfinished business.

An hour or so passed with Annie fetching cups of coffee for the family and renewing parking tickets.

Eventually, Meera walked out of the resuscitation area bleary eyed and solemn.

"He's okay. He's awake but very sleepy. He's asking for Sareeta and Raj."

Sareeta's brother got up and indicated to Sareeta to follow him.

Through the double doors, a uniformed woman at the nursing station nodded toward the closed curtains. Behind them lay Satvinder. He was drowsy and weak. His face looked droopy, weaker on one side. His left arm lay limp next to him whilst his right one was resting on his chest which was slowly rising and falling. Raj sat next to him and touched his arm. Satvinder opened his eyes slightly and saw his son. He looked lost and scared although he knew exactly where he was and why he was there. His pallor was more noticeable than before although he had not bled anywhere. He looked like he'd taken another step closer to death and its greyness was reflecting on him.

"Beta," he said taking hold of Raj's hand. He spoke so slowly when he said, "Your sister needs you."

With that, as well as the shock of seeing him like this, Sareeta finally let the tears fall, spilling out of her heart like a fire hydrant that had burst. The overwhelming sadness flooded her entire being, welling up and presenting itself in sobs so deep that she could barely breath.

"*Na, na,*" wept her father slowly. "*Na*, don't cry. You are my child."

"He's okay, Saru," said her brother, putting his arm around her, "he's okay."

Sareeta sat on the chair next to his face putting his hand in both of hers. It looked to her that he could not move one side of himself but it was hard to tell. He was weak and barely audible. He kept closing his eyes briefly as if she were about to lose him. But he held her hand tight as if to tell her that he was still there. Slowly he pulled her in toward himself with as much strength as he could find. She crouched down to hear him as he whispered to her, "find my sister, bring her back."

Satvinder fell asleep after that, still holding onto Sareeta's hand with Raj blinking back his tears behind her, completely oblivious to what his father had just requested and oblivious to the knowledge that his sister was not who he thought she was.

"We're gonna move him now, to the stroke ward. He's stable."

The uniformed lady was speaking and Sareeta nodded back at her. She let go of her father's hand and went to the waiting area. Jai immediately got up and put his arms around his wife. He kissed her head as his children gathered round.

"He's okay. He's weak on one side but he's still with us," she said. "Mum, they're moving him now."

They decided that Raj would bring his mother home and the rest of them should leave now; there was little more to be done today.

Late the following morning, tired faces appeared one by one in the kitchen. Sareeta had already been to the hospital with Meera for a short time but Satvinder was sleeping so they had come home again for breakfast and to get him some clothes. Meera was back in the annex, finding pyjamas and a dressing gown in the hope that the hospital staff would dress and wash him today.

However, experience had also advised her that it was unlikely that much would be done that day other than to leave him resting in bed in the hospital gown. Sareeta had taken her coffee to the patio, where Dharam was already snoozing in Jai's hammock, and looked over the lake, the morning sunshine warming her feet. She knew she needed to tell the family what had happened.

Jai was the first to join them.

"Shall I make you some tea?" he asked.

It was his morning ritual, since they had first married. Jai always made her morning cup of tea, regardless of which country they were in, regardless of what state of heart they were in, Jai always made her morning tea.

Clearly, she had a coffee mug in her hand but still she said, "Yes, please."

She would no more have refused his tea than he would have denied making it. He came back with two cups of steaming tea and sat down next to her having glanced briefly at his son quietly snoring away.

"Did you sleep okay?" he asked although he didn't need to ask since he always knew when she had not slept.

She'd slept some but not deep. She felt that kind of tiredness that penetrates deep, the kind that allows you to function off adrenaline alone but knowing that if one stops for too long, one would just fall into a heap and not get up for days. She had experienced many episodes of tiredness like this when she was a junior doctor in England with no set hours restriction, a new mother with a baby that refused to sleep more than 3 hours a night and in the days they had first emigrated to Canada with two small children and no idea if they would be able to make a future.

Today, she felt the same, a kind of overwhelming fatigue laced with a fear of the unknown.

"I'm okay, sweetie, let me make you an omelette," she said.

Just as Jai made the tea every morning, Sareeta made him two eggs every day. Jai had some very odd health beliefs like never eating anything charred (something he'd read in the Daily Mail), artificial colouring was very bad for oneself (even though he had grown up on coloured tandoori chicken and bright orange *jalebis*) and eating fresh fish was as good as an elixir of youth.

But two eggs every day was something that Sareeta had not denied him, not because she verdantly believed in their health benefits as he did ("My grandfather had two eggs every day, my darling, and lived until 100!" he would explain to her) but she just liked to do it; it made her homely yet outgoing.

"Dad?" he asked, nodding to the egg suggestion.

"He's sleeping. He's stable. Darling, we need to talk about something."

"Oh yes? Dad?"

"No. Yes. Kinda."

Kiran appeared through the double French doors leading from the kitchen to the patio deck, looking beautiful although unusually casual. The lateness at which they left the hospital that night had made her opt to sleep at the lake house but she'd had to borrow her sister's pyjamas. Not silk, like her own, she was wearing cotton flowery pyjamas and a pink vest, her hair was tied loosely in a topknot. She had no makeup but still her complexion was flawless.

"Hey, guys, how is Nana?" she asked rubbing her eyes.

Dharam also stirred at the sounds of his sister's voice and started to sit up.

"He's okay, he's stable. Now what do we need to talk about, Pumpo?" Jai asked Sareeta. 'Pumpo' being one of the many nicknames he had given to her over the years, along with '*gol guppa*' referring to a brown round crispy snack and *'moti-sali'* literally meaning 'fat sister-in-law'. Had Jai's great love and passion for his wife not been evident every day, she may have become offended at his nicknames, but she actually came to love them and in a strange way, they edified not nullified her.

"Well, maybe not now, we'll talk later," Sareeta replied, indicating, not so subtlety to Jai, the presence of his children.

"It's the photo, isn't it, Mama?" Sareeta should not have been surprised; Kiran was a sharp girl and could also read her mother like a book. "You know something about the photo." Dharam, at his point, just looked baffled.

Sareeta thought briefly. Her nature was, and had always been, very open. She didn't like secrets, she didn't like conspiracy and she didn't like her children not knowing things that affected them. In the past, her openness was something in herself that she had not liked; she wished she had a better sense of self-control.

But she had come to accept that she was who she was and, although she had perceived her openness as a weakness, it had become her strength. She remembered back to when their old housekeeper had stolen from them. Sonia had been a baby and Kiran and Dharam had been small. But one day the housekeeper was there and the next she wasn't. Jai had felt strongly that they should just make an excuse for her absence but Sareeta had thought differently. She had sat them down and explained that the housekeeper had taken things from the house that were not hers and so she could not be in the house any more. Kiran picked up straight away that she had stolen.

"Did you call the police, Mama?" she had asked. "Is she going to prison?"

Dharam had sat there wide eyed looking at his sister for guidance. *Not much has changed over the last 20 years*, Sareeta thought to herself as she saw the same look in Dharam as he stared at his older sister not quite knowing what she was talking about. Kiran quickly bought him up to speed on the photo situation and then both looked at her.

Sareeta took a deep breath. She knew that what she was about to tell them would change their lives as it had hers but probably not as much. She knew they would have a multitude of questions and different opinions. She predicted that Kiran would want to get on a plane straight away and find her, she guessed Dharam would want to think about what would be best for the lost child as well as the family, she suspected that Jai would want to do nothing and tell her that things should just be left as they are now.

So Sareeta started the story. She told her husband and eldest children that their grandfather, Satvinder, was adopted during the partition because his mother had not known whether his father was dead or alive. She told them that he was given to his aunt who had loved and cherished him. She told them that the same aunt who had taken him had been raped by a Muslim landowner. She told them that her child had been abducted and she had been left infertile. She told them that this was why her father had been raised in Kenya and not India. And then she told them that almost twenty years later, her grandfather had returned to India to abduct a child in revenge for the one they had taken from her grandmother. She told them that the child had been given to a servant girl to bring up but her father had returned to Kenya to find her and bring her home. And then she told them that *that* abducted child was in fact her. She told them that Satvinder had brought her up as his own child in England despite knowing that she was not his and kidnapped from a Muslim family. And then she told them he wanted her to find his sister and bring her home.

They all looked at her agog having not spoken a word during her story. And now, she looked down at her hands and then announced, "And I've decided to do just that."

Jai's Breakfast *Masala* Omelette Made by a Loving Wife

Makes one omelette

You Will Need

2 fresh eggs
3 green onions sliced
1 fresh green chili chopped
1 tsp. fresh cilantro – chopped
3 grape tomatoes, or half a regular tomato, chopped finely
1 tsp. salt
½ tsp. chili powder
½ tsp. ground cumin
½ tsp. *garam masala*
Spray oil (canola or olive) or 2 tsps. oil

What You Will Need to Do

Take an omelette pan and spray with oil (or heat 2 tsps. oil in it).

Lightly beat the eggs with the powdered spices and salt and set to one side.

When the pan is hot, add the onion, chili, tomato and lightly soften. This will take about 2 minutes. The onion may take on a little colour but not too much.

Add the egg mixture letting it sizzle at the edges. Draw the edges on and re-disperse the filling until you have a light layer of egg, semi-cooked and evenly dispersed with onion, tomato and chili.

Check the bottom of the omelette; it should be golden brown after about 2 minutes.

Sprinkle over the cilantro and flip the omelette. Cook the other side for about 2 minutes. Jai does not like his omelette soft and slippery; he prefers his omelette well cooked and sliceable.

Serve with 2 rounds of wholegrain toast (and a big kiss).

Chapter 10

Rawalpindi, Pakistan, 1960

"But, *Didi*, what about the scar?" She asked.

Not a baby any more, Baldev Singh and Paramjeet's daughter was now a young woman, Pakistani in all apart from her birth. She knew nothing of her past; the only life she had ever known was that of a servant girl in the *Huzoor's* house in Rawalpindi. Today, despite her young age, was her wedding day.

"By the time he sees it, it will be too late. And you don't know, he may like it," the older servant girl comforted.

She looked down at her chest. Across her breastbone was engraved in her flesh the words 'Pakistan Zindabad!' meaning 'Long live Pakistan'. She could not remember having it done; to her it had always been there. But she had been told that it had been done when she arrived in Rawalpindi, as a mark of ownership to show that she had been won. She couldn't really understand what was meant by that and neither could she gauge at this young age whether it was a blessing or curse. All she knew was that today, a man would see the thick ugly writing raised pink on her otherwise milky white chest because today she was being married.

"Not even a woman yet and being married to such a fine handsome man," she was being told. "You are the lucky one. Just do as you are told and he will treat you well. He has a large family, they will expect you to be good to them, don't disappoint. Remember, already you are here only by the grace of *Huzoor*. He could have thrown you out like a cockroach from the flour but he kept you. *Memsaab* wanted to, always remember that, *Huzoor* has shown you great kindness and now it is time for you to honour him. You are his prize and it is his will that you are now given."

Again, she didn't really understand all of this. Her short life, only 14 years, had seen her doing kitchen chores, helping washing out clothes, helping sweep the *kothi*. For some reason, the *Memsaab* despised her, so she tried to keep out of her way, especially when she had a few minutes to play in the sun. He, the *Huzoor*, was kind to her when she saw him, not the kindness that comes when you fall and hurt yourself; she had never received that kind of attention. He was kind in that he sometimes looked at her and nodded in acknowledgement. Occasionally, he smiled briefly. But mainly, he never spoke badly to her or made her feel sad. Often, the *Memsaab* and her children would taunt her.

"Hey, Gori!" they would yell at her.

Gori was not her name but she knew it referred to her fairer than expected skin, "So ugly you are with that big scar on you and still you walk with your nose high! What you can smell is your own shit, Gori!!!"

She wished she had become immune to the taunts but she had not. She couldn't understand why they hated her so much because she had noted that they did not speak to any of the other servants like that. Perhaps it was because of this that she did not object once to the marriage, hoping that she may be able to escape the tortuous comments that flung her way like the stones of the catapults she saw the boys use. She didn't know much about who she was to marry other than he was wealthy and he and the *Huzoor* were involved in a land dispute.

Despite her lowliness, there was a big turnout for the wedding; some dressed in finery but many were just local farmers and labourers who sat on their haunches awaiting the arrival of the bride. She couldn't see anything, her *duppata* was low over her face and she could see only her henna covered feet. She was guided on both sides by women and girls she did not really know. When the Imam asked her for agreement, she did as she was told to do and silently agreed, someone else mouthing the words, "*kabool hai*."

Only her older companion, the maid by whom she had been brought up, whispered to her as she was led away, "Just remember, this is the best you can expect. Try and be happy, you will find your happiness in his."

Gori was an innocent and she did not know what new tragedy had befallen her. She did not know that she was a trophy of India, embellishment on her chest as proof. She was not aware that she had been given in marriage to secure a property deal. She naively thought that her life would change for the better, thinking she would be free of taunts and verbal whiplashing. She didn't know that she had been traded, taunt for hit, gibe for assault, insult for pain; she had yet to experience all of this.

When she finally laid eyes on her new husband, her shock was so great that she knew not what to say or think; she knew not even where to look so she looked down again. He was immense in girth and stature and he was oily. He was old, older than the *Huzoor*. He grinned a near toothless grin and rubbed his tiny greasy moustache.

"I have wives," he informed her, "I am in need of something young, fresh and firm. You are my prize now. I don't care much for the scar you have, it repulses me. But you are unused. For you, I have given my land so you had better never ever displease me. If you do, I will carve that scar from your chest bit by bit and feed it to the dogs. Now, take off your clothes and lie on your front."

She had never felt pain like the pain she felt that night as he used her like a piece of meat. When he had finished with her and fell into a deep sleep, snores emanating from his sizeable nose like a thunderous bullock cart passing the unfinished road outside the *Huzoor's kothi*, she painfully rose. She went to the bathroom and washed off the blood. She put on some fresh clothes and lay down again. But by the time the sun had risen, she had needed to repeat the cleansing and then yet another time before he finally hauled himself out of the bed to clean himself. Proudly, he picked up the bloodstained sheet, inhaled it deeply and stated 'my prize' before he left her alone to silently sob, the warm tears splashing on her 'Long Live Pakistan' scar.

She had to wash and dress again quickly before her chores started. Flinching with pain, she made her way to the courtyard kitchen where her fellow wives awaited her.

"*Agay*, *Betia-Rani*! You're here, little queen! At last! You think you're just here to lie in his bed and enjoy yourself? What time do you call this, breakfast is already done! Listen, if you're going to live here, let's get this straight. Nighttime, you can be his whore, believe me, we've all been subject to his fantasies. When he's bored of you, he will replace you. But for this work, there is no replacement. Don't expect sympathy, *Betia-Rani*, you missed this morning's labour so you can stay here this afternoon." A *thali* of onions was thrown her way with a small blunt knife. "Here. Peel and chop. We're making *rajma-chawal*."

Gori was not given any food that morning. They talked about her as if she was not present, referring to her as *Betia-Rani*, the child queen, or *Nisaany*, the scarred one. Her entire pelvis ached, she felt bruises on her arms and wrists where she had been held down, bite marks were obvious on her neck and chest. She looked, and felt, like she had been ravaged by some wild pig. For a while, her fingers shook as she tried to peel onions.

"Look," the women taunted, "the *Betia-Rani* cannot use her fingers so well this morning, can she?" and then they laughed. The onion fumes came as a blessing because she was able to cry quietly without further comments.

In the afternoon, after a lunch of *rajma-chawal* for her husband and what she could scrape out of the pot after everyone had eaten, she was put to work again for the evening meal whilst the rest of the women were able to rest from the heat of the afternoon sun. The sun blazed down on her in the shade-less courtyard causing the sweat of her back to stain her *kameez*, paradoxical as she worked on the dry dirt of the courtyard floor. Her scar itched as it often did when she was sweaty. She still felt sore and achy but was also all too aware that come evening time, he may well play with her again.

She felt no better than a dog, like the puppy that the children in the *Huzoor's* house had come by and played with so roughly that it had not survived for long. She remembered how it had howled with the roughness first and then whimpered and then silence as it lay limp on the road. She remembered how the children had first prodded it, then thrown water on it to try and get their plaything to awaken. When they realized it would not, they left it in the street for the wild dogs to take or the night vultures to peck at. She wondered if her fate would be the same; she feared in fact for her very own survival.

The routine of daytime chores and nighttime bondage continued for many weeks, each day breaking her spirit a bit more. The feeling of being a plaything quickly demised to feeling worthless and then feeling entirely insignificant. She was no longer a girl but neither a woman either because she could not understand why any human could treat another human like he did. She had not wronged him, she had not disobeyed him and she couldn't understand the utter contempt he had for her during the day and elevated interest followed by ignorance by night. The words 'you are my prize now' reverberated in her head again and again.

One day she bled heavily with large clots, having not bled for a few weeks and felt terrible pains in her abdomen. She thought that she was dying, and she wished for it too. She was allowed to rest that afternoon and heard the women talk of her.

"She's lost it and that is God's will. This family does not need another runt of Indian blood. Just as well. If it had been born, I would have made sure it didn't survive, or not in one piece anyway!" They all sniggered

What did they mean? she thought and then she realized.

It all came together for her in that moment, she was despised because she was Indian, she was a trophy because she was Indian and she was worthless because she was Indian. Her baby, she realized, was gone but would also have been despised and hated because it too would have been Indian. At that moment, she became a woman. At that moment, she became a mother. And at that moment, she decided she would not die but live. She would not allow any child of hers be killed, or maimed, or have their flesh carved into, or have their body desecrated, or be enslaved. Her child would live a life worthy of being called life.

For the first time in many months, she wanted to live and defy the laws that had governed her since she could remember. Somewhere she mustered the strength to believe that life for her child could be different to hers and an air of defiance came over her such that should have been alien, an innate defiance that refused to accept this existence any longer, at least for her yet to be born child.

The change in her was not visible on the outside; she continued to toil in the kitchen and surrender in the bedroom longing for the few hours' respite in the middle of the night and allowed her body some healing as the sun encroached the horizon. But something on the inside had changed and she took her sufferings as a currency to pay for her future gains. She refused to give any reason for them to have displeasure in her or any credence to their wanton beliefs that she was lazy or ugly or useless or worthless.

In the course of time, she fell pregnant again but this time she knew what it felt like having armed herself with snippets of knowledge from the ladies around her. As the nausea set in and the fatigue took its toll, she took extra care over her eating, her drinking and her body. She lied to him that it was her monthly time and when that week was over, she told him that she had a loose stomach. A year had nearly passed since the marriage so his interest in her had wavered somewhat and she was able to come up with some reason or other until he had satisfied himself elsewhere.

After the first few weeks had passed, her baby was growing inside her. She started to execute her plan, hoarding small amounts of rice, dried beans, pulses and some spices. The small handfuls she took daily went unnoticed as she hid them deep in her armoire hidden amongst the cloths she used for sanitary wear; she knew no one would look there amongst the 'dirty' items. Occasionally, when she thought no one would notice, she elevated the price the *sabzi-walla* had charged and kept the extra rupees, a few *annas* her and there. By the time her pregnant belly was visible and the doctor had been called, she had collected plenty to make a parcel; enough to keep her alive and healthy and feed her growing baby until she reached her destination but not too much to carry.

In the middle of the next night when he snored loudly, she quietly placed all her treasures in the middle of an old *duppata*, securing it tightly and tying it around her waist. Silently and stealthily, she took the big keys hanging on the hook by his clothes and unlocked the *kothi* gates. The air was eerily still but a bright full moon in the darkest ink of a night lit up the paths and gullies. The wild dogs slept calmly under the trees on the side of the road, the bullocks were all safe in their pens. Nothing stirred.

And Gori ran. She ran out on the street, down unfamiliar roads to where the light was less and she was on the road out of Rawalpindi. Her running slowed to a walk. She carried on walking throughout the night until exhaustion and relief caused her to crumple under a big banyan tree as the sun was kissing the world good morning. There she slept for a few hours, grateful for the tree's shade, for the sun's warmth and for a God who had rescued her.

'Pindi *Rajma-Chawal* (Red Beans and Rice)

For Rajma (Beans) You Will Need

2 cups dried Borlotti or light-red kidney beans soaked in cold water overnight
5 cups fresh water
3 tsps. salt
2 tsps. chili powder
2 tsps. ground cumin powder
1 heaped tsp. ground coriander powder
½ cup vegetable oil
2 heaped tsps. cumin seeds
3 medium onions chopped finely
8 gloves garlic crushed into a puree
2 inches ginger crushed into a puree
1 green chili finely chopped
For the *Chawal* (Rice)
½ cup vegetable oil
3 tsps. cumin seeds
2 tsps. salt
2 cups white basmati rice
4 cups water

What You Need to Do for *Rajma*

Take a large pot and put the soaked beans in it. Add fresh water, salt, chili powder, ground cumin and coriander.

Bring to the boil and then simmer until the beans are soft and tender, this takes 1.5 to 2 hours. (This can be done in a pressure cooker and takes 4 whistles or about 20 minutes.)

Meanwhile, in a separate chef's or sauté pan, heat the oil. When it is hot, add the cumin seeds and let them splutter for about 30 seconds, then add the chopped onion.

Cook until they are golden brown. Add the garlic, ginger and fresh chili and continue to cook until it is all dark brown. You may need to add a splash of water if the mixture sticks.

Add the onion mixture to your cooked beans and cook together for 20 minutes. Serve hot with *chawal* and a red onion salad.

What You Will Need to Do for *Chawal*

Take a saucepan or casserole with a lid and heat the oil.
Add the cumin seeds and let them brown slightly.
Now add the uncooked rice and coat with the oil and cumin.
Add the water and salt.
Bring to the boil and then simmer with the lid on until all the water is absorbed and the rice is fluffy.

Chapter 11

Atlantic Canada, 2017

"Sareeta, I don't know what to say. How are you feeling?"

It was a new bright morning and Sareeta had taken solace in the comfort of her closest friend and long-time confidante, Hunsey. The bombshell she had dropped on her husband and children had gone down as expected. After the initial shock of the story had settled in and all the finer details asked, Kiran had predictably insisted that they go straight away to Pakistan to find their lost relative, or the lost child as she had become known as.

"Don't be silly, Kiran, that's madness," Dharam had said to her. "She could be anywhere by now. It was 1947. She'd be…what…70 years old by now! She may not even be alive now."

"That's true, Kiran," Jai interjected. "Things were different back then, this kind of thing happened a lot and that whole generation had difficulties like this. I seem to recall the Indian Government trying to do something about it many years ago, I mean, trying to reunite the abductees with their families. If she was alive, she may well have been reunited although I don't think many were. My guess is we cannot do anything."

"No, Dadda," Kiran had said, "we must. Look, we know she went to Lahore…"

"We *think* she was sent to Lahore," corrected Sareeta.

"OK, so we can start there. There must be some records, some documentation somewhere."

"Lahore is huge, Kiran," Dharam had tried to reason with her. "Needle in a haystack doesn't even begin to describe how difficult this would be. And I doubt there are records, thousands were abducted on both sides and just had to blend in I guess. Even if they were found, many of them couldn't return back to their homeland, they just weren't wanted once they'd been 'tainted' so to speak."

"She was a baby, Dharminder," Kiran retorted referring to her brother as Dharminder after the famous 1970s Indian actor her grandmother was so fond of, she often used this name for him when he annoyed her. Sareeta rolled her eyes. "I doubt she was 'tainted'."

Dharam, ignoring the Dharminder allegory continued. "I'm just saying we don't know enough to find her. And we have to think what is best for her now even if she is alive. She was taken as a baby and may not even be aware. She's probably grown up as a Muslim and after 70 years, would she actually want to know that she's not? Maybe, even if we could find her we should just leave her be and tell Nana that she's okay and her life has been good…if it has been, that is."

"Well, I still think we should try. For Nana's sake. He's asked Mama to find her, it's like his dying wish, sorry Mama, you know what I mean," she glanced at Sareeta's tear brimmed eyes. "I just think we owe it to him and to Mama."

All eyes were on Sareeta, who having already stated that she was going to find the lost child, looked back at her loving family. "I think we should start in Dehra Dun," she had said. "At least we know the Khan family have a presence there. And from that, we can move on."

Now, sitting at Hunsey's kitchen table washed with sunlight, her friend rubbed her hand gently. "Look," Hunsey said, "you know, whatever you do, I'm with you. I'll help with Sonia, Rishi, anything you need doing here. It's a lot to come to terms with and you've done great, honey. I don't know what I'd do in your situation. But I think if the Lord has laid it on your heart to go and find her, find her you must."

Hunsey and Sareeta had been friends ever since Sareeta's arrival in Canada 15 years previously. They had met at the coffee shop Jai had owned when they first arrived and Sonia had just been born. Hunsey's baby had been crying whilst Jai had been on the phone and Hunsey had apologized profusely to him. He, in return, had said that no apology was needed as he too had a baby around the same age who was at home with his wife.

"Wait here," he had then instructed Hunsey, "I'll go and get them."

He had rushed home to fetch them and, as he had thought, Hunsey and Sareeta had become friends instantly arranging to meet for a coffee with their babies and older children the following week. Both, being mothers on maternity leave, they had shared moans about the 'need for external validation', as Hunsey had put it and lamented the 'loss of title' as Sareeta had complained.

After that, they met most weeks, with babies and then without as the babies grew. Over the years, they had shared the joys of their babies becoming young children and now young adults and the losses they had incurred on the journey too. They had both been labelled the 'meanest Mommy in the world' and also the 'best mommy ever', both by their youngest and their older children who had themselves become good friends. And now they found themselves in a place where those titles were fond memories of the years gone but also a time when they could actually sit, undisturbed by 'Mommy!!!!!' and chat about the things that mattered to them.

And since Hunsey was quite an accomplished sailor, these conversations often took place on her boat anchored in various Atlantic lagoons enjoying a cold glass of Nova Scotian wine, a tie that bound them since their giggly visit to the wineries many years ago. The wine was 'their thing' and no matter where or what they celebrated, a Nova Scotian wine was always somewhere on the menu as they pretended to be very gifted sommeliers, where as they were, in fact, just a couple of middle aged women who had visited the wineries once or twice. Their respective husbands often just left them to it and talked about cars. But today, the talk was of a more serious nature, unplanned and requiring more of a counselling type environment. So Hunsey's kitchen table became just that and the two friends talked openly about the future that lay ahead and this time without the wine.

"The thing is," Sareeta explained, "I don't really know how to feel about all this. I mean, I should, and I do, feel shocked. But it still feels like it's someone else's story. And although I know I want to find her, I'm worried about finding me if you get what I mean. I mean if we find the Khan family in order to find the lost child, then actually I'm meeting my own family too, aren't I? Even though I've kinda decided they aren't my family, my dad and mum are my family, Jai and the kids are my family, for goodness sake, Hunsey, you're more my family than they are!" Both briefly giggled. "But they are actually my family and when I see them, and they look the same as me, I may feel different. Then what?"

"I know what you're saying, honey," Hunsey got up to refill the coffee, "but you can't do one without the other. You can't find the lost child without finding your own blood family, can you? You just need to prepare yourself for it and guard you heart." She refilled both cups and sat down again. She reached over and laid her hand on Sareeta's. "Only you know what you can do."

The journey home, alone in the car, gave Sareeta some time to think over her conversation with Hunsey. Sareeta has always found it helpful to talk out her issues because she almost counselled herself in doing so. She knew her friend was right and she could not do the good that she wanted to do for her dad unless she bore the price of seeing her true family for what it was. It was an emotional payoff and she knew it. And she also knew that time was not on her side because she could see her dad was not going to be around for many years to come. But she had decided that it was a risk she had to take and was glad that she had the crash mat of her family around her to cushion the blows that she anticipated would come.

As the big black gates of the lake house approached, she had resolved to go to Dehradun, find the tenants of her grandfather's *kothi* and get some more information before trying to approach the Khan family, or whoever remained there. She wondered if her biological father would still be in Dehradun and she wanted to make sure she had enough emotional armor before she approached him and his family. She would find out where the lost child had been taken and then go there. Piece by piece, she would put the story together and she would find the lost child. And then, well then she would have to see. Dharam was right, the lost child was by now a 70-year-old woman who, if she were still alive, had lived her life, whatever kind of life that was. They would have to think carefully about the next step. But that step was far off and there was much to be accomplished before then.

As she drove up the long driveway, lined with fir trees on either side, Sareeta could see Kiran's car, Dharam's car as well as Jai's. She jumped out comforted by the sight of all the vehicles and glad she had taken enough lamb out of the freezer to make her father's famous '*tariwalla* lamb curry' for everyone. This had to be one of her family's favourite meals which she made in times of celebration and times when comfort was needed, particularly broken relationships, dashed dreams and general melancholy. Rich with tomatoes and ginger and lots of sauce, she and Kiran liked it with rice and yoghurt whilst the others liked it with *rotiayaan* and plenty of them, Sonia and Ash preferring theirs with butter and Jai without. Dharam and Rishi were easy. Annie did not like much meat, not having the carnivorous appetite that most western Punjabis have but she always ate a bit, too polite to express her dislike.

With all of them, she quickly calculated she needed to make the lamb (maybe add potatoes?), rice (*plain basmati*, she thought so as not to detract from flavour of the meat), thirty or so *rotiayaan* should be sufficient (five for Jai, six for Dharam, Ash and Rishi, three for Sonia, one for Annie), a few extra for hungry tummies, cucumber, red onion and tomato salad and *raita*. If Meera was up to eating, and she often had to be coaxed when Satvinder was unwell, she may have a *roti* and some lamb *tari* and *raita*. She would ask her.

She jumped out of the car and up the three steps to the big front door. She could see the dog wagging her tail though the glass panel as she put in the code for the door. She was glad to be home. When life had troubled her, she always felt glad to come through those doors to the safety of her husband's castle. And when all was well, she loved to be out of the house enjoying the spoils of his wealth. When they had married and Jai was penniless, Satvinder had worried about her precious lifestyle.

"She's used to a comfortable life, beta," he had said to Jai and Sareeta thought about it now.

How her father had always been so concerned about her comfort rather than his own, she thought, thinking of the man who hardly wore new clothes, never ventured out to fancy restaurants unless he was made to and much preferred the peasant food of lentils and *chappatis* rather than rich meat dishes.

But his *tariwalla* lamb was, in her opinion, the best in the world. And she knew why too. It wasn't the abundance of fragrant spices or the exuberance of vegetables or even the chunks of lamb leg on-the-bone; it was the big dollop of love he put into every pot of *tariwalla* lamb he made. It was heartbreaking for her to think about her dad now, lying in a hospital bed alone, weak, tired, undignified without his fine red turban and losing his grip on life. She blinked back her tears because she knew if she didn't, they would begin to gush out.

She was glad to see the whole crew in the kitchen. They looked as if they had all recently descended as the kettle was just boiling and Jai was getting the mugs out for tea. It was clear that Sonia and Rishi had been bought up to speed and Sareeta sincerely hoped that it had been done kindly and without embellishment, something that had become a family trait. Sareeta caught the tail end of their frantic discussions.

"…and so we're all Muslims then!" Sonia was asking.

"No, baby-doll," Jai gently told his littlest girl, the least resilient of his crew. He drew her into a big hug. "We are who we were before this all happened and we will continue to be. Your Mama is just having a bit of a hard time and we need to help her."

Jai had a way with his children as if he could see their life from a higher ground. That was the Godliness in him, Sareeta had always thought. He never seemed to melt in the moment they were in but managed to look at it as if it had already passed. And he had a Punjabi saying for each event.

"Your daddy's right, baby," Sareeta added, hugging Sonia tightly.

She then extended her arm to Rishi also, who, although he was the cheeky-chappy of the family was also very sensitive when it came to family matters. Kiran and Dharam huddled closer and Jai enclosed them all bringing his two children-in-law into the scrum.

"We are who we are still. We are Chatwals and we will always be Chatwals. We are stronger than lions by God's grace and we will get through this. My mother always said you cannot separate members of a family any more than you can separate the nail from…"

"THE FLESH!" they all recited back, even Ash and Annie, so many times had they heard this saying from him. It seemed to be the tag line of every family row.

"That's the point, my darling," said Sareeta as the huddle dissipated. "You cannot separate the nail from flesh and yet it has happened to us. We're going to Dehradun."

Papa's 'The Best Ever' *Tariwalla* Lamb Curry

You Will Need (For a Large Hungry Family)

2 kg lamb leg on the bone cut into bite sized chunks (any Indian/*halal* butcher can do this for you)

4 large onions chopped finely in a food processor

1 400 g can of chopped tomatoes liquidized

2 bulbs garlic, 5 inches ginger and 2 large green chilies chopped finely in a food processor

½ cup vegetable oil

3 tsps. cumin seeds

2 tsps. black mustard seeds

3 tsps. salt

2 heaped tsps. turmeric powder

2 heaped tsps. chilli powder

2 heaped tsps. *garam masala*

1–2 litres water to taste

3 medium potatoes chopped into bite size pieces (optional)

What You Will Need to Do

Take a very large heavy based casserole or pot.

Add the oil and when it is hot, add the cumin and mustard seeds. Let then splutter and sizzle for about a minute.

Add the onion and fry until golden.

Add the garlic-ginger-chili mix and continue to cook until the mix is a dark brown adding a splash of water of needed.

Now add the tomatoes and cook until you have a thick *masala* and no more steam is escaping from the pot.

Sprinkle over the dry spices and cook the out for 5-7 minutes.

Now add the lamb pieces and stir on a medium heat for at least 20 minutes.

Now lower the heat and cover the pot going back to stir every 10 minutes or so until the lamb is cooked. This will take 1 to 1.5 hours and a sauce would have formed. (It is okay to eat the curry now as it is if you prefer a stew-type consistency but, by definition, '*tariwalla*' means a more soup-like sauce ('*tari*' meaning gravy)).

Add the water, as much or as little as you like and bring to the boil (potatoes are added here too if you like).

Simmer for a further 30 minutes with the lid off.

Enjoy the meat and rice/*rotiayaan* tonight and tomorrow enjoy the rest of the tari with *parathas* for breakfast.

Chapter 12

The Hotel, Dehradun, 2017

"Anything else I can be getting for you, sir?" the bellboy looked hopefully at Jai as he placed the last case on the case rack.

He had done a fantastic job, he thought, in giving this wealthy westerner a tour of the suite, including the balcony, the two bedrooms and the lounge area. In addition, he had shown him how the TV worked, how to order fresh linen if needed by use of the telephone, how to run the bath taps and set the Jacuzzi function. And then the pièce de résistance, the minibar. He had taken pains to point out the foreign imported whisky and vodka, he informed the westerner that he had personally himself filled the ice bucket and would have, were he not worried about repercussions from his supervisor, poured the westerner a whisky on the rocks.

He had also been very particular to call the westerner 'sir' like they did in the west and not '*Saab-Ji*' which is the term he would normally have used. He was, in his opinion, deserving of a very large tip.

"No, nothing else," Jai replied but did not pay much attention to the bellboy.

He had been aware that the young man had talked a lot and had been reluctant to leave, jabbering on about towels, ice and irritatingly trying to show him how to change TV channels and use the phone. When he had tried to take Jai into the bathroom, he had drawn a line and merely yelled "yes, yes" from his position in the lounge. Kiran had already taken to her room and flopped on the bed whilst Sareeta was busy texting, presumably letting Dharam, Sonia and Rishi know that they had arrived safe and sound.

He removed his wallet from his back pocket and then remembered that he had yet to exchange his Canadian dollars for

Indian rupees. He must remember to exchange a few at the reception desk, despite the abysmal exchange rate. Who used cash any more anyway? It was one of his bugbears, so used he was just using cards for pretty much everything. He rarely kept cash in his wallet although he knew that Sareeta liked the comfort of always having notes in her purse. Predictably, his wallet was devoid of notes, just neatly dispersed credit cards, his driver's licence and receipts.

"Saru,'" he caught her attention, "do you have any change?"

Now, speaking on the phone rather than texting, he could tell she was talking to Sonia.

"Yes, the journey was fine, just long, we're shattered," she was saying as she propped the phone between her ear and shoulder and removed her purse from her bag. She retrieved a $20 dollar bill, ignored Jai's look of consternation, and waved it at the bellboy with a nod of appreciation.

"Hotel is fine, darling," she continued. "Dadda is just sorting out the bellboy and your sister has just crashed." There was a slight pause followed by, "It's pretty much central but the village is, what, about 20 minutes out of town. We'll just rest today and start tomorrow."

There was another brief silence and then "Well, I hope we won't have to come here again, sweetie, maybe just a vacation for you and Rishi to look around. But you just get on with school, *Nani* is there and Hunsey will call round daily. Try not to trash the place. I'll call tomorrow. Give Rishi a kiss from us and tell him to text me the score, I hope he wins this one. Love you, sweetie." And she hung up.

"Everything okay?" Jai asked, still a little sulky over Sareeta's huge tip and look of complete elation by the bellboy.

How many times did he have to tell his wonderful overly generous wife to tip in accordance to the cost of living, $5 would have been more than sufficient.

"All is fine. Rishi is at Lacrosse and Sonia is working on her project. Mum and Hunsey are keeping an eye on things."

"Dad?"

"Sonia says he's not at home yet but later today. I hope mum can cope."

"She'll be fine. The carers will take good care of him; it's good we can bring him home."

In the days following the revelation and the decision to start the search, Satvinder had stabilized. He was able to speak and swallow but was paralysed on his left side. This stroke had been severe and the doctors had warned that significant improvement was unlikely.

"The evidence shows," they had said to her, "that only 5% of patients return to being fully independent after one year with this type of stroke."

She had been devastated because bit by bit she was losing her dad. The proud Sikh man she had held as her hero for so many years, with his fine red turban, tied Kenyan style, his neat beard which had never been trimmed but tied and fixed short, his moustache that curled at the edges, his dark eyes and smile lines, it was all fading.

His dignity was being taken from him day by day, his wonderful astute mind and high intellect was being robbed of him. She took a deep breath and closed her eyes. She could still remember the smell of 'fixo' from his beard mixed with a faint aroma of onions that had been around him so long it was almost part of his natural body odour.

She reminisced about the softness of his hands as he used to brush away her tears when she cried. Oh, to have that time again, just a bit, knowing what she knew now, knowing that it was temporary and would not last forever. Now the smell of fixo and onions were replaced with the smell of disinfectant and barrier creams, the soft hands were dry and papery, the broad shoulders slumped, drooped and would soon disappear.

Why hadn't she treasured these things more? These things that made Dad 'dad'. Why had she taken them all so lightly? Why hadn't anyone told her or warned her or instructed her to treasure every moment?

It had quickly been decided that Kiran would go with Jai and Sareeta to Dehradun. Dharam had to return to work soon (and there was his new wife to think of too), Sonia and Rishi were better off continuing as usual with their school. Kiran had not really needed to go but felt that she wanted to be involved in finding the lost child and, as was typically her opinion, things were less likely to go wrong if she was around. Whatever her reasoning, Sareeta was grateful for her presence.

First class flights to Delhi and then a connecting flight to Dehradun had been booked. The hotel had sent a car to the airport that afternoon and a car with driver had been booked for the next two weeks with a possible extension after that. Sareeta had packed clothes, toiletries and the photo; she didn't really know what else was needed.

The air in India smelled so different from home. It smelled warm, if that were possible, and smoky and spicy. Like the onions on Dad, it was as if all that street food aroma had penetrated the air and had become part of the natural smell of the land. Delhi International airport had changed over the years she had been coming to India and was now a huge modern construction, the international and domestic terminals now linked without the need to exit, hail a taxi and take the 40-minute road journey though Old Delhi.

Despite this, the journey had pretty much worn her out and she felt hot and dirty. Airplane journeys made Sareeta feel flat. The pressurized cabins made her hair flat and her skin dry, then the air conditioning in the terminals added to the lack of life in her hair. To that, the dust and dirt of the streets from Dehradun airport to the hotel added grime to the general flatness. She still looked radiant but she felt flat and grimy and in need of a good hot scrub.

The hot shower revived her somewhat and she had decided not to sleep that afternoon in order to ward off the impending jetlag. When she came out wrapped in fresh thick cotton towels, Jai was in a deep slumber in the bedroom. Peaking onto Kiran's room, she was in much the same state. Sareeta dressed quickly in a cool cotton *salwar-kameez*, one of the few she had packed but was glad that she could wear it without feeling self-conscious in any way. She knew Jai would be immensely happy too to see her in a *salwar-kameez* as, despite 27 years of marriage, he still fantasized about the archetypal Indian housewife, waiting for him at home at the end of a long day with a cup of fresh *masala chai*, simple and elegant makeup, beautiful *salwar-kameez* complete with *duppata* in a colour that made his senses come alive; not a blemish on her skin, no bags under her eyes, no aching back, bloated abdomen and certainly not a hint of a bad mood.

And obviously after she had fed him the most delicious food, she would quietly and demurely await him in the bedroom where she would obviously be the perfect lover too. Where was this wonderful wife she had often asked him, other than in the film *Amar Akbar Anthony*? Most Indian wives she knew were more like *Mother India* than *Mother Earth*, robust, resilient and fierce. The sirens that Jai craved were more a figment of his imagination than an actual nymph but he had invested years in trying to accomplish his dream wife and Sareeta knew full well that seeing her in her Indian raiment would go some way in reassuring him that his dream was still not yet too far away.

With silence in the room, she ordered herself a hot *masala chai* and a plate of *aloo tikki chaat*, her favourite snack. Obviously, she would have loved to have it on a banana leaf walking through Chowpatty Beach on Mumbai's Marine Drive with the Indian Ocean licking her toes. Or maybe whilst walking through the crowded gullies of Delhi's Chandni Chowk market mingled with the scent of fresh *mithai* being made and mini mountains of bright red chili powder and yellow turmeric being sold by street vendors. But today, she would suffice with a white china plate, a thick white napkin and silver cutlery.

She waited patiently for her food relishing the few moments of absolute peace and quiet surrounding her. She had not had much time to reflect on what was happening in her life right now. She had purposely tried to blank out the thoughts of coming face to face with her own blood relatives, fooling herself into thinking that if she did not allow her mind to entertain the new thing, she would be unaffected by it all. But she also knew this was foolish. It would take a miracle, she knew, to come face to face with her own father, mother, siblings, and cousins and just be immune to it all. She had resolved to keep her focus and maybe that's why she needed Kiran with her because being blinkered was one of Kiran's greatest attributes.

Her thoughts were rudely interrupted by the rat-tat-tat on the door. "Room service!" came the familiar voice through the door.

Sareeta hauled herself up, her legs ached now. She checked her hair and makeup in the mirror by the door as was her habit and opened it. The same bellboy stood there with a big grin on his face and a silver tray in his hand.

"Madam," he said, careful to call the westerner's wife 'Madam' and not '*Memsaab*' as he normally would have. "I am bringing this for you myself. I bring the paper with me too, if you are needing to know any special movie and restaurant, please do be letting me know."

Bellboy, waiter and now concierge too, she said to herself. *If only Jai could find staff so multi-skilled in Canada*, she inwardly thought and giggled.

"Thank you," she said and rummaged in her purse. She found a $5-dollar bill and pressed it into his hand. The sheer disappointment on his face was a picture to behold and she did all she could to not laugh out loud.

She opened the huge silver dome and the aroma of chopped red onions, spicy *chana masala* and hot fried potato cake hit her straight away followed by the aroma of the *chaat masala* sprinkled on top. There was something so characteristic about that smell, no matter where in the world you ate this dish. She poured herself a cup of tea and the warmth of the ginger and cardamom mingled headily with the spicy *chaat* aroma.

Food heaven on a plate, she thought as she pierced her heavy silver fork into the soft potato cake, releasing yet more earthy scent. The first taste of spicy chickpea curry, soft creamy potato with a crispy crumb and then heat from chilli and *garam masala*, crunch from red onion and sev, tang from tamarind chutney and then lastly a fresh cool afterglow of homemade yoghurt and cilantro.

Oh my word, would the whole world taste something this divine. God must really enjoy good food to give mankind a dish like this to savor, she thought.

Enjoying every mouthful, swished down with the warm fragrant tea, Sareeta picked up the newspaper. She glanced at the article discussing banning spitting in public places, drones being used to help farmers and the BCCI new reforms. She read with slightly more interest the article about the rise in dengue fever, glad that she had surreptitiously thrown the bug spray into her toiletries bag. She had a look at the classified and entertainment sections, always finding the matrimonial columns amusing knowing that she too had once appeared in them. And then she flicked to the obituaries.

For some reason, Sareeta had a morbid fascination with obituary columns. It wasn't so much that she thought she would recognise a name; it was more what the loved ones had to say about the deceased subject. It pulled chords within her, maybe because she let her imagination run wild with the few words they had written such as 'loving husband to Margaret and good father to Johnny and Sally'. She then imagined how loving he would have been playing with little Johnny and Sally in the yard, building them a treehouse, having water fights, campfires and more. And then he would come in to his doting Margaret, busily mashing potatoes to go with her renowned meatloaf, wearing a tea dress and with perfectly set hair. He would come up behind her, place his hands on her shoulders and kiss her tenderly on the cheek before pinching a carrot from the colander in the sink. From the one line, Sareeta had made a whole life of the deceased and it was perfect.

Her eyes scanned the columns which were not much different to the ones in Canada or England other than a few more religious references. And there she saw it in black and white smudged print. It simply read, *In loving memory of Feroz M. Khan, (b. 10th May 1942) died peacefully at home. Caring husband to Maneeza and father to Khuram and Jehangir. Landowner and farmer. Left for his heavenly abode 10th October 2017. Funeral to be held tomorrow at the family estate at noon.*

Sareeta looked at it in disbelief. Could it be him? Could this really be her blood father? Was Maneeza her mother? There was only one thing she could think of doing right now. The funeral was to be held tomorrow and Sareeta would be there.

Aloo Tikki Chaat Fit for a China Plate

Aloo Tikkis – You Will Need

    3 medium potatoes boiled on their skins and mashed
    1 small red onion finely chopped
    1 fresh green chili finely chopped
    1 tbsp. cilantro finely chopped
    2 tsps. salt
    1 tsps. chili powder
    1 tsps. ground cumin powder

1 tsps. *garam masala*
1 cup fine semolina
1 cup vegetable oil for shallow-frying.

For *Chana Masala* You Will Need

2 cups dried chickpeas soaked overnight in cold water or 2 cans of pre-cooked chickpeas

A pinch of bicarbonate of soda if using dried chickpeas

2 tbsp. vegetable oil (sunflower, vegetable, corn, rapeseed are all good. Olive oil can be used but adds flavour)

1 large onion – finely chopped

½ a bulb of garlic crushed (yes that's 6-8 cloves!)

2 inches ginger – pureed (can be liquidized with the garlic to make a garlic ginger paste)

½ a large can of chopped tomatoes

1-2 fresh green chilies to taste – chopped. Seeds removed if you like (I remove seeds from one and not the other)

2 tsps. cumin seeds

1 heaped teaspoon turmeric

½ a tsp. red chilli powder

2 tsp. salt for boiling the chickpeas if using dried and 1 ½ tsp. for the curry

1 heaped tsps. ground cumin powder

1 heaped tsp. ground coriander powder

1 tsp. *amchur* (dried mango powder)

2 heaped tsp. *channa masala* powder (optional and good but if not obtainable, increase the ground cumin and coriander by 1 tsp. each)

To Make the *Chaat* You Will Need

2 *aloo tikkis*
1 large ladle of the *chana masala*
2 tsps. yoghurt
1 tsp. tamarind sauce
1 tsp. chopped red onion
1 tsp. sev
1 tsp. chopped cilantro
Sprinkling *chaat masala*

To Make *Aloo Tikkis*, You Will Need To

In a large mixing bowl, mix the mashed potato with the fresh green chili, onion, cilantro and spices.

Divide the mixture into 8 equal portions.

With wet hands, form each portion into ball and then a 'cake' (i.e. like a fishcake). Make sure you press the potato together tightly so they do not fall apart when you fry them.

Heat the oil in a chef's pan.

Dust each cake in the semolina and fry on a medium heat until golden brown, turning them over once.

Be careful not them around too much as you don't want these babies to break.

Take out and drain on kitchen paper.

To Make the *Chana Masala* You Will Need To

Remember to soak dried chickpeas in cold a water overnight or for at least 6 hours.

Following this, drain the water and add new fresh cold water, the salt and pinch of bicarb (literally a pinch, approx. 1/8 teaspoon – this will help soften the chickpeas but add no flavour).

Cook the chickpeas – you can do this in a slow cooker for 6-8 hours, a pressure cooker for about 25 mins or boil on a stove top for a couple of hours. We like our *chana masala* to have quite a lot of sauce to I generally would use 1 cup of dried chickpeas to 2 cups of water.

In the meantime, chop the onion, puree/crush the garlic and ginger, chop the chilies and get the spices ready. Open the tomato can, chop the cilantro.

Take a heavy-based casserole or sauté pan and heat the oil.

When the oil is hot (but not smoking), add the cumin seeds – they should sizzle and spit.

Before they turn too dark (approx. 30 seconds) add the onion and stir. Now continue to fry the onion.

When the onion is golden, add the garlic, ginger and green chili. Now carry on cooking until the onion mix is a chestnut brown, quite dark. Now this is important because it gives the curry a good depth and flavour. If it sticks, add a splash of water. This will pick up what has stuck and help the colour progress too. Don't be surprised if this stage takes 20 minutes but it is so worth it.

When you have a shiny chestnut-coloured onion 'mush', add the chopped tomatoes and stir. Now this needs to be cooked until the tomatoes are pulpy and you see the oil separate out again from the onion/tomato pulp (the '*masala*'). When you see the oil around the edges of the *masala*, it is usually a golden and slightly sizzling. When you see this, you know it's time to add the spices.

So lower the heat slightly to medium high and have a cup of water handy if spices begin to stick. Add the turmeric, chili powder, ground cumin, coriander, *amchur*, *chana masala* and salt. Add a splash of water if you get any sticking.

Now cook this mixture for 5-7 mins – the reason for this is to get rid of any 'powdery' taste the spices may have and to make sure they are cooked. Your *masala* should be thick and glossy now and smell amazing.

If you are using canned chickpeas, you can now empty the cans, complete with the liquor from the cans, into your *masala*. Add some water too if you feel you need more sauce. You will need to simmer this now for at least 30 mins to ensure the chickpeas are penetrated with the flavour of the *masala*.

If you have used dry chickpeas, add the *masala* to the chickpea pan (note the other way around from using canned chickpeas). I'm not sure why this tastes better but adding *masala* to hot chickpeas in their stock just does seem to taste better! Bring to the boil and simmer now for 25 to 30 mins.

To Make the *Chaat* You Will Need to

Take a nice china plate.

Place 2 *aloo tikkis* in the centre.

Top each with some *chana masala* – this is really to taste but I like to add 2-3 tbsp. per *tikki* so the *tikki* is covered on the top but you can still see it.

Stir the yoghurt so it is loose enough to dress the *chana masala*, you may need to add a little water if the yoghurt is very thick. To be extra pretty, the yoghurt can be put into a sauce bottle so it can be drizzled over the *chana*. However, you choose to do it, dress the *chana masala* with yoghourt followed by tamarind sauce which can be arranged over the yoghurt in the same way.

Now sprinkle over the red onion, sev and cilantro and finally dust with the *chaat masala*. Serve straight away with a thick white napkin and a heavy silver fork.

And if You Want the Full Experience...*Masala Chai*

You Will Need (Per Person)

¾ cup water
¼ cup milk
1 green cardamom – crushed
½ tsps. Fennel seeds
Pinch *chai masala*
1 tsps. loose black tea

You Will Need To

Take a milk pan and boil the water with the loose tea, cardamom, fennel seeds and *chai masala*.

When it is boiling, add the milk.

Bring to the boil and then lower the heat to a barely simmer.

Simmer for 5 minutes.

Strain into a cup and add sugar to taste.

Chapter 13

Lahore 1978

Ta-ta-ta, rha-ta-ta, ching, ching, shasha. Her foot movements were so elegant and timely, perfectly positioned in the right places as she was taught.

Her feet were ornately decorated with intricate henna designs, her toes a sultry shade of crimson with little jewels on them. Her ankles had thick, high anklets covered in tiny silver bells that made a ring-jing-rang sound as she moved. Her pyjamas tight white and silky, showing off her beautiful shaped calves but only that far before the silver and sequined edge of her *choli* began. Light and flowing chiffon overlay the silky lining, loose over her shapely thighs and buttocks and tight over her breasts. The sequins and silver threads continuous over her pointed breasts reflected the lights sending of chards of sparkle luminescence around the iridescent marble floor. Her arms had been sewn in once her outfit had been put on so they had a beautiful swan-neck like slimness, again adorned with sheer white fabric with the most intricate of silver embroidery leading to her bridal-like hennaed hands. Her low-cut neckline hinted at her ample bosom but the crevice between the shapely mounds were covered with a choker necklace that covered her entire long elegant neck and décolletage. They gave the illusion of lavish unpolished diamonds but were, in actual fact, merely cut glass. More importantly, the jewels covered the ugly scar on her chest that peeped out of the neckline.

Her make-up made her even more fair and lovely than she actually was with pale pink pouty lips, rose blusher and thick *kajol* that extended out and made her beautiful oval eyes more almond shaped than they actually were. The thick mascara framed her beautiful eyes although they did not really need so much emphasis as even without the thick un-smudged *kajol* and equally thick mascara, her eyes were a beautiful long curvaceous shape. Her eyebrows were dense and groomed with a high arch and long length. Her forehead adorned two large glittering *tikki*, one central and a larger one to the side that set off the jewels in her hair which was perfectly coiffured to look soft and sleek although it had been set with plenty of spray.

She danced so exquisitely just as she had been taught many years ago when she first arrived at Lahore's infamous Heera Mandi. It was sexiness mixed with a complete innocence that was paradoxical in its style. She was like a virginal whore who exuded the naivety of one who had never experienced a sexual encounter but at the same time, a woman who knew exactly what to do and how to entice any man; even the most faithful husband could be lured into her embrace. Her specialized bra made her breasts look like two-pointed arrows inviting strangers to visit the cavern that lay between. But it was her hips that made her the most famous of the *tawaifs* in the Mandi, swishy-wishy, swishy-wishy.

'Gori-jan' had become her name, stage name, nickname, whatever one wanted to call it but it was how she was now known. Men came from all over Lahore and farther to sit around her in the dance hall, mesmerized by her beauty, her seeming innocence, her pointed breasts, her swishy-wishy hips and her innate charisma. They knew she was not a whore, she did not sleep with them and she took only the money that was granted to her by her tutor and would-be mother, the Begum Saeeda. But for one onlooker, she would become a mistress, and it was he who watched her so keenly today.

The Nawab had been captivated by her the moment he first lay eyes on her some 18 years ago. Then, she had been no more than a child, maybe 15 or 16 he had thought. Her eyes had lowered naturally when she first came onto the floor as she slowly lowered herself into a seating position, her right leg bent behind her and her left crooked up at the knee. Her *duppata* had covered her head and shoulders like a glowing illuminate tent. When the music started, she lifted her head and he noticed her incredible beauty, her large dove-like eyes, dark and alluring framed with those beautiful long lashes, her high cheekbones and her milky skin tone.

As she began to move, first on the ground and then standing, he couldn't help but be captivated with her flow, her expressions and her perfect swaying, so much so that he could not tell whether she was dancing for the music or the music was playing for her dance. Usually, he only spent an hour or so in the hall but that evening he couldn't help but stay the whole night, watching her, waiting for her, wooing her.

At first, she would not interact with him the way he would have liked; he could tell that she had been instructed to speak to him by Begum Saeeda, and that too only because he was the Nawab. She answered his questions politely until he had run out of things to ask her and then she had quietly taken her leave, leaving him wondering what he could have said to make her stay longer. It had taken him many months of trying to get her to look at him when he spoke, and then to be brave enough to ask him anything. He learned very little about her, only that she had a son and she had been taken in because of her immense beauty and been taught the *Mujra* by the Begum herself. She was lucky to be a good and quick learner and the Begum had been kind to her, looking after both her and her son whilst she was taught.

Over the years, the Nawab had become like sponsor for her although this had taken some time. He would come and watch her and initially just talk. After many months, he touched her. A while later, she semi-undressed for him and lay next to him and only after that, was he able to be her lover. Now, he still came just for her and although she danced in front of many men, he felt that she danced for him alone and the others were the dogs for whom the scraps of her fell. And each time, he would wait for her, make love to her, hold her in his arms and steal away before dawn broke to be back to his own wife and the reality of being the Nawab.

As for Gori, her motives had been plain as she learned about the reality of a tawaif's life. She herself had no need of a lover, a friend, no need of anyone to look after her. She was safe in Heera Mandi and the dance hall, she was well fed and had enough to live on; her life was set. But whilst the boy was having some schooling, she did not know what would become of him. But she knew well that life in Lahore without anyone of any influence would result in nothing better for her son than she had

had for herself, and since he could not follow in her footsteps, she feared his life may not even be as good.

Arriving 18 years previously, pregnant, alone, hungry and dirty, she had headed for the city far from Rawalpindi in the hope that she would find anonymity and some work. But who would take her pregnant and half starved? She had some success in begging, mainly because her swollen abdomen was so noticeable. The Begum had noticed her a few times on the street.

One day, she had simply said, "Come with me, child, let me feed you and the child inside you."

Gori had just followed her. Begum Saeeda had shown her great kindness, she had received a bath, food and bed in that order. She had been allowed to rest. The Begum had advised the others to take care of her and, rather than the taunts she was used to from a throng of women, they had lavished her with love, a feeling that she had never known, making her delicious food that would nurture her growing baby and her.

Lovingly, she was fed sweet *sooji ka halva*, ripe with dried fruits, almonds, cashews and pistachios, earthy *saag* with *makhan*, full of iron to ward off any low blood count, *kadhi* and *pakoras*, abundant with calcium from the rich yoghurt and folic acid from the vegetable *pakoras* to make her baby strong and healthy. She ate with the girls before their evening rituals, as a family ate together, all sitting on the floor and sharing stories like sisters; Gori had never been part of a unit like this and cherished every moment not knowing how long it would last and not daring to ask.

When her time came to deliver, she had plenty of the girls helping her, mopping her sweating brow, telling her when to pant and when to push, telling her how to lie to make the baby come out easier. She heard the strong cry and then cried with them all "Mubarak, Gori-*Jan*!" they cheered, "You have a fine young boy."

She called him *Aatiq*, meaning 'the liberated one'.

Begum Saeeda left her alone for six months to nurse her baby. And then, she came to her.

'Gori-Jan, my child," she said. "You have a strong will and great courage my child. You have a fine son. Now what will you do?" She asked but Gori knew this was rhetorical. So the Begum continued. "I do not know where you have come from, my child, but I know you will not return. I cannot keep you here for nothing. But I can teach you a great skill, my child. You have an indescribable beauty that has been hidden because of whatever tragedy has befallen you. I have seen the scar you have, my child, and I can only imagine why you have it. But that which has been your weakness shall be your strength. God has blessed you with your beauty and your strong spirit. You have come here as you are because you want something better for Aatiq. So now, I shall teach you to use your beauty and your strong will to win the minds and wills of many men such that they long for you. I will teach you to dance and with your dance alone, you will see how you can change your fortune and the future of the child you have born here."

So the tutoring began, six hours a day for the next six months. Lessons in *mujra* dance, in grace, in humility, in servitude and also deception. "You must be able to make him think that you dance for him alone, that you have never been touched and your inner most being desires him only," the Begum had taught her.

On the night of her debut, she was adorned in the most beautiful raiment she had ever seen, her hair washed, oiled, curled and pinned onto her head and she was draped with jewels. Her lips were painted a rosebud pink and her cheeks stained with the slightest hue of peach to give her the illusion of a woman in the first throws of love. And walked out slowly to the middle of the white marble floor. A large circle of men in *kurtas* reclining on comfy cushions and smoking *hukkah* were all around. But she wasn't scared, she lowered herself down and waited for the music. And then she danced, seductively, artistically, passionately. Although every eye was on her and many heart rates had increased exponentially, she knew nothing of it as she swayed and writhed to the *tabla* and harmonium and *sitar*.

When the Nawab heard of her and came to watch her, he had wanted to meet her. She had not objected, considering special audiences to be a part of her job. His insistence each time neither excited nor annoyed her. After a few months, the Begum spoke to her. "Gori-Jan, my child, you are fast becoming a prized possession. The Nawab has an eye for you. What would you like to do?"

Gori kept silent, she did not understand the question as such. Begum Saeeda continued. "Gori-Jan, you can ignore his advances and I can tell the Nawab that I cannot bring you to him. His indignation will pass, I know. But, my child, Aatiq is a boy today. One day he will be a man. Then he will need someone of influence to guide his path and make his way easy. The Nawab can do that. And while you wait, he will make sure that you lack for nothing."

So slowly, she had allowed him to come into her life and into her body knowing that at the right time and in the right season, she would ask him for something in return for all she had given to him. By that time, she knew, she would have made him hers and would be able to bend his will. Not that she felt the Nawab's presence was something to be endured, in many ways he was kind and considerate. He never hurt her and he never insisted on seeing her (and her scar) exposed.

But she did not love him, she only loved her son. Had she not wanted something better for Aatiq, she would not have given herself to the Nawab because, however one looked at it, she was a whore with one client. As Aatiq grew, he asked some questions about the Nawab and Gori knew that he did not like the man who vied for his mother's attention in the small hours of the night. But Gori told him that the Nawab would secure their future. They were unwanted people whose only way of liberation from the life that they lived was so bear the curse of it too.

"We must all give of our selves today, my son," she would say to him. "That God may return blessings tomorrow."

Aatiq did not like it one bit and secretly swore and oath to himself that he would one day he have a big *kothi* and much wealth and his mother would no longer have to subject herself to being the courtesan of the Nawab. Deep in his heart, he harboured hatred for the Nawab and it festered like an untreated wound. By the time Aatiq was a young man, his oath to look after his mother could only be satisfied by the desire he had to rid her of the Nawab forever.

Aatiq worked hard at his studies, not understanding that the Nawab's destiny was to secure a future for his courtesan's son. He wanted to make a future for himself that would afford him wealth and power and he understood that education would be his path into that world. At the same time he sat his entrance exams for medical college, the Dean was having an audience with the Nawab and being heavily encouraged to overlook any discrepancy between the entrance mark and a seat in college for a particular young man.

The Nawab need not have wasted his time since the Dean was not a fellow to be easily influenced, or worse still bribed, and especially not for an outdated would-be imperialistic concept that no longer had a place in modern Pakistan. More so, Aatiq passed his entrance exam with flying colours coming second in the state and 10th in the country. He could have in fact had his pick of medical colleges, away from any rumours surrounding his background, parentage or general raison d'etre.

But Aatiq chose to stay in Lahore because, apart from wanting to remain with his mother, he did, of course, have an oath to keep and his target should remain oblivious and close at hand for the days which were to come.

Sooji Ka Halva for a Soon-to-Be Mum

You Will Need

2 cups fine semolina
½ cup ghee
4 cups water
1 cup white sugar
3 green cardamoms – opened
½ cup assorted dried fruit (e.g. golden sultanas, raisins)
½ cup nuts (e.g. skinned sliced almonds, shelled pistachios, silvered cashews)

You Will Need to

Put the sugar, water and green cardamoms in a saucepan and bring to the boil so the sugar dissolves and you have a fragrant syrup. Set to one side.

Toast the nuts in a dry pan so they brown slightly and release their fragrant oils. Set to one side.

In another pan, melt the ghee.

When it is melted, add the semolina and fry in the ghee until it toasts and becomes a lovey golden brown colour.

Now add the sugar syrup bit by bit, like making a roux. Let it thicken before adding more. Generally, add about ½ a cup of syrup at a time.

Cook for 2 minutes and then add the nuts and fruit and stir well

Serve warm, both temperature and affection, preferably whilst doing a foot massage on mum-to-be.

Chapter 14

Dehradun, 2017

The morning of the funeral was bright and clear with little humidity. The monsoon had passed and with its passing came a more temperate climate with sunny warm days and cool nights. The external temperatures did not usually matter much to Sareeta anyway since she was either in an air-conditioned car, hotel or restaurant but today, she suspected that she may be spending some time outdoors and was glad of the pleasing temperature and lack of mugginess.

Over dinner the previous night, she had revealed her plans to attend the funeral of Feroz Khan to both Jai and Kiran. She had immediately been met with opposition, both father and daughter citing valid but obstructive reasons to not be so hasty. These included the notion that only men attend funerals, that the odd family of three would stick out like a sore thumb, that it was an inappropriate time to try and get information about a historical event that is likely to have been buried in family history and the most obvious, the entire inappropriateness of being reunited with her family under such circumstances.

But Sareeta would not be deterred. She was tired of not doing what she wanted to do in life because of the inbred mentality of 'what will it look like?' All she knew was that she had been given the seemingly miraculous opportunity to see her biological family with her own eyes and start her quest to fulfill her father's wishes. However, a part of her knew Kiran and Jai were more objective than she had the capability to be so they had agreed that they would attend after the funeral rites had taken place and pay their respects to the grieving widow, Maneeza Begum, and take things from there.

They had imagined all kinds of ways to make themselves acceptable but unnoticeable at the funeral, considering how to dress, act and introduce themselves. They thought about making themselves cousins from England or the US, long lost relatives who just happened to come across the obituary, even relatives of previous tenants who had gone abroad and been lucky. But each story just became more entangled as they imagined the questions that they would be asked. In the end, Jai, who was the least in the family opposed to confrontation, encouraged them all just to be truthful.

"If anyone asks the connection, we'll just say Mama is the grand-daughter of a landowner who was friends with the deceased's father. It's not a lie and hopefully the questions will stop there," he had stated. "Pumpo, are you sure you want to do this? You know, I'm sure we can hire an investigator to get the information we need, maybe even to find Dad's sister full stop."

"No," Sareeta had replied. "Dad has asked me and I want to do it for him. This is a start for us; let's see where this takes us."

"Mama, I'm here for you no matter what, okay?" Kiran had said unusually gently for her. "Just be prepared, I think it's gonna be hard for you to see them all."

So this morning, whilst Jai and Kiran were still sound asleep, Sareeta sat on the balcony overlooking the city bustling away with street vendors and tradesmen, making the most of the cooler climates that lured tourists and residents alike out of their cubby holes and into the heart of the local economy. She drank her hot *masala chai* quietly and resolved in herself to make sure that her dying dad at home would remain her father no matter what she felt today. She tried to tell herself hard truths and old clichés like a dad and mum are more than those that give birth to your existence, the Khans could have found her had they really wanted to just like Satvinder had, her life had been exceptionally good thanks to Satvinder and Meera and would her life had been so good in the Khan household anyway? But in the end, she wondered what it must be like to lose a child. She thought of how she would feel if Kiran had been taken from her and reappeared over fifty years later. She could not imagine, but she knew her life would not be the same.

By the time Kiran and Jai rose form their slumber, they had missed breakfast and opted to head out to the market instead for some street food. Standing at the kiosk now, they munched on crunchy *aloo* and spinach *bhajias* and hot mint chutney, enjoying all the sensations of crunchy, soft, sweet, hot, sour, all one delectable mouthful. Kiran and Sareeta devoured the crispy morsels whilst Jai scrutinized each one asking the same question for each, "Is it safe to eat?"

"So we'll pay our respects to his wife and then try and speak with some of the extended family, right?" asked Kiran, finally deciding just to ignore her father's overly anxious questioning and eyeing of each *bhaji*.

"Well, let's just see what happens, Kiran," replied Sareeta a little nervous now of her eldest's 'go get 'em' attitude.

"Kiran," Jai warned, "Let's just take it slow, sweetie." By now, he'd decided to ignore his own hypochondriasis too.

The driver of the roomy SUV Jai had hired had no problem in locating the Khans' *kothi* as, although Dehradun had expanded considerably since the 1960s, some things did not change including the celebrity-like status of the old families there. As they arrived, they could see the dusty road lined with cars well before they arrived at the gates. Sareeta had begun to feel nauseous. She would have liked to think it was the *bhajias* but she strongly suspected it was impending uneasiness of unfamiliarity that was fast approaching. Nonetheless, the driver managed to navigate his way right up to the big iron gates of the *kothi* and stop the car.

"*Saab-ji*," he spoke to Jai, "*Yahaan teek hai*? Is it alright for me to stop here?"

"*Teek*," said Jai. "Just wait here. Are you ready, Saru?"

Tentatively, she got out of the car. Dressed in a simple *salwar-kameez* with full sleeves, she took off her sunglasses and put her *duppata* over her head. Purposefully but slowly, she walked through the gates trying to gauge if she had a sense of being somewhere familiar. But she did not.

The courtyard was full of men, perhaps they had returned from the mosque or the burial, she was not sure. Some turned and looked at her with Jai and Kiran in tow because no matter how much one tried to blend in in India, tourists always look as such. Sareeta kept her focus forward walking up the three marble steps into the spacious marble-floored foyer. Exquisite antique furniture lined the room which was itself was adorned with hardwood and glass mirrors; Sareeta strongly suspected that much of this hand carved furniture was from the mountainous regions of Pakistan. The vast crystal chandelier hanging centrally was not lit but even so, the sunlight reflected off the crystals making the whole room shimmer. A few women were in there dabbing their eyes and being comforted by younger women. The activity intensified around oversized, intricately carved hardwood double doors. Jai nodded toward them and Sareeta made a beeline.

More women were gathered and she could hear stifled sobs, uncharacteristic of the Indian funerals she had attended but she was aware that Islam did not permit wailing at funerals. Jai seemed to hold back and she looked anxiously at him. "It's women here, darling," he said, "I'd better wait outside, you go in with Kiran."

Kiran took hold of her hand and led her forward. It was difficult to see the focus of the sobs throughout the mass of black clad aunties, cousins and sisters but slowly Kiran edged her way forward. Through dark covered shoulders and heads, Sareeta laid eyes on an elderly woman sitting on a straw *charpoy* that was completely out of place in the grandeur of the drawing room. Two ladies who looked to be in their late forties or early fifties sat on either side of her. The elder was leaning against one who had her arm around her and was rocking her gently side to side as she wept. She wore a simple dark brown *salwar-kameez* and had a *duppata* draped over her head which she was using to dab her eyes periodically. She was tall, even sat down and had light brown, almost hazel eyes. She was slightly rotund but even so, did not look like she was a woman who enjoyed eating. Sareeta could not help but stare at the widow, her mother.

"Mama," Kiran whispered, "Are you okay? Shall we go?"

"No, I'm fine," said Sareeta and took a step forward. She knelt down so she was face to face with Maneeza Begum. "Salaam alaikum aunty-*Ji*, we, that is my family and myself, are very sorry for your loss."

Maneeza Begum looked straight into the eyes of the woman in front of her.

So striking, she thought, *very beautiful*.

She looked at her more intensely trying to put a name to the face. She looked very familiar, this lady in front of her but she did not know from where. She was obviously not from here in Dehradun and her clothes, mannerisms and slight awkwardness showed her that she was a foreigner. But Maneeza had never been out of India and rarely left Dehradun itself over the past few years. Had she come as a visitor to the house before she wondered, was she a foreign relative? Her eyes, the same colour as her own, and skin tone made her think they must be related but she could not be sure. Elderly, yes, but she had no memory problems and was in fact renowned for her memory for faces. But even so, she could not place this lovely woman in front of her but she did look very familiar.

"Thank you, *beti*. May his soul rest in peace. From where have you come?" she asked hoping that the answer may enlighten her.

"From Canada, Aunty," Sareeta looked carefully for a reaction but none was forthcoming other than Mrs. Khan looking at her just as intensely as before. Her eyes were the same colour as Sareeta's, not too brown, not too hazel. She had high cheekbones, just as Sareeta did. Even her facial hair growth was in the same pattern as Sareeta, although the latter took great pains every three weeks to wax herself back to nudeness. It was not like looking in a mirror exactly but there was such a familiarity without any foundation that it was unnerving, like the proverbial white elephant in the room.

"Oh, such a long way, *beti*," Maneeza replied, "I am thankful." She hesitated, unsure of whether to ask her next question. "Are you family, *beti*?"

"Not as such, Aunty, but I am the grand-daughter of someone you may remember, who used to live here. Sardar Balwant Singh."

Maneeza went visibly pale, "Balwant Singh is no friend of this family and less so my husband."

She looked Sareeta straight in the eye. The truth of who she was became as apparent as when the Apostle Paul's scales cleared in front of his eyes and he could see clearly. She paused briefly and had a good look at Sareeta before saying, "I wondered what had become of you."

The women on either side of her had by now stopped their snivels and looked utterly confused, looking between Sareeta and Maneeza for some explanation of the odd statements.

"You look like life has treated you well enough," Maneeza Begum continued. Again, she paused and then her eyes became thin and she said in hushed tones "But if you have come here now to stake a claim on any inheritance, there is nothing for you here, child. The estate belongs to my sons now."

Sareeta did not know what to think, it had never occurred to either herself, Kiran or Jai that her timely appearance may suggest she was gold digging.

"I…I…haven't," she stammered. "No…please don't misunderstand me…I have come for…I mean, I've come to ask you something. I didn't know how else to find out. I don't want anything from you…I just need to know what happened to her…to the baby." Her last statement was slightly more assured.

"Mama, let's go," whispered Kiran before Maneeza Begum's gaze fell upon her. Kiran instinctively lowered her eyes.

"You have a beautiful daughter," Maneeza said looking at Kiran. "There is nothing I can tell you and your daughter is right, you should leave now."

"I'm sorry…I'm sorry," Sareeta could feel herself beginning to weep as Kiran deftly put her hand underneath Sareeta's elbow and helped her up. They left whilst in the corner of her eye, Kiran could see the two daughter-in-laws on either side of Maneeza Begum begin to bombard her with questions.

Struggling to keep composed, Sareeta hurried out with Kiran's hand still latched into her elbow. In the courtyard, Jai was chatting to two men in their late forties. He had a knack of being all things to all men. Having grown up in India, he was not as awkward as Sareeta. He looked, not so much a foreigner, but more a native that had made his fortune abroad, a true representation and not an uncommon phenomenon in India these days. He managed to appear affluent and internationally educated and yet at the same time be like an old college friend.

Prior to his marriage to Sareeta, he had a long-standing Pakistani girlfriend and so was really quite fluent in Urdu as well as Punjabi as well as Hindi. It was hard for a stranger to tell whether he was Muslim, Sikh or Hindu although, in fact, he was none of the above. Out of his periphery, he could see his visibly shaken and upset wife being ushered out hastily by his daughter.

Quickly, he took his leave and walked over to them as quickly as he could without being too obvious.

"What happened, darling-*Ji*?" he quickly led her before she broke down into huge sobs. "*Na, Na*, darling," he said, putting an arm round her other side and aiding Kiran in getting her off the premises and into the SUV, "Not here."

Safely in the car, Sareeta broke down. "She thought I wanted money, she thought I'd some here for his money," she sobbed, "I didn't even think of it, I never thought of it."

As the driver quickly sped off as instructed by his customer, Kiran filled Jai in on what had happened. Sareeta was too emotionally spent to add much. She was not only shocked by the accusation but deep down inside, she had wanted, and maybe even expected, a tearful joyful reunion. It was naïve, she knew. It was also unfair to Meera and Satvinder and she knew that too. But somehow, deep within, she had thought her biological mother had thought about her every day longing to be reunited with her. But she suspected that the truth was more like the day she had been taken, she had died to her mother and father. They had not looked for her much, they had not longed for her. And when confronted with her, she was little more than an embarrassing family unpleasantness that had stained the otherwise impeccably perfect Khan family history. She hardly heard what Kiran was relaying, she was consumed by the reality of what had just happened. And in the same way the revelation that she did not belong to Meera and Satvinder had sent ripples through her psyche that had taken time to resolve, the truth that she was nothing to her biological mother shook her to the core and she could not overcome it.

She could hear the other two exchanging questions and answers but did not really know what they were discussing until she heard a statement from Jai that brought her focus back immediately.

"And then they told me where I could find her."

Potato and Spinach *Bhajis* with *Pudina Chutney* Worthy of the Street

You Will Need for the *Bhajis*

2 cups finely chopped potatoes (cubes approximately 3 mm each)

1 cup finely chopped white onion (the same size as the potato)
2 cups finely shredded spinach/green Swiss chard
2 cups gram flour
½ cup water
1 tsp. salt
1 tsp. chili powder
2 tsps. carom seeds
1-litre vegetable oil

For the Chutney You Will Need

2 cups fresh mint leaves (soft stalks can be included)
1 cup cilantro leaves (again soft stalks can be included)
3 garlic cloves, 1-inch ginger and 1 small green chili chopped finely – food processor is a good tool here
2 tbsp. fresh natural yoghurt
2 green onions
1 tsp. *chaat* or *dahi masala*
1 tsp. dried mango powder (*amchur*) or juice of ½ a lemon
1 tsp. ground cumin

To Make *Bhajis* You Will Need to

Place the oil in a *karahi* or wok and heat to medium hot. Whilst this is heating, place all the *bhaji* ingredients into a mixing bowl, preferably a lightweight one.

Mix together well by squeezing the mix through your fingers – this is messy but well worth it as it will ensure that all the spices are well mixed, the vegetables well disbursed and you will get a feel of the consistency of the mix.

Check the oil is hot by dropping in a pinch of mix, it should sizzle gently and rise straight to the top,

Now, take small portions with your fingertips – about the size of a walnut.

Compress slightly with your fingers to make the 'walnut' hold together as much as possible and use you thumb of the same hand to push the 'walnut' off and into the hot oil.

Repeat the process until you have between 8 and 12 *bhajis* in the oil.

Deep fry for about 10 minutes until golden brown and crispy.

Remove with slotted spoon and repeat until all the mix is gone.

This mix makes about 30 to 35 *bhajis*.

For the *Pudina* Chutney

Place all ingredients into a blender and whizz to a puree.

Enjoy hot *bhajis* with the chutney as a dipping sauce, preferably eaten from a bag or paper cone made out of newspaper! (Oh and with the smell of the city behind you.)

Chapter 15

Lahore, 1985

"Clamp." The surgeon held out a blood-covered glove to the operating department assistant who deftly placed it in his hand. "This one is a bleeder," He added, immediately clamping off a small squirting artery.

"Okay, I think this is done. Aatiq, you can close." The surgeon nodded at the young resident stood on his right and turned round to de-glove and de-robe.

The sound of relief could almost be heard in the operating room as the double doors swung shut and he exited. The surgeon was well known to be a ruthless and harsh man who spared no humiliation in his theatre. A place on his firm was both feared and coveted as one would need the fingers of a seamstress but the heart of a lion. Any inaccuracy, mistake or less than perfect performance, stitch or plan would result firstly in the droll humiliation (usually without eye contact) followed by a complete disinterest in that resident's future progress. It was true, once the surgeon had made a decision on whether the young resident in front of him was ever going to be anywhere near as competent as him, he would either be left in a state of uncertain suspension or completely disregarded. The latter was very obvious, the former less so.

Aatiq had, so far, remained fortunate. His career in cardiothoracics was developing nicely; he had become well respected and highly thought of by his peers, despite his unsavory and unusual background. Amongst the young nurses, female doctors and even the older matron, Aatiq was a pleasure to behold with his tall good looks, fair skin and almond shaped eyes. His beautiful chocolate coloured eyes surrounded with thick luscious eyelashes, strong jaw line and quiet mysterious demeanour made him somewhat of a delightful puzzle. He was extremely bright, quietly self-confident and generally luscious in all respects.

He would arrive early on the wards to the swoon of the night duty nurses and check on all his post-operative patients before the 7:30 ward round would start. The notes were always handy but he knew his patients well enough not to need them. His almost photographic memory, and genuine interest in each patient, allowed him to reel off any result straight away without the need to check once again in the notes. More so, his uncanny wisdom, despite his lack of experience, in the field allowed him to have already implemented a management plan that left the surgeon merely nodding his head and moving to the next patient.

The surgeon had, over the past year, become very used to finishing his ward round at a little after 8:15 and enjoying his customary cup of hot chai much earlier than expected. Initially, he had been unsure of how to use the extra time he had before theatre started, too less to go home for a quick rendezvous with his wife, and too long to merely have extra time to sip his tea.

However, he was accustomed to Aatiq's brilliance by now and there were days when he wondered why he even bothered doing his post-theatre rounds; he was fully convinced that Aatiq was more than efficient in both pre- and post-operative care. Increasingly, he was taking over in the theatre too with his eye for microsurgery, a blessing now that the surgeon himself had to resort to varifocal lenses.

The surgeon, for fear of being made redundant too soon, continued his daily ward round, occasionally adding an interesting comment about some new piece of research that the department should consider piloting. At 8:15, he would retire to his office where a peon would bring his hot tea. The extra 45 minutes he had been left with he would now use not to complete any paperwork or read any correspondence, he did not even use it to read the newspaper. When he was sure that the peon was on other duties and his staff were busy getting theatre and the patients ready, he would close his door lightly, lower his blind, sit back comfortably in large worn leather captain's chair, put his large feet up on the desk in front of him and have a sizeable nap.

On this particular morning, Aatiq, having successfully finished the operative list, checked the post-operative patients in recovery and also on the ward and decided he could afford to head home early. His flourishing career had allowed him to afford the rent on a small Lahore apartment and it had now been nearly two years since his mother had left the Dance Hall.

Still not yet 40 years old, Gori-*Jaan* could have still had a few years of dancing ahead of her but on no level was this now needed. Aatiq's reputation could not have stayed unsullied for long once, as a working doctor, his mother continued to dance. The Nawab had himself passed on unexpectedly a few years previously which had saddened Gori-*Jan* more than she could have anticipated. It wasn't that she loved him and felt the loss as a widow would, it was more the loss of an old friend who had given some stability in the unpredictable tapestry of life. She had felt he was like an anchor, a constant in a future that she had learned not to trust.

Of course, she had not been able to express any of her grief. For one, Aatiq's scorn for the Nawab had only become more obvious as he had grown older and privately Gori-Jan had worried over what her son may do to the Nawab had nature not taken the upper hand. In addition, it would have been entirely inappropriate for her to outwardly mourn the loss of her sponsor; the official grieving was strictly the place of the formal widow and the Nawab's family.

The news had come to her from the Begum Saeeda one crisp cool winter morning as she sat oiling her hair as she did most mornings before washing. She had been aware that the Nawab had not been to see her for 2 nights and had merely assumed he had family commitments that had kept him away. She never questioned his comings and goings; she knew she had no right over him as such. But she had felt oddly unsettled in herself too over the last two days, as if a great flood was coming toward her. Gori-*Jan* had tried to ignore the feeling, attributing it to the change in weather instead or the shifting of the moon.

The Begum had sat down with her. "Stop what you are doing, child, and look at me," she had said.

Gori-Jan had raised her almond shaped eyes and looked into the Begum's eyes, knowing that the messenger who was to explain her sense of foreboding had arrived. "The Nawab has passed to eternity. His heart has stopped beating."

Gori-*Jan* looked down at her hands again and nodded. After a silence, the Begum spoke again, "Perhaps you would prefer not to dance tonight."

Gori did not look up but spoke, "May God bless him and give him peace in eternity. I will dance," she continued to oil her hair as the Begum took her leave.

Aatiq was already aware of the Nawab's demise having been the resident in the emergency room when he had been brought in. He had recognized him on the gurney immediately but did not make it obvious to the arrest team around him; he was there to lead the arrest and planned to do so. Aatiq did not fail in in his duty as such, he had given oxygen, checked serial ECGs, delivered a shot of epinephrine, managed the CPR and all else that was expected. But had he given the patient his very best judgment, his very best efforts and his very best life-saving skills? For such a talented young doctor, it was doubtful. For someone like the Nawab, one would have expected a sense of urgency that was not forthcoming in this case. Perhaps the Attending Consultant should have been notified sooner, the epinephrine given quicker and more often, the CPR more vigorous. Perhaps the time of death should not have been recorded so soon. Life was indeed cheap in Lahore but for some it was cheaper than others and the Nawab should not have been in that category.

Aatiq had not mentioned anything to his mother when he returned home after shift that night but he did begin to formulate his plan to bring an end to her dancing days and move from the only home he had ever known. This was far from easy for him as he had been loved, cared for and nurtured by all the women in the Dance Hall, a son to all of them and a grandson to the Begum Saeeda. He had massaged her aching legs as a young boy and been fed by her very hands when his mother was dancing. In the middle of the night, when he had nightmares, it was often another bosom that cradled him and rocked him back to sleep. When he fell and scraped his knee, his tears would be dried by other soft hands.

His graduation from medical school saw the biggest feast ever heard of in Heera Mandi and he already had a host of informal female patients around him wanting him to heal their various aches and pains. He loved them all dearly as they loved him and the thought of leaving them made him very sad. But equally he knew what sacrifices his mother had made for his life to be elevated from that of a servant to that of a King and it would only be accomplished when the ties of their undistinguished past were cut.

Within a month, he had secured a small apartment near the hospital and Aatiq with his mother Gori-*Jan* moved out of Heera Mandi. The Begum Saeeda had wept, not unusual for the other dancers but she was a stoic woman who had always given the impression that the girls were her business and not her family (a paradox really since the bonds that tied them all together were stronger than many family ties). Still she wept as she pressed a small box into Gori-Jan's hands. "For Aatiq," she said, "when the time comes." In it, Gori found a small gold set for a new bride.

Now two years on, they were settled in the apartment having had no further contact with the dance hall and Heera Mandi, a fact that the Begum must have been fully aware of when she had pressed that small box into her most celebrated dancer's hand.

Gori-*Jan* soon settled into a routine where she woke early in the morning and prepared breakfast for her son and herself whilst he caught the last shards of the early morning dawn deep in slumber. After he had taken his leave for the hospital, she would wash, dress and say her prayers. She then went to the *sabzi* market to buy vegetables for that day, bright green firm okra or shiny purple brinjals, firm white cauliflower or deep orange-crimson carrots. Sometimes, in season, she would by *laukis* for *koftas* and fresh yellow-fleshed sumptuous mangoes which she would slice for him in the evening or puree for mango *lassi* when it was too hot for chai.

Aloo gobi was Aatiq's favourite *sabzi* so, at least once a week, she would prepare the crisp cauliflower and fluffy potatoes with extra ginger, hot green chilies and just-ripe but still tinged with green tomatoes. He would arrive home at lunchtime, hungry and tired to the aroma of frying vegetables and soft puffed *chapatis*. After lunch, he would sleep before going back to the hospital in the evening whilst she prepared the evening meal.

Gori-*Jan* kept herself private from the rest of the apartment block, not caring, or daring, to speak to anyone. She wanted Aatiq to be free of her and her past and she did not want anyone to ask questions. Lahore was a big enough city for them to remain anonymous and they were now far from Heera Mandi. Those who did find her familiar would be too embarrassed to admit that as, unlike the Nawab, the working classes perceived Heera Mandi more as a red-light district to assuage the carnal pleasures of man rather than the home of the most ancient and erotic art form.

She had come to lead a very quiet existence. She should have felt lonely but her short life had been filled with so many acquaintances that she felt she had enough memories to keep her company whilst Aatiq was away. Soon it would be time for him to be married and she may then embark on another chapter of her life. For now, the solace was appropriate for her.

On this day, when she arrived back from the *sabzi* market, she was surprised to find Aatiq already at home resting on the sofa in the small lounge, a medical journal covering his eyes. "*Aare,* beta," she enquired, "Are you okay?"

"I'm fine, Mama," he sat up. "I just came home early. What did you bring today?"

"Your favourite, *puttar*, *aloo gobi*. Are you going back?"

"After lunch, this evening."

Aatiq resumed his snooze as his mother unloaded her goods in the kitchen placing the cauliflower, potatoes, onions, ginger, garlic, chilies and tomatoes on a large *thali* and taking it to the veranda. There she sat with a small knife on an old *charpoy* and began to prepare her vegetables whilst listening to the gentle hum of Aatiq's snoring and the fan-wafting warm air over his face.

How life had changed for them both, she thought. Strangely, she felt no bitterness over her past. The scar in her chest, the taunts she had been subject to her during her younger years, the years endured as a house slave and general sex toy, the weeks she had slept with the sun beating down on her swollen abdomen hoping her body had enough reserve to nurture her growing baby. The years spent as a dancing girl convincing gentry that she was swaying to the beats of their hearts alone, the comfort of knowing the love of someone who was not free to love her and finally, the utter peace and tranquility she felt now as Aatiq's gentle breathing played the backdrop to her rhythmic chopping.

She continued cutting absent-mindedly until a slip of the knife cut her finger and crimson blood dripped onto the snowy white cauliflower. Red on white, life on death, love on hate, blessing on curse. Such was her life, such was her fate. And she was content. She was happy.

Aloo Gobi for *Heera Puttar* ('Diamond Son') Made by Equally *Heera Mama.*

Aatiq himself likes this with *chappatis*, pickle, cucumber and onion slices and yoghurt. It is a dry dish that is simple in its flavours, in that it isn't too complex. The few spices enhance the flavour of the vegetables and really makes a dull cauliflower sing! And (although Aatiq would never do this!) left over *aloo gobi*, at room temperature in a toastie or a wrap with cheddar cheese…is divine!

Now the quantities cannot be exact as sizes of cauliflower varies and some people like more potatoes, less tomatoes, loads of ginger etc. So below is an 'average' but alter as you like. The dish is about the vegetables and not the spices to think of the spices as an 'enhancer' rather than a sauce for a curry – when you make it, you'll know what I mean!

You Will Need

1 fresh head of cauliflower – prep by tearing and then cutting the florets onto bite size pieces. Then take the inner leaves which are a pale green colour with a white stem and cut then up too into thick-ish shreds – they taste delicious

3-4 medium potatoes – to be honest, it doesn't really matter how much potato you use, it's all to taste, but generally after chopping my cauliflower and putting it in a medium sized colander, I fill the rest up with cut up potatoes. Cut the potatoes into bite size pieces smaller than the cauliflower because you add both at the same time, but the potatoes take longer to cook (so they need to be smaller)

1 medium white onion, sliced into half moons

1 bulb garlic (8-10 cloves), sliced

A good chunk of ginger, about 1 ½ to 2 inches depending on how much you like. Julienne (we like loads so generally I'd have about ½ a cup of ginger julienne!)

2-3 green chili sliced thinly

3-4 good sized tomatoes, firm and just ripe (often slightly green tinges are best) – about 1 ½ cups worth – cut into chunks (8-12 chunks from each tomato)

½-1 cup vegetable or sunflower oil. Mustard oil is also good and imparts a flavour that works well.

2 tsps. cumin seeds
2 tsps. salt
1 heaped tsp. chili powder
2 heaped tsps. turmeric powder
2 heaped tsps. ground cumin
1 heaped tsp. ground coriander
I heaped teaspoon *garam masala*
Chopped cilantro to taste
Have a cup of water handy

What to Do

Take a heavy based *karahi*. Don't use a casserole for this because the vegetable primarily steam-fry rather than steam so you don't end up with a soggy heap for cauliflower and potato.

Heat the oil in the pan until it is hot and add the cumin seeds. Let them spit and splutter and then add the onions

Fry the onion until they are golden. Then add the garlic, ginger and chillies and fry with the onions until the garlic begins to brown – about 5 mins.

Now add the tomatoes and cook until they are pulp and the oil has separated – it should be a lovely orangey/golden colour.

Now add the cauliflower and potatoes and stir.

Add all the spices, except the *garam masala*, now and stir/toss until the potatoes and cauliflower are completely coated. Take your time with this because all the vegetables need a good coating and the process of continuously moving them in the pan is the 'frying' part – you'll get a better flavour. Typically, I'm doing this for about 10 mins. Add a splash of water if there is any sticking but just a splash – remember this bit is the frying. Depending on how much is in the pan, you may need to add a little more oil too.

Now, lower the heat to as low as possible, cover the pan and leave to 'steam'. During this stage, check every few minutes that there is enough liquid to steam. Typically, I look at about 5 mins, add a couple of tbsp. water and close the lid again. Try not to stir any more as the cauliflower can break up and you end up with a mush.

After 12-15 mins, check the vegetables are cooked with a sharp knife (or a mouthful!).

Now sprinkle over the *garam masala* and cover again off the heat for a minute or so

Uncover and you should get a heady aroma from the *garam masala* (*'khushboo'*). Sprinkle over the chopped cilantro.

This is good with a flat bread or as a side dish with a lentil/bean meal

Alternatives

So this recipe is good for most vegetable-based dry dishes.

Eggplant and Potatoes

Now you can use eggplant and potatoes cut up raw just instead of the cauliflower and potato and it tastes good, you may need to add more oil as eggplant soaks a lot of it up BUT…

If you cut the eggplant and potatoes into even sized cubes and deep fry them first, it tastes amazing! Add a couple more chopped tomatoes too and more cilantro. It isn't too greasy this way as the hot deep-frying oil 'seals' the vegetables so they are soft and fluffy in the middle and silky on the outside.

Okra and Onion

I love this dish. There are no potatoes in this, just okra, onions and tomatoes. But you need the same amount of okra as onions so generally, I would use about 4 cups of okra (cut into ½ inch pieces) and then the same amount of onion (i.e. 4 cups cut up into half moons).

Carrot and Pea

This is a great dish because it has that natural sweetness which marries well to the heat of the spices. *Garam masala* and carrot also work well together (in fact carrots roasted with some *garam masala* taste good!)

For this, cut the carrots into batons and then small cubes so they are roughly the same size as a pea. Use frozen peas and add them after the carrots have been steaming on their own for about 15 minutes. Add the peas and continue on a low heat for another 10 minutes. This is good with just the carrot and peas but sometimes potato cubes are also added, cut to the same size and put in with the carrots.

Chapter 16

Dehradun, 2017

It was true to say that, after her encounter with the Khan family, Sareeta wept the entire way to the hotel and continued for most of the evening.

She could not describe the range of emotions that consumed her: shock, disappointment, disbelief, anger, grief and hatred to name some. She felt exhausted, homesick and utterly sick. She questioned if she should give up and go home. This entire experience was becoming too painful for words but she was so tired she could not even think rationally. The numbness that she had felt previously would have been welcome today, but that comfort had gone, and she was left with a mass of entangled feelings that she couldn't seem to get clear in her head. This was not an entirely unfamiliar feeling for her; there had been times before when she had felt she was carrying around a basket of tangled dirty laundry in her heart and head and all she could see was the mass. She'd needed some loving support from her friends and family to help her sort out the emotions into more concrete ideas that she could begin to manage, rather than they managing her.

But in some ways, these feelings were also new to her. Sareeta had been a more confident woman once, excelling at almost anything she did. She was not used to being needy, she was used to being needed. She wasn't used to taking support and comfort, she was use to giving it. She was the confidante, the reliable friend, the 'go-to' woman, the true mother figure. And here she was, a crumpled, lost mess, sitting in a hotel room, wearing a hotel bathrobe, no longer knowing who she was and what she wanted. Nothing at this point felt familiar or hers; it was as if she was watching someone else's life from a distant position.

It had been two days since the funeral now. Jai had found out from the men in the courtyard that there had indeed been a profound effect on the Khan family during Partition. Initially, he had merely had polite discussions with the men, how sad it was that Feroz-Bhai had passed on, what a loss to the family and community, how much he had done for the community, how much he would be missed. As the men grew more confident around Jai's general air and relaxed informal attitude, they asked him questions about himself.

"*Bhai-Saab*, we haven't seen you before, are you a relative?" They had tentatively asked.

Jai had smiled at them with a look that had left them intrigued. "Who do you think I am?" he had teased them.

With some people, the teasing could have been misconstrued for impropriety at a funeral, especially that of such a respected individual. But Jai had a way about him that very rarely caused offence. His demeanour, and use of colloquialisms, had caused them to warm to him immediately. It was obvious that he was not from Dehra-Dun or even India now. He looked like a wealthy man who lived abroad but still someone who valued and respected the land which raised him. He wasn't teasing them, and they all felt that they should remember him, a slight embarrassment on their parts.

"*Bhaiya*, I should know who you are but I'm afraid I do not. Are you from here? Are you a relative?" one of the gentlemen had replied.

"No, no, my friend, I am not from here. My wife has family from here and wanted to pay her respects. I am merely the chauffeur!"

At this, they all laughed and the atmosphere relaxed again.

"But since I am not really known to the family, I can see he must have been a very important man. An old family, it seems."

"Oh yes, *Bhaiya*," the younger man spoke with confidence, "The Khans have been here for so many generations. We own much land here and around. We are one of the few Mughal families left in this state."

"Is that so? Very good," Jai had replied. Feeling they had an avid listener to whom they could boast the longevity and wealth of the family, they continued.

"Oh yes, *Bhaiya*, you do not know how much of the land is ours. Some say you can walk from here to Patna on land owned by the Khans!"

"You lost none during Partition?" Jai asked innocently.

"Of course not, *Bhaiya*! It was Firoz-*Bhai's* father who protected it. How could he give it up? This was the family legacy." The younger one was animated in his boasting by now.

"But how? I thought land was just plundered and taken."

"It was, *Bhaiya*, but not to us," the older man joined in, "You see, Rizwan *Thaiya-Ji* knew very early he had to be respected; so many of our people were fleeing, respect was everything, the most valuable commodity. He did some things, to ensure his place in society. No one bothered him much after that."

"Things?" Jai asked curiously

"*Hahn, Bhaiya*, things. You know, not things to be proud of but things that were needed," the older one had lowered his voice and looked hastily from side to side as if he may be overheard.

Jai leaned in, "I heard he took a child."

The men huddled in toward him, looking swiftly around them before speaking. "Where does Bollywood come from brother if not from our own stories? He took his best friend's wife, burned his *kothi* and sent the child to 'Pindi to our cousin. After all, if you yourself put your head in the mortar, why fear the pounder. No one messed with him after that."

Jai and Kiran had spent the last couple of days trying to obtain visas for Pakistan ready for the next part of their journey which would take them to Rawalpindi. Ordinarily, this would have taken a couple of months but they were acutely aware that this was not an option for them; they were already feeling the pulls of the business fending for itself at home. They were also aware, having had private discussions about her whilst she slept, that Sareeta simply did not have a will strong enough to allow this matter to persist for too much longer. On the other hand, they also knew that it was deeply embedded in her to restore the equilibrium to her family, particularly her father.

It wasn't that Jai had many influential contacts in the Pakistani High Commission, or the Indian one at that, but he did manage to speak to a few people higher up the immigration food chain, pay the humongous fee and secure visas pretty quickly. The fact that they were Canadian and not Indian citizens helped enormously, and it was still true, even now, that a bit of extra wealth and a couple of political contacts managed to get the heavy stone rolling faster. There was little left for them in Dehra Dun now. Sareeta was lost in her own world and withdrawn. Try as they might, Kiran and Jai could not coax her out; they could only ensure that she ate, she slept and she knew that she was loved.

That evening, Jai insisted that Sareeta dressed and that they went out. The streets of Dehra Dun were busy as commuters had made their way home, changed and collected their families to head out again for delicious food and one of the many eateries or fresh sweetmeats. Jai reminisced about his childhood days, his father coming home late from the car showroom where he was head mechanic. Jai and his brothers would have been playing cricket in the dirty gullies rather than studying; his mother, who was well past the stage of getting frantic over the three boys' misadventures, would be in the kitchen anticipating the arrival of her husband, ready to make hot *chapatis*. At the sound of his scooter, the three boys would run in the house and quickly sit on the floor, hot, dirty and gleeful. Quickly, they would get out their school books just as he walked through the door and start reciting important historical dates or mathematical formulas they were supposed to memorize.

"They sat when they heard me, didn't they?" his father would say to mother as he walked through the door and saw them.

"What else?" she would reply.

The boys were terrified of their father, in a good way that was lost on Kiran's generation. He would tower over them and berate them for giving their mother a hard time. Jai could remember the smell of diesel on his hands and the slight aroma of whisky in his breath as he tried to convince his wife that he had come straight home and, of course, he hadn't had a drink with his colleagues. Eventually, he would relent. "Okay, just one peg. One peg only, my sweetheart, would you deny me that?"

The boys would look up at him wide-eyed.

"Satnam," he would say to his wife, "Go and put on something beautiful, get ready. Boys, go and wash, let's go."

The boys would quickly rush off to wash whilst mother would argue with father about the meal already being made, how tired she was, how the boys had homework to do but it was always to no avail. Dinner being made had little effect on father, neither did her fatigue. And the boy's homework? Well, he would have a quiet word with the principal in the morning, who was one of his customers anyway so knew how things worked.

It was all just part of the dance: father would insist on taking his family out, mother would bring up the same excuses why not (with the same lack of conviction) and they would all end up on his scooter speeding off toward town. It was a well-rehearsed and well-loved script. Father would be driving with the little one between him and steering. The two other boys squashed behind father with mother perched on the end, side-saddle, wedging the boys in.

Sometimes, he would take them to buy mother a new *salwar-kameez* or sari, sometimes the boys would get toys or books and sometimes, it would be a plate of *chana* and rice off the street followed by hot *gulab jaman*. But by far their favourite was trips to Moti Mahal for the infamous butter chicken, moist fleshy chunks of chicken cloaked in thick tomato gravy laced with melted butter, cream and cilantro. Hot in the *handi* with sumptuous pillow-like *naans*. They would feast and shop and go to bed late. Father would take them to school in the morning with some *mithai* for the principal, advising the boys would complete homework tonight and just to overlook today. The principal would smile and nod and tell the boys to get to class before having a chat with father about an extra oil change or engine tune. All was balanced, all was well.

Jai reminisced because he could no longer live out those days, his mother and father had passed on and his brothers were scattered over the world, both with families of their own. He so missed those days, the simplicity of cricket in the gullies, the smell of diesel and whisky, the melt of butter chicken, the warmth of the air on his face, the anticipation of new toys, the promise of a restful sleep. Life had become too complicated, too busy. Even for his own four children, they would not know those smells or sounds because Jai's 'garage' was an office, his hands smelled of Jo Malone hand wash, not diesel. His scooter was a Maybach. The toys were IPADS and not kites and the mere thought of regular helpings of Moti-Mahal's butter chicken, he was sure, put extra plaques on his arteries before he even tasted it.

But tonight, he needed that comfort and that familiarity and he wanted to share that intimacy with his wife and his eldest, just once. He insisted Sareeta wore something beautiful and told Kiran to get washed; they were going out. He had given the driver a night off and had planned on them taking an autorickshaw to town, the nearest he could get to the tightness of the scooter, the warm wind on his face. The bellboy had suggested a place for butter chicken (although it had taken Jai some convincing to make him understand that he did not want another five-star establishment, just a family place where working men would take their children). They were all ready to leave and Jai was ready to return to his childhood delight when the bell of their suite rang. Sareeta had just stepped out of her room in a baby-pink raw silk *salwar-kameez* with rose-gold embroidery over the bodice, looking more like the Sareeta they were all used to. She just heard Jai open the door and a woman's voice, assured and mature speak.

"I've come to see my daughter," she said.

Jai stepped aside. In the doorway, wearing a dark *salwar-kameez* and *duppata* over her head, stood Maneeza Begum.

Butter Chicken *(Murgh Makhani)* Reminiscent of a Childhood Spent in Moti Mahal

You Will Need

    1 cooked tandoori chicken cut into 10-12 pieces
    1.5 kg ripe red tomatoes
    250 g butter in 3 portions, 100 g, 100 g and 50 g
    2 tsps. vegetable oil
    6 green cardamoms – bruised
    2 slivers mace
    2 cloves
    1 dried Kashmiri chili
    1 heaped tsp. crushed garlic paste
    2 tsps. salt
    2 tsps. vegetable oil
    2 green chilies sliced thinly

1 heaped tbsp. ginger-garlic paste
1 heaped tsp. chili powder
1 heaped tsp. ground cumin
1 tbsp. dried fenugreek leaves
½ tsps. Green cardamom powder
½ cup cream (single)
1 tbsp. fresh chopped cilantro

You Will Need to

Chop all the tomatoes into 8 pieces each.

In a large sauté pan, melt 100 g butter with 2 tsps. oil. When hot, add the chopped tomatoes and stir.

Now add the bruised cardamoms, mace, cloves, Kashmiri chili, garlic paste and salt.

Stir well and lower the heat and cover, cook for 20 minutes or until the tomatoes are broken down and pulpy.

Pass the tomato mix through a sieve into a bowl so the puree comes through and the skin/husks/seeds are in the sieve; you can throw this away.

Clean the pan and add 100 g of butter and 2 tsps. oil. When it melts, add the green chilies and ginger-garlic paste. Cook for 5 minutes until the paste is brown.

Now add the tomato puree back into the pan.

Add the chili powder, cumin, fenugreek seeds and green cardamom powder. Stir well.

Bring to the boil and lower to a simmer.

Add the cream and stir.

Add the last 50 g butter and allow if to melt into the sauce.

Add the cooked chicken portions to the sauce and heat through.

Sprinkle over the fresh cilantro (and a drizzle of melted butter or cream if you like)

Enjoy with *pilau* rice of fluffy pillow-like *naans*...and a couple of aspirin 81 in case a coronary occurs.

Chapter 17

Dehradun, India, 2017

It was a shock to say the least, not only to see Maneeza Begum standing in the doorway of the hotel executive suite, but also to hear her refer to Sareeta as daughter.

For a few seconds, there was complete silence whilst all four of them stood and stared and tried to take in the reality of what was occurring. The atmosphere was electric; Jai, Sareeta and Kiran dressed as if going to a party whilst the widow stood solemn and staid at the entrance. It felt wrong; it was as if Sareeta had not been mourning, as if the entire encounter at the funeral had been a casual affair. Had Maneeza come an hour ago, she would have seen the mess that was her daughter with her tear stained face and dishevelled appearance.

Maneeza appeared not to be fazed by the appearance of the three in front of her; in fact, she hardly noticed what they were dressed like. The last two days had sent her mind reeling into over-drive. Fifty-two years ago, she had lost a child. For fifty-two years, she had tried to forget that her daughter even existed, she had daily quashed the bitterness that could have consumed her thinking about how the sins of her father-in-law had stolen her happiness, had taken from her the one thing that she treasured more than anything else in the world. For fifty-two years, she had put on a face of devoted wife, loving mother, society matriarch whilst inwardly she was crushed and hollow.

Did anyone know how much of herself she had spent on self-control rather than tearful outbursts? Could anyone anticipate how devastatingly destroyed a mother could be to not lose a child as such, but have a child taken? She had called her daughter, her first born, her *dil-de-tookra*, a piece of her heart and when she was stolen, Maneeza literally felt a piece of her heart had been torn off her and thrown to the lions.

For fifty-two years, she had kept quiet, knowing that the expectation on her was to continue the family way of life and uphold the Khan name and respect.

And now, her *dil-de-tookra* was here in front of her again.

After Sareeta had left the funeral, her two daughter-in-laws had questioned her fiercely. How strange it was, Maneeza had thought, that these two women could change instantaneously from weeping kittens to dancing cobras. All their tears vanished immediately as they tried to tease out of her some nuggets of family gossip which they had heard rumour of through the community for years. Maneeza, as she had done for so many years, managed to block out the encounter for the rest of the day whilst mourners came and paid their respects; it was her duty and she always carried out her duty. But in the quiet of the night, when exhaustion should have carried her comfortably to sleep, she was consumed by the image of the enigmatic woman who had knelt at her feet, so familiar and yet such a stranger.

By the morning, her sons had predictably been filled in on the happenings of the day before. At breakfast, they approached their mother direct whilst their wives stood haughtily in the corner watching, their faces partly obscured by their *dupattas*.

"*Amma*," they had said, "she is no daughter of yours and no sister to us. Did you ask yourself why she comes now? *Amma*, we cannot allow her appearance here to change anything; it is not the way this family is. You must forget what happened. We must carry on as before."

Nothing more had been said; it was the usual way after the men had spoken their piece. The servants were instructed to bring fresh *puris* to eat with the steaming potato curry already in front of them, refill the pickles and yoghurt over and to ask the kitchen to prepare hot *chai*.

Maneeza pushed her food around her plate, unable to eat. She considered what her sons had said. Of course, given the way the family was, they were right. The Khans were not people to indulge in romantic notions. All the actions of each individual were carefully carried out (or not carried out) to the benefit of the family and not the individual. Each member had their role and all parts must work together for the better good of the unit. No one married simply for love, the family married into other families to bring dynasties together. No one endeavoured to start a new venture; the family would decide what was needed and assign its undertaking to one member. The women never went out alone, the children never considered only their siblings as brothers and sisters, even the servants had a pedigree familiar to the family as many had worked through generations. There was a clear and definite hierarchy, established systems and ways of operating. There was no instability, no question without answer and no surprises.

Until two days ago.

Maneeza had questioned and questioned herself over what to do. It was ingrained in her to forget what had happened for the sake of the family but she could not, she simply could not. Fifty-two years had not been long enough for her move on from what happened and consider her daughter as non-existent. She had to see her, and she had to make sure that no one knew.

That evening, she had waited until after the evening meal of lentils, vegetables and *chappatis*, a simple meal as the family was officially still in mourning. When her sons and daughter-in-laws had retired to their quarters, thinking that Maneeza herself had retired, she called her maidservant. Rehanna had been with Meneeza Begum since she had first come to the Khan residence as a young bride. She had helped dress her and bathe her, make sure that her hair and makeup were immaculate. But more so, since Rehanna's mother had herself been a maidservant to the wife of Rizwan Khan, she was able to advise (and ensure) that the new bride paid heed to what was expected of her.

When her mother-in-law had ordered the new bride to wear clothes fitting of her new status, it was Rehanna who had known exactly which outfit was needed for which occasion. For visiting elders, something primrose or peach that showed off her fair skin and fair eyes, but demure in its image. The fabric and subtle embroidery should reflect the wealth of the family as should the carefully selected jewellery, small diamonds set with morganite on rose gold. For a more elaborate affair, the outfit should be a brighter colour, magenta or cerulean, heavily embroidered with an array of golden bangles; there were no glass bangles in this household other than on the servants from time to time.

Rehanna had guided her skillfully during those early years. And when the baby had been taken, it was Rehanna who Maneeza secretly bared her soul to with inconsolable sobs and wailing that came with a grief that could only be understood by another mother.

It would be Rehanna who would now act in secret for Maneeza again, going out onto the street after nightfall and summoning a taxi. Stealthily she would huddle her disguised mistress into the back seat making sure that her face was hidden. Only Rehanna spoke to the driver, instructing him to drive direct to the hotel (Rehanna had found this out too from the other servants who had connections in the city). On arrival, the taxi*walla* was told to wait and she would return quickly. Swiftly, she perused the reception area and her eyes fell on a bored-looking and overworked bellboy. Approaching him, she pressed 2000 rupees into his clammy palm. "*Bhai-saab*, I'm looking for a western family, a tall distinguished man, in his fifties with a wife and grown up daughter."

The bellboy looked at the little bundle of 500-rupee notes in his palm. "Executive suite, fifth floor," he replied and grinning, placed the notes in his pocket.

Rehanna scuttled back out to the taxi and relayed the message to her mistress. "I'll wait here, *Memsahib*," she said, "but please be careful."

Maneeza covered her head, chin and mouth with her *duppata* loosely but surely and walked swiftly to the lifts, keeping her eyes low. Only the bellboy himself noticed her but he was too enthralled with his good luck to be that interested, thinking about how he could now partake in the game of cards that was to take place very late that night in the bowels of the hotel.

Now, with Sareeta in front of her, her look softened. The stern face that she had so easily adopted two days ago was replaced with, not kindness or even resignation, more a look of absolute fatigue and exhaustion. Fifty-two years of pent up grief seemed to appear on her face in that moment. Lines around her eyes became deeper and greyness surrounding became darker. Any trace of youth was gone and an old tired woman starred at Sareeta. But there was a great compassion and peace in her eyes which now watered as the two women just looked at each other.

"My daughter," she finally said stumbling at the words such was the choking in her throat, "my daughter. I'm sorry."

With that, she took Sareeta's hands in her own and held them to her mouth and tenderly kissed them whilst her tears fell on Sareeta's skin. "I should have found you."

Sareeta gently led the old woman to the couch to sit before either of them fell under the weight of emotions raining down on them both right now. She didn't know what to say right now, she often had a very delayed emotional response although it would have been fitting right now for her too to be tearful. Maybe it was the physician, or the mother, in her that did not allow her to have any kind of demonstrative emotional release right now, although she was aware that her heart was beating rather rapidly and she was shaky. "Kiran, can you get Aunty some water, let's sit."

"I don't know what to say, Aunty-*Ji*," Sareeta began. "This is hard on all of us. But please, just tell me what happened?"

"What can I say, *beti*," Sareeta noted the use of her word 'daughter' again. "Many things happened in 1946, 47, terrible things. I was told how my own family, your Nana, took us all from our beautiful home in Delhi one night. I have four sisters and two brothers, your *masis* and *mamas*. They are not all with us now. We were small children but we knew how things were changing. An army vehicle came; your Nana was very influential and wealthy. My mother took what she could, I remember a big trunk in which she put her gold, some clothes, a few photographs but that was all. Our Delhi house was magnificent and we left everything.

"It took days to get to 'Pindi. We were squashed into a small place, in that army jeep. Sometimes, the jeep was stationary for hours and we had to keep so quiet. My sister told me that I had my mouth tied with Mama's *duppata* to stop me from crying. When we arrived our relative's house, we had one room to ourselves. Your Nana lost everything and we started again.

"Rizwan and my father were cousins so when the proposal came, my father accepted quickly. I was very young but with five daughters to marry and all our wealth gone, he knew this was a blessing from God.

"I was 19 when you were born and you were the most precious thing in the world to me. When you were taken, I wanted to die. Every day I wanted to die."

Maneeza broke down into heavy sobs and Sareeta took her hand. "Your father changed that day. He couldn't be immune to what had happened no matter how much he wanted to. He had to try. He went to the *kothi* and he tore it apart, he tried to find out what had happened, where you had gone but in the end, he had to let it go. We became strangers, he in his own world and me in mine. We were told the family had to be thought about, we were told sons were needed to fill the hole that was left by you. We were told to carry on and forget. I knew he could not any more than me but there was no choice given to us."

"Why didn't you find me? You must have known where I had been taken. Didn't everyone know Baldev Singh had gone to Kenya?"

"My sorrow lies there, *beti*. We all knew and yet none of us could admit to knowing. To some, justice had been served and Rizwan's sin atoned for. 'At least it was a girl,' they said. But to me, my heart had been ripped out and there was nothing I could do. Who could I fight? Where could I go? I begged your father to go and find you. I knew he knew where you were. But he could not, call it weakness, call it pride, whatever it was, he closed up his heart and mine with it. All I could do was mourn you like a child killed. And even that I couldn't do it outwardly. Name and respect were everything, my loss was my burden to carry and mine alone."

"I need to know what happened to my grandmother's child." Sareeta asked. Somehow, it wouldn't penetrate her that the story she heard was her story. Self-preservation perhaps or maybe just a need to focus on the task in hand.

"My father's relatives in 'Pindi had taken the child in, she was in the same house where we stayed too when we arrived but I didn't know who she was. She was with the servants there. My Aunty and cousins despised her but Uncle Shiraz was kind to her. He married her young. Some say it was to secure a land deal, she was very beautiful. But I think he did it to save her from his wife and children.

"Her husband was not a good man and I heard she ran away after a year to Lahore. There were many rumours about her. Some said she had become a prostitute, others that she had married a rich Nawab who had fallen for her beautiful looks." Maneeza looked at her hands and Sareeta knew that she knew the truth.

"You know what happened to her, don't you? I mean more than the rumours."

Maneeza looked up at her, eyes mirrors of each other, two hearts yearning for redemption and peace. Two weary souls, victims of a man's world, victims of hatred, jealously, greed.

"I know exactly where she is, *beti*. I know everything."

Aloo Purees with Pickle and Yoghurt for Breakfast, Brunch…Or Any Time of Day

You Will Need

For Potato Curry

3 large potatoes, cut into quarters, boiled in their skins and then skinned.

2 medium onions sliced thinly

1 tbsp. finely chopped garlic

1 cup chopped canned tomatoes

½ cup vegetable oil

2 tsps. cumin seeds

1 tsps. salt

1 heaped tsps. chili powder

2 tsps. turmeric

1 heaped tsps. ground cumin.

2 cups water

2 tbsp. fresh chopped cilantro

What to Do

Cut the cooked potatoes into bite size chunks and set to one side.

Take a large *karahi* or sauté pan.

Heat the oil.

When hot, add the cumin seeds and let them sizzle and release their earthy aroma.

Add the sliced onion and brown.

Add the garlic and allow that to brown too (it takes less time that the onions so make sure the onions are nearly golden before adding the garlic).

Add the tomatoes and cook until pulpy and the oils separates from the tomato-onion mix.

Add the spices and stir well, you may want to add a splash of water to prevent any sticking.

Now add the cooked potatoes and coat well. Lower the heat and continue cooking for 5 minutes until the potatoes have taken in the sauce.

Now add the water, stir again and bring to the boil.

Lower the heat and simmer for 10 minutes until the potatoes are bathed in the sumptuous glossy sauce.

Sprinkle with cilantro and serve hot with purees.

For Purees

This makes 12-14 purees

2 cups *chapatti* wheat flour

Enough warm water to make a pliable soft dough, about 2 cups.

1 litre cooking oil

You Will Need to

Mix the flour with the water a little at a time until you have a soft and pliable dough. Knead for at least 5 minutes and rest for at least 10 minutes

Whilst waiting, place all the oil into a deep *karahi* or wok and heat to medium high. To test if it is hot enough, take a tiny pinch of dough and drop it in, it should sizzle and rise straight to the surface. If it does this, the oil is hot enough to start deep-frying – fish your 'test-piece' out. Heating the oil takes about 10 minutes on the stove.

Roll a piece of dough into the size of a golf ball and start to roll out into a thin round disc; it should be about the size of a large saucer.

Drop the disc into the hot oil. It should sink, then rise and fill with air. Turn it over and cook the other side; both sides should be golden brown. Each puree takes about 3 minutes to cook.

Repeat the process until all your dough is used.

To Serve

Place 2-3 purees on a plate (or even better stainless-steel *thali*) with a good ladleful of potato curry, a good dollop of fresh yoghurt and some good *achar* (pickle) on the side. Maneeza favours mango but her sons like chili, whatever works for you!

Chapter 18

Lahore, 1990

It was a quiet and understated ceremony, unusual for a prominent doctor but anything else would have felt unusual to Aatiq, who had aimed to live his life true to himself alone.

Undoubtedly, his wife was beautiful and intelligent and from a wealthy family; he could have had the most resplendent of weddings. Selina was the third generation of doctors in her family, well groomed, well brought up and very privileged. She had admired and adored Aatiq from a great distance throughout medical school but his aura was such that many admired but few knew. Aatiq had a close circle of male friends and very rarely took the company of females.

Their love story had been a brief one. She was his junior colleague at the hospital and through some engineered one-on-one tutorials, they graduated to swift greetings in the canteen and then longer chats during coffee. Soon Selina had managed to turn Aatiq's heart and no sooner had he admitted to himself that this aspiring cardiologist would make him a suitable wife, and importantly his mother a very suitable daughter-in-law, he arranged to meet her father and asked for her hand.

Selina's father was in two minds over the proposal. On the one hand, Aatiq was well known for being a brilliant young man, certainly an individual with a great medical future. On the other hand, no one knew anything much about his past, his upbringing and his family. There were many rumours about Aatiq's family and he knew not whether to take heed or not. Selina herself was prime marriage fodder, intelligent, beautiful and a good daughter. He had received many proposals for her, from friends, relatives and those who had heard of her. He had resolved many years ago that she would only marry another doctor because she too was brilliant and had a very good future ahead of her.

But Aatiq was not the typical suitor for her. Clearly she was enamoured with this man, a look that her father had not seen in her when presented with other suitors. She didn't 'light-up' as such in his presence but a serenity came over her that was difficult to describe. It was as if she had a found a place for herself in this turbulent life. She appeared somehow more beautiful, more content, more intelligent even; everything she was, she was more of when Aatiq was around. Selina's father chuckled to himself as he was well aware of Selina's stubborn and determined nature and wondered if she would display more of these too when Aatiq was with her.

Although family matters bothered him somewhat, it did not take him too long to reach the decision that Aatiq was the right man for Selina. His calm demeanour would balance her exuberant one, his contemplative attitude toward issues would complement her rashness, his strength of mind would help her in her weakness of conviction over certain things and certainly, his good judgment would override her stubbornness. Yes, Aatiq was a man of sound character and Selina's father was sure he would provide a comfortable and honourable life for his eldest daughter. She would not grow too proud nor too weary. And as for family matters, well in Lahore when the turn of the century was fast approaching, should not any man be happy that his daughter had chosen within her own culture a man with a modicum of good potential. The days of dynasties being married into each other were gone and even if there was a less than perfect background, a good solid marriage with a successful husband would soon quieten wagging tongues.

Finally, the day came for Selina's family to visit Aatiq's mother in her home. Laden with dried fruit and clothes offerings, the entourage left the big house in central Lahore and travelled to the apartment where he lived with his mother. Aware that apartment living was vastly different to the home with servants Selina was accustomed to, they ascended the two flights of stairs to Aatiq's home. Pleasantries were exchanged at the door before the wedding party entered in the small apartment where they managed to find seats tightly squeezed next to each other. Gori-Jan brought out tea, savouries and sweetmeats whilst Selina's mother paid close attention to the apartment décor, size of rooms, areas of dampness and Gori-Jan herself.

Selina's mother, much like Selina, was used to a comfortable life but, unlike Selina, showed a fullness in her bosom and tummy that reflected many years of good food and little need to move. She noted immediately, not only Gori-Jan's immense beauty, but also her svelte figure and took a dislike to her straight away. She did not say much to her daughter's future mother-in-law, well, nothing positive anyway. She picked at the snacks laid out, muttering that the sugar content was too high and her husband should avoid them, the tea had too much milk for their tastes and definitely, the fried goods were off the menu for her family. Selina's husband tried politely to make light of her comments, chuckling to his hosts saying his wife was always overly concerned about his health and that she ought to bear in mind that for generations their people had enjoyed these sweet and spicy delicacies.

Despite her attempts to refute the union, Selina's father had his mind made up. There was something undeniably charming about Aatiq's mother. She was stunning and youthful; it was clear to him that she had given birth to her son at an early age. But even beyond that, she had something alluring about her that brought out some emotion in him which he could not vocalise, but nonetheless he knew he should be ashamed of. She was simple and yet astute, shy and yet charming. He could see where Aatiq got his charisma from.

Tentatively, he asked about Aatiq's father to which Aatiq quickly responded. "My father is no longer with us and has not been for a long time. We are content now with what we have," Something in his tone indicated, but not aggressively, that there was nothing more to add to that. It was not the most satisfying of answers but Selina's father knew that it would have to suffice.

Later at home, Selina's mother tried again to convince her husband that the lack of knowledge surrounding the family, and the father in particular, was in no way a satisfactory situation. "We simply do not know enough about the boy's background," she lamented. "How can we be sure that they are our type of people? And as for her, well, I hardly think she would fit into our way of life. Are you even sure she is his mother? She looks very young to me."

"They are a well-suited couple and his family relations are of little consequence. He is decent and hardworking. I see no issues with his mother, she was perfectly pleasant and your behaviour toward her, my dear, was not very gracious. You heard Aatiq, his father died when he was young. She has raised a fine young man, and that seemingly on her own. I cannot see any issues her. We will fix the date for the near future."

And with that the decision was made. Selina's mother knew very well she had little chance of him changing his mind. She sulked for a few days which he overlooked. A date was set for one month. At the request of the couple, there was a simple ceremony and a meal to follow. This too grieved his wife who felt she had been robbed of the months of planning, extravagant outfits, expensive jewellery. The years she had spent planning her daughter's wedding were reduced to two modest outfits, a simple gold set and one wedding meal. She felt belittled, cheated and embarrassed as she sat at the head table pushing her *keema muttar* around the plate.

For her part, Selina was ecstatic with the agreed union and the haste at which her father had planned the wedding. She tolerated her mother's sulking, acutely aware that this was not what she planned for her eldest daughter's wedding. Selina had grown up amongst society weddings and parties but had rarely enjoyed them. She was not one for spending hours at the beauty parlour, the hair salon and the tailor. She found her empty-headed contemporaries tedious and dull, much preferring to be surrounded by her medical journals and political commentaries. The wedding of her dreams was indeed a simple affair with her family and few girlfriends. Her mother would have liked many days of parties and feasting, she knew, but she was content with her and Aatiq's favourite dishes, *aloo gobi* for him, *keema muttar* for her. Kebabs had to be present for her father and obviously, a good biryani. Even for her mother, she insisted on soft sweet *gulab jaman* but knew that this would not make up in even a small way for the festivities she had been denied. Selina took solace in her father and new husband's contentment and the promise of a future that could be entirely hers, not ruled by a man who would decide how she should dress, how she should act, what she should do.

After the wedding, Selina moved into the apartment with her husband and mother-in-law. She had no apprehension about her new living quarters and quickly took to the routines of married life. She had been warned that her role as daughter-in-law was just as much a role as that of wife; she had been groomed to expect to adjust, learn to keep house and serve her new family. But her married life never transpired like that. Gori-Jan took to her as a mother to a daughter, happy to teach any skills she wanted to learn in the kitchen or household but having little, if any, expectation of her. She found, on her return from a long shift at the hospital, a hot meal waiting for her and Aatiq. Her mother-in-law had often retired to bed by the time she returned and Aatiq was sometimes at home waiting for her, or she would wait for him.

Gori-Jan rarely interfered with the new couple's time together and they were very happy. It was not long before Selina fell pregnant with their first child, following which she returned to work whilst her mother-in-law took care of their son. It was a happy life and looked destined to stay that way. But pleasures in life ebb and flow like the tides that are governed by the moon and it was not long before heartache struck the trio and changed their lives forever. By the time a second child was born, Selina was all but an orphan having lost both her parents in a short space of time. And now, her family was no longer society weddings and parties, but the all too common business of working and raising children.

Life continued as such for many years, always looking forward with anticipation, both husband and wife enjoying and resenting change as their babies became children and then teenagers and then adults themselves. The past was all but forgotten. It would have carried on as such had an elderly man a long way off not insisted in his last days that memories and events be raked up in order to bring a broken family together. Unbeknownst to Aatiq, Selina and Gori-Jan, three Canadians were making their way to Lahore to be reunited.

Keema Muttar for a Simple Wedding Feast

You Will Need

500 g ground lamb
1 tsp. vegetable oil
2 tsps. cumin seeds

2 medium onions finely chopped
2 tablespoons ginger-garlic paste
2 green chilies finely chopped
1 tsp. tomato puree
1 cup water
2 tsps. salt
1 tsps. chili powder
1 heaped tsp. ground turmeric
2 tsps. ground cumin
2 tsps. ground coriander.
1 cup frozen peas
1 tsp. chopped fresh cilantro to garnish

What to Do

Take a casserole or saucepan with lid and heat the oil.

When hot add the cumin seeds and allow them to sizzle for 30 seconds and release their aroma.

Now add the onion and brown. When golden brown add the ginger garlic paste and chilies and continue to let the mix darken.

When the mix is a chestnut brown – add the tomato puree and water and cook out for a few minutes until the oil separates from the *masala*.

Now add the spices – salt, chili powder, ground turmeric, cumin and coriander.

Let the spices cook for a minute and then add the ground meat.

Stir continuously on a medium heat for 10 minutes adding a splash of water of you get any sticking.

Now lower the heat and add the peas.

Give it a good stir and cover.

Let the peas and meat cook – about another 15 minutes – in their own juices. Again, add some water if there is sticking. This really depends on the juices exuding from the meat, a lean ground meat may need more water that a fatty one.

Now sprinkle with the fresh cilantro and serve hot with *chappatis* or *naans* and a good party!

Chapter 19

Lahore, 2017

What Maneeza had revealed to Sareeta was invaluable in their quest. She did indeed know everything that had happened to Gori-Jan, some through idle chit-chat in the extended family but mostly because she had made it her business to always know, as if she felt she needed a family-held insurance policy that she knew one day she would need to cash in.

She knew that Gori-*Jan* had neither become a prostitute nor a Nawabi, she knew she had become one of the most well-known and well-respected dancers in Lahore. She knew that the Nawab himself had taken to her and become her patron. She knew she had given birth to a brilliant son who was now one of the most revered cardiothoracic surgeons in all of Pakistan. She knew he had married into a respected Lahori family and they had two grown up children. She knew that the successes of Gori-*Jan's* son had blotted out the shadows of her own past.

But it was also true that, although a past could be camouflaged, it could never be erased. Maneeza had felt no pity for Gori-*Jan* and for what she had been through but neither did she ever feel a complete detachment from her situation. She could see parallels. They were not lives that had gone two separate ways but they were somehow inextricably bound to each other, like extreme opposites that, despite the vast difference in experience, had left them with the same scars. One inflicted by the prison of expectation, honour and wealth, the other by the trappings of poverty. Like fascism and communism, so extreme yet so similar.

Sareeta had asked, although she knew it would be a lame answer, why Maneeza Begum had not done anything to reunite Gori-Jan, especially when she knew the pain of losing a child.

Maneeza had simply replied, "Sub Khuda k Hath mein hai," (all is in God's hands). Sareeta knew well the resignation in her tone having experienced the same melancholy resignation in many conversations she had had with her parents.

Sareeta questioned what would happen now, to her and Maneeza. By now, the old lady was composed. She had taken both of Sareeta's hands and put them to her eyes.

"My eyes have seen you, child. That is enough. But when I take my last breath, please come that I may find rest in eternity." She had left after that, leaving Sareeta on the couch reflecting on all the things she had heard.

A strange peace had come over the turmoil she had lived with for so many weeks; the clouds had broken and sunshine bathed her face. She could breathe easy; she knew her place again. Her mother had let her go but let her go with blessing. There was no compulsion for her to be reconciled, to know a new family, to question her heritage. She could be who she always believed she was, Sareeta the Indian Canadian, born to Satvinder and Meera, retired physician, mother of four. Raised Sikh, now Christian. She doubted that her's and Maneeza's story was over, but she felt the intensity lift and a calmness that made her feel she was able to treat this newness in her own history with the respect and time it needed.

But now, the question was not to pursue her own anxious thoughts but to find Gori-Jan and bring her to Satvinder before time ran out for him. It was not hard to locate Aatiq, a quick Google search revealed the hospital where he spent most of his time. She could clearly see how brilliant he was, his name either the primary or associated with many foundation papers and prominent research articles in Cardiothoracics.

The question was how to approach him. She wondered what he knew and what he would want to know. Would he be willing to reunite brother and sister or would he be resistant? Would he even see Sareeta? Would Gori-Jan be in a position to travel and would she want to? Would she even know about her origins or would Aatiq, there was so much to consider and so much that could potentially go wrong, she could feel the weight of it all discouraging her.

"Well, Mama, we've come this far," Kiran reassured her. "All we can do is take the next step and see what happens. What is it you used to say to me, Mama? One step at a time, baby, one step at a time."

Jai had changed the flight tickets from Rawalpindi to Lahore easily and they were due to fly the day after next. No one felt like feasting on butter chicken any more, they all just fancied a pizza and beer and knew there was a place right next to the hotel.

As they stepped out into the warm air, no one spoke much. The hour was late, all three were emotionally spent. Revived with Indian style *masala* pizza and some cold beer (imported, of course, Jai did not trust Indian beers), their tongues loosened and the three were able to reflect on the evening's activities.

"I can't believe she came," started Kiran, "I mean, I was there, Mama, when she told you to leave the funeral; it was so bitter."

"The Indian psyche is very complex, Kiran," Jai started. "My mother always said you cannot separate the nail from the finger. Family is family, it may suffer but it cannot be broken. Maneeza came because she is your mother's mother and she will always be."

"But where does that leave *Nani*?" asked Kiran referring to Meera at home.

"Well, she is my mother and your *Nani* and that is never going to change either. It's a different kind of love, one that doesn't come from obligation or expectation. That's why it is so special. Nothing is going to change with Mum and Dad. Nothing will ever change that."

"I don't get it though," continued Kiran. "Why would she come here, say all that she said and then just say 'make sure you make it to my funeral'? Does she want to know us or not?"

"Oh, Kiran. You are a western girl. I wouldn't expect you to understand! The Indian mother is unlike any other. Her life is not just about her husband and her kids and doing what is best for the family unit. There's the whole extended family and society to think about and then all those other things, like what is expected, family honour, righteousness, justice, putting the family first. You know where it comes from, I mean where it was cemented?"

"I have no idea, mother," Kiran rolled her eyes at her mother. She knew that it would be one of Sareeta's strange theories about the human condition.

"*Mother India*. The film, *Mother India*. She is the archetypal Indian Mom who put morality over motherhood. It changed how mothers perceived their role and what a mother's role actually is. If you ever want to understand your *Nani's* foibles or Maneeza's at that, just watch that film." Sareeta had herself found it hard to understand why her upbringing had been different from her friends when she grew up in England.

Why they had taken long treks to visit relatives rather than go to the local social club. Why it was imperative that they went to Punjabi lessons at the temple although they all spoke English at home. Why when they were invited for dinner, the women would all start cooking with the hostess rather than politely wait until the food was being served.

She had come to understand it slowly over the years; these were gestures of underlying principles. No mother was merely a mother to just her own children, she was a mother to all the children. No mother's child was more important than doing what was right and any child that brought shame on himself had brought shame to the entire family. Honour was imperative, morality principal and the Indian way to be preserved.

Her children had been brought up quite differently. Individuality was valued and each child was different. All of her children had different needs and different motivations. Kiran often needed to be reined in because she was so self-assured and confident. Dharam had need more coaxing because he lacked confidence. Sonia was stubborn but her stubbornness could only be melted by acts of love and Rishi often had difficulty in taking anything seriously. They could not all be treated the same even if she was trying to accomplish the same thing in all of them. And their needs did indeed come utmost for her, much higher than any expectation placed on her by outsiders.

Nonetheless, she could understand Maneeza's desires to not let Sareeta infiltrate her family and at the same time, her need to have a relationship with her. Things in the east were never as black and white as the west and the indulgence in melancholy was as much a part of the female psyche there as the need of salt in food. She understood, even if she found it hard to agree.

"What will you do, Mama? I mean with Maneeza?" Kiran questioned, her eyes hunting for a waiter to deliver her another delicious pizza.

"I don't know. Maybe I'll write to her when we get home, maybe I'll call if I can get her number. Maybe I'll leave things as they are I don't know."

"Pumpo, maybe just leave things. For now, anyway. Mum and Dad need you more," Jai interjected.

He adored his wife but he knew that her capacity for compassion could leave her very hurt. He had lost count of the number of times she had just given her heart away to a new friend or someone in need and had been left crushed at the end. He remembered how when they had first arrived in Canada, her eagerness to make a social life for her children and for them had caused her to lavish kindness and love on complete strangers, some of whom had become great friends but many who just remained acquaintances – he had always felt it was quite unbalanced. Despite all their years of marriage, this was one thing in her that he had never seen changed and he knew well that she would pour herself out on Maneeza and was doubtful that Maneeza felt free enough to return that love. He would have to help her.

Early the following morning, Sareeta, Jai and Kiran left Dehra Dun and headed for Delhi to connect to Lahore. Sareeta could see her journey reaching a culmination. She was tinged with both anxiety and anticipation, a sense of completion and a sense of foreboding. She hoped to meet her aunt and her cousin and to somehow, in some small but not insignificant way, atone for some injustice that had been done to her family some 70 years previously. She hoped that, for her family, she could undo the atrocities of the 1946 partition and show the world how strong the cords that bind families are. She hoped she could restore to her father what he had lost, not only the years living incomplete but all he had given up to make her world a better place. She hoped she could do all of that.

But that would have been too perfect a tale. As the Boeing tires hit the hot tarmac at Lahore international airport, an eminent cardiothoracic surgeon sat in a colleague's office trying to internalize the magnitude of the news that was being delivered to him. His brief but extreme weight loss had not been without reason, neither had the change in his bowel habits, neither the bloody diarrhea he had experienced. The changes in his body he had been experiencing had indeed been caused by his worst fear.

The cancer had spread too fast and too aggressively to be amenable to surgery. The end of his days was near and he had to tell his wife, his children and his mother.

Pizza – *Desi* Style

You Will Need

4 ready-made round *naans* or 4 ready-made pizza bases.
I quantity *masala* tomato sauce
4 cups shredded cheese – a mix of cheddar, mozzarella and *paneer*
Assortment toppings such as chopped green onions, sliced bell peppers, mushrooms, red onions, chopped tandoori chicken, chopped chicken *tikka*, chopped *sheek kebabs,*
Chopped green chilies
Chopped cilantro

For *masala* tomato sauce

I tbsp. vegetable oil
1 finely chopped white onion
1 tbsp. garlic-ginger paste
1 can crushed tomatoes
2 tsps. salt
½ tsp. chili powder
½ tsp. turmeric
1 tsps. ground cumin
1 cup water.

You Will Need to

Preheat oven to 450 degrees Fahrenheit

To make the sauce, heat the oil in a sauté pan. When hot, add onion and fry until golden. Add the ginger-garlic paste and continue to fry until all is chestnut brown. Now add the crushed tomatoes and cook for approximately 20 minutes in a low heat.

Add the dry spices and a cup of water to prevent the spices from burning and continue to cook for another 10 minutes until you have glossy fragrant pizza sauce.

Place a *naan* or a pizza base on a baking sheet and spoon over 1-2 tsps. of sauce to taste.

Liberally sprinkle over a cup of cheese mix.

Top with vegetable and meat of your choice.

Finally sprinkle over chopped green chilies to taste and the cilantro.

Bake for 10 minutes or until golden and bubbling.

Serve immediately with a cold beer and the anticipation of wanting another.

Chapter 20

Lahore, 2017

Gori-*Jan* was silent. She was still. She stared at Aatiq and Selina who had tears slowly progressing from the caverns of her eyes to the crevasse of her breast. Aatiq looked defeated. His shoulders slumped, his face was grey, his eyes hollow. Gori-*Jan* stared deep into his grey-brown eyes looking for fear or despair but she found nothing. They were empty; he had nothing to give.

The road outside the big house was usually noisy and congested which some of the neighbours despised. But Gori-*Jan* had come to consider the white noise comforting. Today, she couldn't hear it. She couldn't hear anything but the beat of her own heart as it pumped rhythmically in her chest; the same as yesterday and the day before and before that, long before she had heard today's news which should have stopped that beating. The big clock in the hallway carried on ticking extra loud ticks, like her beating heart, it was as if it had not heard what Aatiq had just said and merely carried on with its work, unaware of the devastation that had hit its family.

"Ami," wept Selina, "Say something."

Poor Selina, Gori-*Jan* thought.

The poor girl who adored her son as much as she herself did. Who had sacrificed so much of her own potential to give him the comforts only a wife could bring him. Who had raised his beautiful children and turned her back to the gossip and backchat of the privileged Lahoris regarding his heritage. For what? She thought. In her prime now and on the brink of having her husband to herself for their twilight years, she would be alone.

How would she take it, Gori-*Jan* wondered. Would she withdraw from the world like Gori-*Jan* herself or would she find her place, however unconventional? One thing Gori-*Jan* knew for sure was that she would not embrace widow-hood like she embraced being a wife and mother, it was doubtful that her usual assured attitude would prevail.

"There is nothing that can be done, *puttar*? You are sure?" She spoke because Selina needed to hear her, but she knew the answer.

She watched him shake his head slowly, his head and eyes lowered, his delicate skillful hands enfolding his wife's pale soft palm.

"How long?"

"Maybe six months, Ami. Maybe a bit longer."

"And the children know?"

"Yes, Ami, we told them yesterday."

Gori-*Jan* nodded.

"Work?"

"They do not know. I will tell them this week. Then I will be at home for what is left."

Again, she nodded.

"Selina, my daughter, you are a brave and strong woman. But you will need strength only God himself can give you. You must ask for His grace and mercy on you at this time."

Selina sobbed heavy tears on her husband's hands.

"*Na, na, beti*," Gori-Jan coaxed, "He gives and takes away. All is in His hands."

The afternoon was quiet. Gori-Jan had taken to her room where she lay on her bed staring at the ceiling as reality slowly set in. Her son was dying, the core of her soul was being extinguished, her constant was leaving. Aatiq was more than a son to her; he was her very light and her raison d'etre.

She had lived because of him, she had breathed because of him and she fought life's battles only because of him. It had only been him that had given her any motivation to push through and push on when really she should have just resigned herself to a life of servitude in a big house on the outskirts of Rawalpindi with the other wives there.

What would she do now? Would she inwardly die too? She could see that happening. Or rather, she could not see how she could continue to live when her very light was gone. Already she could feel the darkness setting in like a big flood she could see in the distance advancing rapidly toward her. Her breath became deep and heavy as the grief began to accumulate in the pit of her stomach. She could feel it, rising up in her from stomach to chest to throat. And then, it erupted in heavy wails as she emptied herself, vomiting out her pain in sounds that words themselves could not express. She wailed and sobbed and cried and wept and lamented. It hurt, oh it hurt. Eventually, she wore herself out and fell into a deep slumber waking only when the sun had dipped and darkness engulfed her room as it had her whole being.

With trepidation, Gori-*Jan* stepped out of her room and made her way to the living area where the family were all assembled. The children, young adults now, and Selina, all with red puffy faces sitting close to their father. Food had been made but no one had eaten it. Empty teacups strew the coffee table. Tissues dotted the surrounding like large lumps of confetti. Aatiq, on seeing his mother arose. "Come and sit, Ami," he said.

Her grandchildren got up and embraced her and Selina made her way to the kitchen to fetch tea.

"You will all be comfortable," Aatiq continued as he looked as his family. "The house is free and my pension is plentiful. You children are working now too and we have plenty of savings. I do not want you to worry about your futures. But…" he looked at his children, "you must take care of your mother and grandmother now. I have some time but I will become weak and they will need you. Do you understand?"

They nodded somberly.

"Life is like a cricket match, my children. We have played and won many times. But sometimes, one wicket remains and the fast-bowler is ahead of you. You must still face the ball and aim for that six. Never lose that hope, my children, never lose heart my young ones. Face the bowler, stare him in the eye and when that ball comes that sounds your defeat, hit it, hit it hard, hit it with all the strength you have left in you because only through hope will you defeat your adversary."

The next morning, Aatiq's driver drove him to work as usual. He had cancelled his theatre list that morning and arranged to meet the hospital director, an accomplished and talented gentleman.

"Good morning, Aatiq," he said rising up as Aatiq stepped through the door into his office. "Please take a seat, can I get you anything?"

"No. I'm fine, thank you,"

"So what can I do for you, my friend? Your email sounded very urgent."

"Omar, I have some bad news. I have been diagnosed with metastatic colonic cancer. It is inoperable, extensive and disseminated."

"Oh, my friend! I can't believe it!" Omar half-sat half-fell into his chair.

"My family all know and I can have some palliation," Aatiq continued himself taking a seat now. "But I don't have a lot of time left and I want to spend what I do have left with my family. You understand, of course?"

"Yes, of course, I do. But can anything be done? Were you diagnosed here? Shall I speak to Mr. Khan in Colorectal?"

"It was Khan that diagnosed me, Omar. He did everything himself and all very quickly but it is too late. I have a very aggressive form. I am at Dukes 4 already."

"Aatiq, I am so sorry. Can anything be done abroad?"

"Here in Lahore, nothing. Khan is looking at whether there is any experimental treatment that I would qualify for, maybe in the US or he mentioned Canada, but he is doubtful. I have told my family that I am dying. I do not want to give them any false hope. Maybe if Khan hears something…well, I don't know. It is better for them to prepare their minds and be realistic. It's better for all of us."

"Oh, I wonder if that's what that email was about. A doctor from Canada contacted me wanting to get in touch with you, I'll forward you the mail right away. Aatiq, what can I do?"

"There is nothing, Omar, I just need to leave as soon as possible and be with my family. Can you do that?"

"Of course, my friend."

"There are a few patients that I need to operate on this week, whom I have seen through but no one else."

"Of course. Just let me know what we can do. Shall I inform the department?"

"Yes, I think so. But maybe after this week."

"Whatever you want, Aatiq. Can I do anything for Selina or the family?"

"Not for now but I will let you know." Aatiq arose. "Thank you, Omar. I will of course keep you informed."

With his boss now being in the picture and having granted him immediate leave, Aatiq had to concentrate on preparing for life ahead or what little life he had left to prepare for.

He returned to his car and went home. Walking through the door, he smelt the aroma of frying cumin seeds, garlic and ginger.

Tarka daal, he thought to himself and smiled briefly. *How ironic.*

Selina always made his *daal* with extra turmeric and garlic heralding their anti-cancer properties. And here he was now riddled. No amount of turmeric could help him now but he knew this was her way of loving him. His appetite had waxed and waned over the past few weeks, sometimes hungry but full quickly and sometimes so nauseous that the smell of food was enough to suppress any appetite he may have had. But today, he felt okay and he wanted to eat the food of his wife's hands knowing he could not do so for much longer.

Making his way to the kitchen, his phone in his pocket bleeped. A forwarded email had arrived from Omar. Aatiq had been a little surprised when Omar had mentioned the email from the Canadian doctor as he had been under the impression that Mr. Khan, his friend and colorectal surgeon, would do all the liaising for him.

He opened the mail:

Dear Hospital Director,

My name is Sareeta Chatwal and I'm a retired physician from Canada. I am trying to get in touch with one of your cardiothoracic surgeons, Mr. Aatiq Hussein for a very important manner. It is a personal matter but I am hoping you will be able to help me. I look forward to hearing from you.

Dr Sareeta Chatwal

How strange, he thought to himself. 'Retired physician', no tag to the name and a generic email. Perhaps she was a retired Oncologist.

Quickly, he tapped out a short reply:

Dear Dr Chatwal,

I thank you for the email you sent to the hospital director who has forwarded this on to me. I can be contacted on the above email.

Regards
Aatiq.

In a Lahore hotel, not far off, Sareeta sat in the foyer whilst Jai checked the family in. Her phone bleeped in her handbag. She got it out and read the email.

Not long now, she thought to herself passing the phone to Kiran to look at, *not long now at all*.

Tarka Daal with Healing (But Not Life-Giving) Properties

For *Daal* You Will Need

2 cups yellow *daal* (split *moong*)
1 cup red *daal* (*masoor*)
6 cups water
½ cup dried fried onions
2 tsps. salt
2 tsps. ground turmeric
1 tsps. chili powder
1 heaped tsp. ground cumin
1 heaped tsp. ground coriander

For *Tarka* You Will Need

½ cup vegetable oil
2 tsps. cumin seeds
6 cloves garlic thinly sliced or finely chopped
2 inches ginger finely chopped
1 green chili finely chopped
For garnish
1 tbsp. chopped fresh cilantro
1 heaped tsp. *garam masala*

For the *Daal* You Will Need to

Put all ingredients in a pressure cooker and stir well. Cook for 20 minutes. Alternatively, this can be done in a slow cooker (6 hours on high) or on a stovetop – bring to the boil and simmer for 45 minutes or until all lentils are soft.

For the *Tarka*

Heat the oil in a *karahi* or frying pan. When hot, add the cumin seeds and allow them to sizzle and splutter for 30 seconds.

Now add the remaining ingredients and fry until the garlic and ginger are golden.

Whilst the *daal* is on a low simmer, poor the *tarka* over the top and stir well.

Garnish with chopped cilantro and sprinkle with *garam masala* which will release a warm and comforting aroma as it is heated by the *daal*.

Enjoy with *chapatis* or rice, pickle and yoghurt and feel it doing your soul good.

Chapter 21

Lahore, 2017

Lahore in the fall was beautiful. The days were still sunny and warm and even at night when the temperatures dipped, it wasn't so cold that town's folk stayed in. The air often smelt of burning coals as the street vendors still roamed with their carts laden with sweet, spice, salt and crunch enticing locals and tourists alike.

Gawalmandi Food Street was awash with young and old, families and couples, friends and singletons lazily sitting at long tables with plates of sizzling kebabs and *tikkas* in front of them. The air was smoky but not so much that it stung the eyes. The smells of all the offerings intermingled storming the senses with aromas that were so distinct and yet just seemed to become lost in each other. Food for the rich, the poor, the middle classes. Snacks, meals, sweet treats, all elevated from their lowly street positions or brought down from their fine-dining positions to fill the stomach and soothe the soul. The people, poor, rich, middle class, like the food, all equal under the moonlit sky on Gawalmandi that night.

There were many stories on the street that night, in the midst of their telling. A young couple meeting in secret to expedite their passions, the housewife with her young brood who had awaited her husband's return from work all day to savor the treats of this street tonight, the married couple who were trying to avoid the impending argument brewing between them.

Jai sat scrutinizing the food in front of him, picking up his pieces of chicken and questioning whether or not they had colouring in them making them that glorious shade of burnt orange and picking off any bits that were too charred for the likings of his health fantasies. Sareeta and Kiran, well used to his health foibles by now, politely ignored him as they tucked into their plates of *tikkis*, kebabs and fried fish.

"So show me again what you sent him, Mama," Kiran said between mouthfuls.

"Here," replied Sareeta passing her daughter the phone.

She read it out loud. "Dear Aatiq, thank you for your prompt reply. What I need to talk to you about is a rather personal matter so I'm wondering if we could meet in person? I am in Lahore for a few days so can meet you wherever you feel is best. Kind regards."

"He's suggested the hotel foyer at 3 pm tomorrow."

"Are we all going?" Kiran asked.

"You know what, I think I'd like to meet him alone. Are you both okay with that?" Sareeta looked searchingly at Jai and Kiran, pleased to see that Jai too had decided to take his chances and eat the food in front of him; he seemed to be enjoying it now he had convinced himself it was safe.

"I don't think that's a bad idea, Saru," he said, "I mean, I know this is no immediate relative but this is your cousin kind of. And I think more than the direct association, this is Dad's family and he has commissioned you to find them. You're going to have to explain the story and hopefully he will take it well. I wonder if he even knows about his family history. And of course, let's hope Maneeza is right in the information she has given you about them."

"Yes, although when I looked at his profile on the hospital website, it does seem to match up with what she said about him. I think I'll just have to be brutally honest with him and see what he says. I've got to say though, I am a bit surprised that he agreed to meet me so readily without knowing anything – he didn't even ask me what the meet was regarding." Sareeta looked perplexed.

"Well, you doctors are a strange breed," Kiran retorted sifting through the assortments on the plate deciding what to take next, "I think that if a random doctor wanted to meet with you, you'd do it too."

Three pm the following day arrived very quickly. Sareeta had thought carefully about what to wear, wanting to look non-threatening and friendly, and what to say. She had chosen a pale yellow *kameez* paired with jeans, simple daytime makeup and a smart tote bag. She had decided to tell Aatiq first a little about herself and her family and her dad. She would ask him if he knew anything about the family history. If he did, that would make the conversation somewhat easier. If not, she may have to just ask if she could meet with his mother to pass on greetings from her father. But she also knew it was all well and good to plan out these conversations but experience had taught her that really there was no planning and she would just have to see which way the conversations went. She hoped that Aatiq was a kind man without any bitterness or arrogance, but then again, he was a surgeon and she knew she may have to battle a bit of an overinflated ego too.

She arrived at the hotel early and chose a seat near the entrance of the foyer, an arrangement of a three-seater sofa and two plush armchairs, all in a very stylish ochre print, surrounding a glass-topped coffee table. She drank sparkling water in a tall glass with a slice of lime. Anxiously she watched the set of three glass-panelled double doors that opened by the same doorman at frequent intervals.

A couple came in, *maybe honeymooning*, she thought. A gaggle of fifty-something glamorous ladies passed through, laughing and talking loudly to each other. *No doubt a weekly kitty party for the well-off*, she thought to herself. Various staff members in smart suits and gold badges rushed through from time to time. A tall, distinguished-looking gentleman came through on his own, likely to be in his sixties and Sareeta thought that may be him but he was quickly greeted by another gentleman and they obviously knew each other well.

She waited. And then at 3:03, a man about her age entered. He was tall and fair and very good-looking with grey-brown eyes. He was thin, almost gaunt but handsome. He wore a grey suite, cream shirt and burgundy silk tie, nothing elaborate but obviously expensive. He had a gold watch and smart shiny shoes. He carried himself proud and was confident. The doorman knew him, opening the door for him with no hesitation and referring to him as 'Dr.-*Saab*'.

Sareeta instinctively rose to greet him. He scanned the room briefly and set his eyes upon her. They were kind eyes, she thought to herself, but the darkness beneath them and the fine lines surrounding them indicated that he was tiring of something, no doubt his work.

"Dr. Chatwal?" he asked extending a hand, "I'm Aatiq Hussein."

"Yes, that's me but please call me Sareeta," she replied.

He had a silky voice, comforting and deep. And his teeth were straight and white. She imagined that he had a lovely smile, although he did not smile at her fully that moment.

"Sareeta, of course," he said. "Can I get you anything else, some tea perhaps?"

"If you are having some then I will join you," she replied.

Aatiq called over the waiter who had chosen to loiter near their table anyway and ordered a pot of *masala chai* for two.

"Well, it is very good to meet you, Aatiq. I have been looking forward to this for a while."

Immediately, she felt embarrassed by this comment. It may have been welcomed in Atlantic Canada but she knew that her colloquial attitude may be misplaced here. He didn't know who she was or why she had come, why she had been looking forward to him, he probably thought her crazy and over-familiar. Even her tone was one that perhaps should not be extended between the sexes in Lahore, especially between herself and a stranger. He did indeed look at her oddly now.

"Oh, I'm glad," he said a little awkwardly. "Khan must have told you more than you needed to know perhaps."

"Khan?"

"Mr. Khan, colorectal? From the Hospital? About my case?"

"Your case?" she said, slowly trying to put the pieces together.

Instantly, she decided just to be quiet and let him reveal his story. She was immediately aware that there was a misunderstanding here and, given the already sensitive nature of her intended topic, she did not want to upset the delicate balance.

"Yes, my case. He must have told you I am at Dukes 4 already? Here only palliation is the option for me but maybe you have something else in mind?"

"Go on," she said

"Well, it is inoperable but Khan mentioned experimental treatments? Forgive me for asking but your email did not give much away. Are you an oncologist?"

Sareeta sighed a deep and heavy sigh. Now it was Aatiq's turn to look confused.

"I'm really sorry, Aatiq. I'm so sorry to hear that you have cancer and it's so advanced. And I'm really very sorry to tell you that I'm not here about any treatments. I'm not an oncologist. I'm not even here in a professional capacity."

"Oh," replied Aatiq, he looked really perplexed now. And also thoroughly disappointed.

"I'll get to the point, Aatiq. Oh gosh, how am I going to start this?" She was rubbing her hands together and looked at the ceiling.

Her task was now 100% worse and she had to be very cautious, knowing instinctively that given the gravity of what he had just revealed, he may just up and leave the second she started her story. Sensing her anxieties, and having warmed to her instantly just because of her sunny disposition and mature beauty, he put a hand over hers. She looked into his eyes. "Just talk," he said, "I'll listen."

Her beating heart stilled, her dry mouth moistened, her pent-up tears stayed pent up. "It's quite a story, Aatiq, but I think we'll find our way through."

Plates of *Tikkis*, Kebabs and Fried Fish

Kebabs
For Kebabs You Will Need

1 lb. ground lamb (shoulder and leg meat mixed is ideal)
1 tbsp. finely minced ginger
1 tbsp. finely minced garlic
2 finely chopped green chilies
1 small onion finely minced
1 tbsp. fresh cilantro finely chopped
2 tsps. salt
1 tsp. chili powder
2 tsps. cumin seeds
1 tsp. smoked paprika powder
1 tsp. ground cumin
½ tsp. ground coriander
½ tsp. green cardamom powder

You Will Need to

Mix all above ingredients together thoroughly.

Have a bowl of water handy to wet your hands, this allows you to shape the kebabs without the mixture sticking to your hands.

Kebabs can be made over a thick skewer (sheik) which can be bought from most middle-eastern or Indian hardware shops and some grocery stores. If you have these, take a golf-ball amount of mix and shape around the skewer so it is about ½ cm in diameter all the way round and about 6 inches long – you may need to add a little more mixture. Be sure to press the meat well into itself and around the skewer.

Broil on medium high turning when brown until the kebab is cooked – about 15 minutes.

If you have no skewers, shape golf-ball amounts of mix into sausage shapes or patties and cook in the same way.

Chicken *Tikka*
You Will Need

6-8 chicken breasts sliced into bite size chunks
1 cup natural yoghurt (or enough to coat all the chicken)
2 tsps. salt
1 heaped tsp. chili powder
1 tbsp. ginger-garlic paste
2 heaped tsps. ground coriander
2 heaped tsp. ground cumin
2 tsps. smoked paprika
Squeeze lemon juice (1/2 a lemon should be fine)
1 tbsp. tomato puree

You Will Need to

Mix all ingredients together and leave to marinade for as long as possible, preferably overnight but at least 2 hours.

Thread chunks onto a skewer or spread on a baking sheet

Broil on medium high turning occasionally, until cooked though and slightly charred, about 10 minutes.

Fried Amritsar Fish

3-4 fillets firm white fish – tilapia, halibut, hake, haddock, sea bass are all good choices – skinless and cut into bite size chunks
Juice of 1 lemon
1 tsp. salt
1 tsp. turmeric powder
4 tbsp. all-purpose
2 tsps. chili powder
2 tsps. salt
1 litre vegetable oil
1 lemon cut into half
1 tbsp. chopped fresh cilantro
Sprinkling *chaat masala.*

You Will Need to

Mix the fish with the lemon, salt and turmeric and leave to steep for 20 minutes – this allows the fish to firm up a little.

Heat the oil in a *karahi* or wok (or deep fat fryer) to medium hot.

Drain the juice from the steeped fish.

Mix the flour with the chili powder and salt and toss the wet fish in the flour. Coat well with the seasoned flour.

Drop the piece of fish into the hot oil and cook until golden – about 10 minutes.

Drain off on kitchen paper and squeeze over the lemon, sprinkle with cilantro and *chaat masala* and eat hot.

To Serve

Place a selection of the above on plates with a bowl of tamarind sauce, mint chutney and, of course, ketchup!

Chapter 22

Foyer, the Hotel, Lahore

"My father is a great man, Aatiq," Sareeta started. "He's 70 and he's just had a big stroke. He's very sick right now but before that, he was a brilliant man. He came to the England in the 1960s with twenty pounds as a student and by the time he left to join me in Canada, he was millionaire. He was in the international Who's Who for his work in telecommunications. He had dinner with Bill Gates and Princess Anne. And just before he left, he was awarded an MBE by the Queen for his works for charity, bringing racial groups together. But to meet him, Aatiq, you would never know. He's such a humble man. He wears the same clothes he's been wearing since I was a teenager and drove a regular family car. When I converted to Christianity, he never stopped me; he even dropped me off at church every week. And when I got married, my goodness, you should have seen my wedding! He spared no expense and gave the most lavish five-day party. He was always there for me and my husband, Jai, and my kids. I couldn't have asked for a greater man for a dad...or a friend. And now he's really sick, I think his end days are near. He's told me something really significant...which is what I need to share with you."

Aatiq said nothing, simply looking at Sareeta knowing the story that was unfolding was not a simple family tale but not quite anticipating the gravity of what he was about to be told. Sareeta stared back at him in silence for a split-second wondering if he was going to interject. But he didn't, so she continued.

"My son got married very recently, I have four children. The wedding was in Canada but the girl's family are originally from Kenya; they are a Gujarati family. They brought with them their old nanny. She knew my father from their days in Kenya, my mother and father both grew up there. Is this getting complicated? I'm not sure how much to tell you."

"No, I'm following it fine. Just carry on," he replied kindly.

"Well, she had an old photo with her. It was a photo of my dad and my grandparents and a little baby. We have the same photo at home, except the one I have at home doesn't have the baby in it. Anyway, this photo was given to my eldest daughter at the end of the wedding, the photo with the baby that is, who showed it to me. When I showed it to my father and mother…well my life changed a lot. And I think yours will too.

"It turned out that the baby in the photograph was me. My parents, who brought me up, are not my biological parents. It turns out that I was abducted as a baby and taken to Kenya and then to England where I was brought up by the people who I had always considered as my parents. I've only just found out so you'll have to forgive me if I am unclear on all the details."

"It must be lot to take in, Sareeta. But how does this involve me?" Aatiq asked.

He asked in such a way that, although the question itself could be construed as a little aggressive or inpatient, it did not come across as such. He didn't even give the air that he was frustrated with her convoluted tale or wanted her to get to the point. The way in which he said it was almost as if to encourage her, to show her that he was interested and that he wanted to know the whole tale and help her out. So she carried on.

"I was abducted as an act of revenge, Aatiq. I mean, I was a few months old and this was in 1966. I was taken from the Khan family, a family of wealthy landowners in Dehra Dun in India. I have just found my biological mother but I didn't find her for me. I found her to find you."

"Oh?" said Aatiq frowning.

"Well, more than you, Aatiq, I came to find your mother."

"My mother?" Now Aatiq was looking surprised and more than a little concerned.

"There's no way to break this gently so I think I'll just tell you. My father and your mother are brother and sister."

"Pardon?"

"Well, they're kind of brother and sister. My dad considers your mother as his sister, very much so."

"Sareeta, now I am lost. How can this be? Your dad is an Indian who grew up in Kenya and then moved to England. My mother is Pakistani."

"Well, I don't think she is actually. I mean, my father tells me that your mother was the one that I was avenged for. Oh gosh, this is hard to explain."

"Well, please try, Sareeta. At the moment, this sounds like a Bollywood movie." Sareeta could sense his demeanour was changing and she had to get to the point quickly.

"As I understand it," she continued, trying hard not to make eye contact now, "Your mother was kidnapped by a Muslim family, the Khan family, in Dehra Dun in 1946, during the partition of India and Pakistan. She was a baby and she was taken to protect the Khan family's honour when all the atrocities were going on. They did it, as I understand, to protect their land and ensure no one would mess with them. She, your mother, was sent to Pakistan, Rawalpindi I believe. I was abducted twenty years later to avenge her. It was my grandfather's friend, Rizwan Khan, who took her, your mother that is. And it was my grandfather, well, the one I always thought of as my grandfather, who took me."

Aatiq had gone visibly grey, more so than he had looked before.

"My father," Sareeta continued, "is very sick and he wants to see his sister. He wanted me to find her and to bring her to him. I've been looking for her, and you, for a long time. Before it's too late."

Sareeta could feel a dampness in her eyes and she blinked furiously to stop the tears from falling but it was to no avail; they trickled down her cheek. She brushed them away firmly with the thin two-ply embossed napkin siting under her teacup. Her chai had gone cold, as cold as the fondness that had exuded from Aatiq just moments before. He leaned back in his armchair and took a deep breath in. He put his fingertips together and looked at the ceiling. Sareeta was still perched at the edge of her seat and didn't want to move back. She sat there, looking at Aatiq, looking at the floor, looking at her hands. It seemed like hours before he spoke but it can't have been more than a few minutes.

"Sareeta, my mother is a good woman who has had a difficult life. She has fought for her very survival in this world and has always put me and my needs first. She singlehandedly raised me and put me through school and medical school. She married me in Lahore high society although she has never been in that society. She has never brought shame to me although some may have considered that we should have been a very shamed family.

And now, she is in a place where, if she had thought life had nothing left to throw at her, I get ill and she has to come to terms with reality that she is going to outlive her son. Even if what you are saying is true, and I just don't know what to think right now, this news would destroy her. She has accepted her whole life that she has no family, other than me, no heritage, no knowledge of where she has come from or how she came to be. And she's done just that, she's accepted it. She's not bitter, she hasn't searched and she hasn't fantasised. She's just lived as good a life as she could. I don't think I want to tell her about this Sareeta, I'm sorry."

"Don't you think she would want to know, Aatiq? Don't you want to know?"

"I don't think I do. We have made a life and family for ourselves. I have a wonderful wife and two wonderful children and I have enjoyed a good career, respect, honour, they've all become mine through my own efforts. I don't think we need anything more now."

"But, Aatiq…"

He stood up to leave. "Look, Sareeta, I'm sorry that you've come all this way and I cannot help you more. I hope you can explain to your dad. And I hope you have a safe journey home."

"Aatiq, please, let's talk."

"There is nothing to talk about. You seem like a very good person, Sareeta, and you obviously love your father as much as I do my mother. We both need to do what's best for our own. I know you'll understand why I'm taking this stance. All the best to you. I must leave."

And with that, he walked briskly toward the doors and through them.

Sareeta sat stunned.

"Can I get you anything else, madam?" the hovering waiter came and cleared the cold chai and pot.

"No, just the bill please."

"No need, madam. Doctor Sahib has an account here. Maybe something *mitha* for madam?"

He was offering her something sweet, she must have looked upset, too upset to him, she thought.

"No nothing, thank you," she got up to leave, grabbing her bag.

The doorman, anticipating her leaving, had already signaled her car. She put on her dark sunglasses, to shield her eyes from the sun and the onlookers from her red-rimmed eyes. Silently, she got in the car. "*Challo*," she said to the driver, "Let's go."

Something *Mitha* (sweet) to help with an upset
Mitha Seviyan (Vermicelli in Sweet Milk)

You Will Need

1 cup vermicelli pasta broken into small pieces about the length of rice

2 tbsp. unsalted butter

2 cups 3 % milk

1 cup coffee cream

2 green cardamom pods crushed

½ tsps. nutmeg

1 cup sugar

You Will Need to

Take a heavy based casserole and melt in the butter. When melted and frothy, add the dried vermicelli pasta and stir.

Cook for 2-3 minutes until the vermicelli turns a golden brown.

Add the milk, cream, sugar, cardamoms and nutmeg and stir well.

Bring to the boil and then simmer, stirring frequently to prevent sticking, until the pasta is cooked – about 8 minutes.

Serve hot, with sympathy and a box of tissues.

Chapter 23

Khan Residence, Dehra Dun, 2017

It had been a few days since Maneeza had seen Sareeta at the hotel. The mourning period was also over and things in the Khan household were returning to normal.

No one had found out about her late-night escapades; Rehanna had kept the secret well and had managed to restore Maneeza back to her quarters without arousing suspicion. Hunger had caught hold of her and Rehanna on the way back. It was highly unusual for servant and mistress to eat together, but that night they had become sisters, comrades and friends. In the darkness of the kitchen that night, as Maneeza relayed the conversation to her faithful friend, they feasted on a plate of Bombay *aloo*, fried to perfection, and mango pickle. They sat, dissecting the conversations and the deciding on the future but Maneeza didn't feel at peace or at ease with what had happened, something in the entire equation was missing and she could not quite work out what.

Maneeza had thought long and hard before she picked up the phone in the days that followed. She was torn between the comfort of having made peace with her daughter, Sareeta, and knowing that the girl had had a good and wonderful life, and the discomfort of being embroiled once again in a turn of events dictated by history. She could well anticipate what Sareeta's trip to Lahore would achieve…nothing. She had known long enough what her own people were like and how their minds differed from the west. People here were just more accepting of what life events had chastened them and saw little value in retribution. Many comforted themselves in the notion that all would be restored to full balance and justice would be served in God's time. But just as many undertook their burdens graciously with the caveat that they were paying the price for the sins of their ancestors or themselves. There were even those who believed that burdens, like flagellation, were prescribed by God.

Whatever the reasoning, the culture around her was not one to want to put things right or restore losses, especially if there was no family pressure to do so and no face to lose. And in this case there certainly was not. Maneeza understood what Sareeta's heart was about; she understood that the girl had an innate sense of justice and a pure love for her father, even an innocence about her that assumed that everyone wanted the same. But the world, especially in India and Pakistan, just did not operate like that. She could guess that Sareeta had found the surgeon-son but the outcome would not be what Sareeta had wanted. It was doubtful that, even if the surgeon had agreed to meet her, he would agree to aide and abet her in confronting Gori-*Jan* of her true origins.

She was not sure what drove her to make that phone call or why she even felt so responsible for the situation that was unfolding. Was it an underlying guilt, was it a sense of duty, was it out of love for a desperate daughter? She did not know, perhaps all of the above. What she did know though was that she felt inextricably linked to the problem and therefore a yearning to be part of the solution. Gori-Jan would be her age, a woman of maturity who had seen the world change and had fought to keep her place in it. If anyone could make her understand what had happened, it would be Maneeza.

It was not hard to find the number for the residence in Lahore; high society in Lahore made most families connected in less than seven degrees of separation. It was not through her connections to Aatiq though, but through his wife's family; a call to a cousin here, an old friend there and very soon, she had the number of Selina written on the pad next to the phone. Her telephone calls had also unearthed the news that the surgeon was extremely sick and almost definitely dying.

Now Maneeza found herself staring at the number trying to muster up the courage to make the call. What would she say? How would she say it? Who would she speak to? Eventually, she dialed the number.

"Hello?" answered Selina after a few rings.

"*Quon bolre*? Who's speaking?" Maneeza asked.

"Selina. Who is this?"

"Selina, *beti*, I am calling from India, I am a friend of your family. How are you, *beti*?"

"I'm fine, thank you, aunty. How are you?"

"I'm well. I heard about the terrible news to your husband's health. It must be awful for you all."

"Thank you, aunty, we are coming to terms with it."

"Yes, very hard for you all. Alas, sickness comes with age, daughter. When we come of that age, we are all defeated. But he has you, and his mother. I was wondering if I could speak with your mother-in-law. If she is free?"

"Erm, yes, aunty, I'll just fetch her," Selina was a little surprised.

She did not know any aunty in India, well, not one close enough to call the house directly. And more so, she had been daughter-in-law to Gori-Jan for over twenty years and had never known her to have a call from India; in fact, she very rarely received personal calls at all. Selina took the cordless phone to Gori-Jan's room where she was resting. "Ami, you have a call."

Gori-Jan, looking equally perplexed at the news that she had a call, took the phone off Selina.

"Hello?" She said.

"*Bhien-Ji*, sister," Maneeza started, "I am calling from India. We have not met for many, many years but as a child I knew you."

Gori-*Jan* kept silent but dread began to fill her being.

"I knew you when I was growing up in Rawalpindi. You lived in my Uncle's house for a while. My Kaka, Shiraz Khan."

Gori-Jan went as white as her name suggested and the dread in the pit of her stomach grew. It had been many years since she had heard mention of Shiraz Khan or 'Pindi.

"I know what you went through back then and I have not called to haunt you or upset you. I have called that you may know the truth that you should have known many years ago. I am aware of what your life has been like and how things are for you now. I too have had a life which has been shaped by the events of the past and my husband's family and have had losses. I have recently been reunited with my daughter who was taken from me. She found me after fifty years but she was not looking for me, she was looking for you. She has come to find you and to give you hope. But this is what I know about what she has to tell you. I hope you are ready to hear about this," she paused, and on the other end of the line, Gori-*Jan* sat down on the edge of her bed, her hands shaking as she clutched the white cordless phone to her ear.

"You were taken from an Indian family during the partition of India and Pakistan, *Bhien-ji*, in 1946 and you were sent to Pakistan. You were just a baby. Your parents did not know where you had gone. The times were such that so many bad things were happening that you were just another child taken from their family because of all the hatred that existed back then. But your family calls out for you now and that is why I have called."

"I don't understand," said Gori-Jan. Her heart was racing within her.

"My daughter has come from Canada to find you. She herself was taken from me and brought up by a man who is your brother. He calls for you now."

"My brother?"

"You have a brother, *Bhien-Ji*. He has kept this a secret for so many years but the time has come for the secret to be unearthed and for you to return to your family, to the family that bore you and cherished you and had you stolen from them."

Maneeza was crying now, tears of relief, tears of joy that were not hers to shed. But she felt loosened, unchained from the ties that had bound her for her whole life. "You are a child of India, *Bhien-Ji*, not of Pakistan. You are from Dehra Dun and you are a Sikh. You have a heritage, you have a family."

Now Gori-Jan started sobbing. How many years had she yearned to hear those words? How many times had she imagined that someone would find her and tell her something? How many times had she hoped against hope that there was some story, some reason, some explanation for her existence? And now, here, pieces of the jigsaw were being given to her by a stranger. Pieces, pieces, pieces of her life given to her so she could start to put it together, so she could begin to understand, so she could begin to have a foundation. Could anyone have ever understood what it was like to be a building without a foundation, to be a tree without roots, to be a person without birthright? Did anyone know what it felt like to search for your ancestors in your head and your heart and know nothing, to feel nothing? And now, after seventy years, she had some hope.

"Tell me, tell me, *Bhien-Ji*, where can I find him?" she pleaded desperately with Maneeza, "Tell me."

"Sareeta, my daughter, will find you, *Bhien-Ji*. She has come to find you and to take you home. May God give you justice, my sister, for what you have suffered. And may you find rest now in the comfort of your family."

With that, Maneeza put the phone down, tears running down her face but with a lightness in her heart and freshness in her spirit. She felt aglow, as if the light that had been extinguished when her baby had been taken was suddenly turned on again and she could see, she could finally see. Seeing Sareeta had not been enough, being reunited with the daughter she had lost had not been enough for her but now, now she felt free. She felt she had changed the balance of the scales and had put right what her father-in-law had made so wrong. She felt strong, the weariness had gone, the peace, for which she had searched and grown accustomed to not having, had come.

Gori-Jan ran from her room to the foyer to find Selina and share the news, the wondrous news that she had a brother and he wanted to see her. Still clutching the cordless in her hand, she ran calling out for her daughter-in-law. She stopped dead in her tracks at the end of the corridor as she entered the foyer. She was unprepared for what she saw in the middle of the room. Lying on the white marble floor with blood oozing from the seat of his pants, lay her son in the arms of his wife.

Bombay *Aloo* (Potatoes) Fit for a Midnight Snack and Post Event Dissection

You Will Need

2 large potatoes, peeled and cut into bite size cubes
½ cup vegetable oil
2 tsps. cumin seeds
2 tsps. salt
1 tsps. chili powder
1 heaped tsp. turmeric powder
2 fresh green chilies sliced.

You Will Need to

Take a *karahi* or heavy based sauté pan and heat the oil.

When hot, add the cumin seeds and allow them to sizzle and splutter for 30 seconds,

Now add the rest of the ingredients and stir thoroughly.

Lower the heat and allow the potatoes to sauté until cooked – you may need to add a splash of water of there is any sticking.

Cook until potatoes are tender and slightly crispy.

Serve on a sharing plate with a couple of forks and a large spoon of pickle.

(If you're feeling very indulgent, add a fried egg…or two).

Epilogue

Atlantic Canada, One Year Later

For the time of year, the weather was surprisingly warm. The sun and clear blue sky reflected on the lake giving it a pearlescent blue hue which was unusual, even on the brightest of days. The sun had warmed the deck and made the mahogany wood feel as warm as the reddish tinge in it would imply. It was perfectly still and so quiet. A gentle sizzle could be heard from the kitchen as Sareeta flipped over the last of the *dosas*. Not familiar with South India, making this staple breakfast dish had taken her some years to perfect but Rishi and Dharam enjoyed them immensely so she had taken the time this morning, being Dharam's wedding anniversary weekend, to make the crispy rice pancakes filled with soft, slightly spiced, fragrant potato filling, coconut chutney and spicy *sambhar dal*. She was looking forward to the arrival of Annie and Dharam for brunch, Kiran and 'poodle' would be on their way shortly, Sonia and Rishi were in their rooms getting ready.

Sareeta felt great that morning. She felt loved, cherished, motherly, womanly, as if all calm had been restored after the tumultuous year. She and Jai had shared moments of passion the previous night with such intensity, she felt like he completely engulfed her in his unending hunger to be one with her. The years had been kind to them. There had been times when their marriage had felt like a chore, something to endure and battle through because they would never not be married. Looking back now, these had been times of extreme external pressures, times when jobs had been at risk, money had been scarce, children had been needy, futures had yet to be built, parents had been ill or worse.

But those times had also passed. The sun and risen and set every day, the seasons had changed and Jai and Sareeta had found themselves standing in new plains with renewed strength and understanding for each other.

Now, Jai and she were in a great place. Mature in their awareness of each and their needs, lives filled with passion for the other expressing itself in bedroom intimacies and stolen caresses, looking forward to a quieting of their days as their children became more self-dependent. Sareeta reflected on how blessed her life had been despite the unusual turn of events.

Satvinder's health had improved greatly over the last year with lots of input from physiotherapy, speech and language and, of course, his wife Meera. He was able to walk slowly with a tripod cane and, although fatigue wore him down, he was able to spend time with his children and grandchildren. Meera still lived for him, sometimes crushing him with kindness and fuss that only a wife could deliver. But usually she just provided for his needs, helped him dress, fed him and kept him positive.

When Sareeta had returned with Jai and Kiran a year earlier with the news that they had found his sister but the family had decided that reunion was out of the question, he had suffered. He had wept for days, finding no comfort in the words uttered by his daughter and son-in-law that she was well, that she had a comfortable life, that she had borne a son who was an eminent surgeon, that she had two grandchildren and she was happy. It was only after the months had passed and the cool grey evenings and given way to the warmth of the buttery sunshine as summer approached, could he begin to feel a lifting in his spirit and some relief that she had been okay…in the end. Eventually, he had begrudgingly accepted that, despite his feelings for her, she had not felt the same. History had worn her in a way that it had not worn him. She had resigned her life to the tossing of the waves, eventually finding herself in a place of calm waters whilst he had always felt an undercurrent, a pull by some source higher than he wanting the restoration that had been denied to him and his family for so long.

The family piled in in now, one by one. First Jai, looking and smelling gorgeous on a lazy Saturday mid-morning. He came up behind Sareeta as she was filling dishes with the brunch feast, slipped his arms around her waist and kissed her gently on the neck. "Good morning, Pumpo," he whispered in her ear, "How's my wanton mistress this morning?" Sareeta gently tapped his backside.

"Behave yourself," she said. "She's fine, by the way. Can you help get the plates out? I think we'll eat outside."

"Agh," Jai resigned. "Always going back to being mama when your children are around! Yes, I'll get the plates, my dear, anything else?"

Sareeta began to reel off a list of implements, condiments and refreshments she wanted on the table whilst Jai tried to frantically take it all in. Luckily, Rishi and Sonia lolled in through the kitchen French double doors at that moment.

"No, he *is* Kaiser Sosay! Don't you get it?" Rishi was debating with his sister. "It was all just a story!"

"I completely don't get it! So is Kaiser Sosay dead or not? Who blew up on the ship? What happened to the long hair and super bod? It's so stupid!" Sonia was saying.

"Ahh, great film. Fantastic film! Definitely in the top 10," Jai joined in. "Maybe Mum and me will watch it tonight? What do you think, Saru?"

"I'll watch it again with you, Dad," jumped in Sonia, "I really don't get it!"

"Dippo!" exclaimed Rishi under his breath

"Hey!" came from a back-turned Sareeta.

"Be nice!" from Jai

"Watch it, Bozo!" from Sonia

"Now stop fighting you guys and help Dad get brunch ready," continued Sareeta, reading off the list again.

The clattering began as cupboards were opened to retrieve juice glasses, champagne flutes, teacups, side plates, dinner plates and small bowls just for the *sambhar*. The fridge door opened as a jug of juice, one full, one with room to add champagne were retrieved, a clanking at the cutlery drawer as spoons and forks were gathered.

"So when did Prince Dharam get back?" Rishi asked holding a bunch of napkins between his chin and chest, hands full of glass wear.

"Just put the glasses down, Rishi," scolded Sareeta, "He got back last night."

"Late honeymoon, mama! When I get married, I'm leaving straight away before you guys can all decide to join me!"

"Er, few issues with that, bro," started Sonia. "a) no girl in their right mind would marry you...unless she was blind...or stupid...or both!"

"Be nice!" piped up Jai from the deck

"b) even if someone of stupid enough to marry you, I don't know what kind of honeymoon an unemployed surfer bum can afford and c)," she continued before either of her parents could shoot her down, "I can't think of anything worse in my entire life than being stuck on some beach island with you and your new flavour of the month."

"Okay, guys, that's enough now!" said Sareeta firmly.

She had given up playing referee between her younger two. Kiran and Dharam had been through the same continuous sparing but, like Rishi and Sonia, she knew that they deeply loved each other, cared for each other and actually enjoyed each other. They spent many a weekend, as they had done last night, in the confines of each other's company, chatting and confiding in one another, their actions speaking louder than their words. It was true to say that if there was anything significant happening in either of their lives, the other would know well before Sareeta would. Jai would catch up eventually, usually though the grapevine.

"I'm just saying," said Rishi, "I thought he was going after a few months but it's been a year. What happened?"

"Annie couldn't get vacation. He was speaking to Kiran about it a lot though. I think changing their plans to tour India was good for them though; she must have convinced them. It's good to be in touch with your roots. They sounded like they were having a good time when I Skyped them. I'm sure they'll tell us all today."

The conversation continued whilst Satvinder slowly made his way in with Meera tentatively following him, arms outstretched in case he toppled back.

"Slowly, just go slowly," she was muttering to him. He made it to the kitchen table and sat down for a rest.

"Is my Prince here yet?" he asked Sareeta.

"Not yet, Dad, would you like your tea here? We're eating on the deck."

"Yes, I'll have my tea here. And your mother will too."

Sareeta poured two cups of tea as Jai wandered back in from the deck. Bending down to Satvinder so they were face to face, he took Satvinder's hand."

How are you today, Dad?" he asked gently, aware of his father-in-law's increasing frailty. "Remember, the elephant has passed, just the tail is left."

Satvinder nodded. "I know, Beta," he replied, "always so optimistic."

It was 10:45, Dharam was coming very soon. *Kiran should have been there by now*, thought Sareeta looking at her watch.

What a year for her, she had thought. No sooner had she arrived home from India, she had announced she was expecting her first child. Now, seven months into her pregnancy, she was blooming, front heavy with puffy ankles and aching joints. She waddled around the office refusing to give a date for the start of her maternity leave and desperately trying to find appropriate outfits to wear. She had given up wearing her trademark stiletto heels many months ago but even her pumps were now showing signs of stretch. She had spent many an evening lying on Sareeta's comfiest couch rubbing her swollen belly getting Ash to rub her back, her feet, get her drinks or food or magazines or remote controls. Sareeta had cooked for every craving she had, including desires for Gujarati food like her grandmother made, rice pudding like she had as a child and pizza with very odd toppings (none stranger than the tuna fish with banana phase).

Currently, it was chocolate butterscotch ice cream which Jai had to travel a few miles to get, Sareeta had kept at least three tubs in the freezer; she was indeed the darling of the family and the first to be with child.

She had not seen much of Kiran over the last two weeks; when she was at the lake house, she often waddled out of the room to take a call. Sareeta had made a mental note to ask her eldest if all was well but for now was assuming she had a lot of work on, especially since Jai was taking much more of a back seat. Still it was unusual for Kiran to be late, especially for a family get-together such as this. Sareeta grabbed the cell from her apron pocket and quickly texted her daughter "Are you en route?" But just seconds later heard the front door open and Kiran's lighthearted banter in the foyer as she got Ash to pull her sneakers off. Waddling through the Kitchen doors in a polka dot smock tunic and leggings, she still looked very gorgeous despite her girth and general new-found plumpness. "Mama, you wouldn't believe how much this baby kicked last night, I'm exhausted!"

"Go and have a lie down outside, sweetie, your dad, Rishi and Sonia are already out there. Where's Ash?"

"He's just getting some stuff from the car. Nana here?"

"I'm just here behind you," replied Satvinder; the position of the kitchen table was such that her back was to it since walking in.

Kiran waddled over and kissed him on the forehead and put her arm around his shoulders. "You should wear something nice today, Nana," she whispered to him.

He looked back quizzically at her but did not say anything; he was quite used to his eldest grandchild commenting on his simple attire.

What a happy day it was becoming, thought Sareeta fully aware that these days may not last for many years to come.

Satvinder was aging with every new health insult and Sareeta knew Meera could not live without her husband; they were entwined with each other like a clematis that crept around an oak tree.

It had taken Sareeta many months to get over the guilt she had long felt for not being able to reunite Satvinder with his sister and she probably did not feel completely guilt free even now. She wished she had another plan when Aatiq had put an end to any discussion. Many a time she had thought about re-connecting with him but he had been so adamant on that day that under no circumstances would he allow her to contact his mother. She wondered if she should try and contact his wife but, in a very unsatisfying way, she did understand why he took the stance he did. And she did appreciate that he had very serious health problems that took precedence.

Sometimes she had wondered if he was still alive and if she should find out but it still all felt very raw to her and she did not know what she would do with any news about it; perhaps it was better for them all just to move on she had convinced herself. Still, she wished she could have done something. Jai had been her strength when she was so distracted in her thoughts that she missed the punch lines of their conversations; he had been patient with her, knowing her well enough by now to know what she was pondering on.

"Saru, don't beat yourself up," he would say, "It's not your fault. Seventy years of thinking you are someone else is a lot to give away. We all just need to get on with what we have here. But if you want me to, I can try calling Aatiq."

She would always reply in the negative, tempted as she was for another shot. Returning empty-handed to Canada had felt like it had when she had gone for interviews for medical school, given her very best, and been left without a place offered to her; she had felt helpless, guilt-ridden and at a loss all in one go. It had felt similar but worse because now she was carrying her own disappointment as well as her father's. Today though, she felt, was not a day to think about the sadness and frustrations of the past year but to enjoy having her whole family around her, the anticipation of a new baby and the joys of hearing how Dharam and Annie's adventures in life were progressing.

All the cooking done and Satvinder now outside with Meera and the rest of the family, Sareeta took off her apron and headed to the deck where Jai was pouring out tall glasses of Mimosas and short ones of orange juice. She sat down in a comfy cane armchair her face warming in the sunshine. A car could be heard pulling up outside the house, good, Dharam and Annie had arrived. Kiran pushed herself up to stand, belly first, much to the protests of Jai who told her to sit back down and he would go. But she was already waddling off in the direction of the front door to greet her brother. Just like Rishi and Sonia, Sareeta thought, like a pair of scissors, often at opposite angles but woe betide anyone who tried to come between them.

Sareeta could hear mumbling from the foyer and voices she did not recognize. Had Dharam brought company with him, she wondered. She got to the edge of her seat ready to stand up to meet the guests, whoever they were. The mumbling got louder and caught the attention of Jai, Satvinder, Meera, Rishi and Sonia; Ash started smiling.

The family looked toward the patio doors between the kitchen and deck and silence fell. Kiran walked in, closely followed by a very elegant elderly woman with grey-brown eyes, a much younger woman, equally as pretty and about Sareeta's age with Dharam and Annie following behind, both with glistening eyes.

No one said a word.

Kiran knelt down in front of her grandfather whose eyes were already full to the brim with tears as he looked at the two unknown women.

"Nana," she said, "meet your sister."

The End.

Dosa for a Family Brunch and to Line the Stomach for a Big Surprise

You Will Need for *Dosas*

3 cups rice
1 cup split *urad dahl* (black and white)
½ cup *powa* (flattened rice flakes)
1 tsp. coarse semolina (optional but makes the *dosa* extra crunchy)
Water for soaking and to make batter
1 tsp. vegetable oil
1 tsp. fenugreek seeds
2 tsps. salt
Vegetable oil for pan-frying

You Will Need to

Place the rice in a bowl and cover with water, leave for at least 6 hours (or overnight) to soak. Do the same with the *dahl* (in a separate bowl).

Drain the rice and *dahl*.

Place the rice and approximately 1-cup water in a food processor and blend to a paste. Do the same with the *dahl*.

Mix the two together and leave to ferment overnight in a warm place. You should notice bubbles on the batter the following day.

Now add the salt, fenugreek seeds, oil, *powa* and semolina if using, and mix thoroughly. The mix is ready to cook with now but can be left in the fridge for up to a week.

Before cooking, add enough water to make a batter as thin as coffee cream (or crepe batter).

Heat a *tawa* or flat griddle and brush with oil.

Take a ladle full of batter and spread quickly over the hot griddle – it should be as thin as a crepe.

The *dosa* should only take 1-2 minutes to cook; there is no need to flip it. The underside should be a lovely golden brown and ready to fill with the potato *masala*.

Potato *Masala*

You Will Need

3 large potatoes (yellow flesh are good), pre-boiled and chopped into small pea-sized pieces.
2 tbsp. vegetable oil
2 tsps. cumin seeds
1 tsp. black mustard seeds
1 tsp. fenugreek seeds
2 tsp. white *urad dahl*
2 dried Kashmiri (red) chilies
10 curry leaves
2 tsps. salt
1 fresh green chili finely chopped
1 tsp. turmeric powder
½ tsp. chili powder
Up to ½ cup water
1 tbsp. chopped cilantro

You Will Need to

Take a *karahi* or large sauté pan and heat the oil.

Now add the cumin seeds, black mustard seeds, fenugreek seeds, *urad dahl* and dried chili. Let them all sizzle for a minute and then add the curry leaves.

Now add the chopped potatoes and spices and stir well.

Add enough water to make a moist *masala* and cook through until the consistency is soft and velvety, a perfect contrast to the crispy *dosa*.

Cook for a minute or two. Add the cilantro and stir through.

Sambhar

You Will Need

2 cups pre-washed *toovar dahl* (if it is preserved in oil, wash thoroughly in a colander a few times). (Note: these are also known as yellow pigeon peas)
4 cups water

2 tsps. salt
2 tsps. turmeric
1 tsps. chili powder
2 tbsp. vegetable oil
1 tsp. cumin seeds
1 tsp. white *urad dahl*
1 tsp. black mustard seeds
1 dried Kashmiri chili
1 onion finely chopped
2 fresh tomatoes finely chopped
½ cup green beans chopped to bite size pieces
½ cup peeled and chopped zucchini/marrow/similar squash. Chop into bite size pieces.
Juice of 1 lemon (or tamarind juice) or to taste.

You Will Need to

Place the *dahl*, water, salt, turmeric and chili powder in a pressure cooker and cook on high for 20 minutes (you can also do this on the stovetop, boil and simmer, or slow cooker on high for 6 hours). At the end, what you would hope to see is all the *dahl* dissolved and a sunshine coloured 'soup' in the pan. At this stage, the *dahl* looks bland and tastes as such...but wait, the magic is about to begin!

Take the oil and put in a *karahi*/sauté pan. When hot, add the seeds and chili and let them sizzle.

Now add the vegetables and cook through until the vegetables are soft and the tomato has broken down.

Pour the vegetable mix into the *dahl*.

Now add the lemon/tamarind and taste. There should be a slight tang to the *Sambhar* so add more lemon/tamarind if needed.

Coconut Chutney

Just buy it!
Or
½ cup grated fresh coconut
½ cup natural yoghurt
½ tsp. salt
½ tsp. chili powder

Mix all together and serve.

To Assemble the *Dosa*

Take a hot *dosa* and whilst on the *tawa*, fill with 1-2 tbsp. potato *masala*.

Fold it over (or even roll the *dosa*).

Place on a plate and serve with a bowl of steaming *sambhar* as a dipping sauce and a spoon of coconut chutney.

Enjoy 2 (or 3) with lots of family, friendship and celebrate God's goodness!

Glossary of Terms

Aare	Colloquial term meaning 'hey' or 'hey there'
Aloo	Potato
Begum	Madam (Urdu)
Beti	Daughter
Bhabi	Sister-in-law
Bhai	Hindi term meaning brother, usually refers to older brother
Bhagwan	God
Bhajias	Fritters made up of vegetables and chickpea flour
Bharat	India
Bhien-ji	Respected term for older sister
Biji	Respected term for mother when she is older (elderly)
Biryani	Layered rice dish, usually with lamb or mutton, for feast days/special occasions
Chai/masala chai	Indian tea made with tea leaves boiled with water, milk and sweet spices which may include ginger, cardamom,

	fennel seeds and cinnamon. Often with sugar added.
Challo	'Let's go'
Chana/Chana masala	Chickpeas/ chickpea curry
Chapati	Unleavened flat bread, also called roti. Everyday staple starch.
Charpoy	A wooden framed cot with rope mattress
Choti/Choti-saab	Little one/ younger master
Dahl	A curried lentil dish, there are many types made with different lentils
Dada	Paternal grandfather
Duppata	The scarf worn with a *salwar-kameez*
Gori	Fair one
Gujarati	From the Indian state of Gujarat
Gulab jaman	Hot desert of doughnut balls steeped in sugar syrup
Gurdwara	Sikh place of worship
Handi	Deep dish, bowl like, often stainless steel used for both cooking and serving curries.
Huzoor	Master
Inshallah	God willing
Jalebi	An Indian deep-fried sweet meat, usually bright orange in colour

Ji	Term for respect as in Pita-ji, Saab-ji. Can also mean answering in the affirmative, i.e. 'yes' or 'really?'
Kadhi and pakoras	A yoghurt-based curry with chickpea flour vegetable dumplings
Chacha	Younger uncle
Kanchi	Slang term for young girl (teenager)
Kirpan	Sword or dagger, one of the symbolic '5 Ks' carried by Sikhs
Kothi	Large residence
Kurtha	Shirt-like top worn by men
Laukis	An Asian gourd
Maafi karo	Forgive me
Makhan	Butter
Makki di roti	Flat bread made with corn (maize) flour and served with sarson ka saag
Mamma	Mother's brother
Mammi	Mother's brother's wife
Mandi/Heera mandi	Market/diamond market
Masi/Masis	Mother's sister/s
Memsahib (or memsaab)	Mistress/Madam. Used as term of respect
Mithai	Sweet meat
Mubarak	Congratulations

Mujra	Classical dance performed by tawaifs in the dance halls
Musalman	Hindi term for Muslim
Naan	Flat bread made with plain flour and yoghurt
Nana	Maternal Grandfather
Nani	Maternal Grandmother
Nawab	Landowner/wealthy man
Nawabi	Wife of Nawab
Nayhe	No
Parathas	A fired flat bread, usually stuffed with potato ('aloo'), cauliflower ('gobi'), daikon raddish ('mooli') or cheese curds ('paneer'). Sometimes unfilled.
Pindi	Rawalpindi
Pyjami	Pants worn under a kurta or kameez, usually slim as opposed to a salwar
Parjai	Older brother's wife
Pilau rice	Rice dish cooked with seasoned water and other ingredients
'Pindi	Shortened version of Rawalpindi, a city in Pakistan.
Pita-Ji/Papa-Ji	Respected term for father
Paranda	A type of hair accessory with coloured tassels, usually plaited into the hair.

Puri/puris	Deep fried bread/s often served for breakfast with potato or chickpea curry
Puttar	Son or child
Rajma-chawal	Beans and rice
Rani	Queen
Rotiayaan	A type of flat bread
Saab/Saab-Ji	Sir
Sabzi	Vegetable or vegetable curry
Sabzi-walla	Vegetable seller
Salaam alaikum	Greeting (Arabic but used worldwide amongst Muslims) meaning peace be with you
Salwar	The pant part of traditional dress (*salwar-kameez*) – usually loose
Salwar-Kameez	Traditional outfit comprising a tunic and pants
Sari	Traditional outfit for women comprising approximately six yards of patterned fabric wrapped and folded around the body in a particular way
Sarson, sarson-ka-saag, saag	Yellow mustard leaves, leaves made into a curried puree
Sat sri akal	Greeting of Sikhs roughly meaning 'true is the name of God'
Sharia	A set of Islamic laws – refers
Sherwani	An elaborate men's outfit comprising heavily embroidered coat dress and

	slim pants, usually reserved as wedding attire or for festivals
Sikh	One of the three majority religions in India, Sikhs being characterized by five religious symbols ('5 Ks') and wearing of the turban
Sooji ka halwa	Sweet dish made of semolina, butter and sugar syrup. Often with added dried fruits and nuts
Tandoor	Clay oven, traditionally heated with coal/wood
Tandoori	Refers to food cooked in a tandoor
Tari/Tariwalli	Gravy/with gravy
Tawaif	Dancing girl
Taxiwalla	Taxi driver
Teek	Fine/okay
Thali	Stainless steel tray
Thaiya	Father's older brother
Yaar	Term meaning friend, usually used between young people